LAUGHING CAN KILL YOU

A HAZEL ROSE BOOK GROUP MYSTERY

MAGGIE KING

Cover Design by Mariah Sinclair

Interior Design by Tina Glasneck

Print: ISBN 979-8-9852318-1-6

To my sisters in crime, with appreciation

ONE

R andy Zimmerman was dead.

Or was he?

Call it horrified fascination, but I couldn't take my eyes away from the grim scene before me: Randy, sprawled facedown on the floor in front of a coffee table. The big toe of his right foot protruded from a hole in his sock. An overturned wine glass lay by his left hand. A red stain—wine? blood?—created a Rorschach-like pattern on the white area rug.

As of two days before, I hadn't even met Randall Zimmerman, Esquire. Since then, we'd not only met but had fought in public.

He sure looked dead.

Tarrant's Café was an old drugstore turned restaurant in the heart of downtown Richmond, Virginia. Lots of dark wood, brick walls, European-style paintings, and crystal chandeliers created a soothing background for its upscale offerings—or would have had I not been so rattled by my publisher.

Lucy Hooper, my cousin and closest friend, sat across from me. We often met for lunch, as she managed a downtown staffing firm.

Tucking my hair behind my ears, I tried, but failed, to smile.

"They dumped me." My voice caught. "Lucy, they *dumped* me."

"What? They *dumped* you? Who dumped you?"

"My publisher." My eyes filled.

Lucy pulled a tissue from her purse and passed it to me as a couple of tears rolled down my face. "Tell me what happened."

"Let's order first." I picked up the menu and scanned it briefly before putting it down.

Our server, a sweet young woman whose name I no sooner heard than forgot, took our orders. Once she glided away, Lucy waved her hand in a go-on motion. "What's up?"

"Sam called me this morning with the news." My agent, Sam Barker, had negotiated the contract for my debut romance and had represented me ever since. I took a sip of water before continuing. "Even though sales weren't great for my last title, I didn't think they were bad enough for Blasey Publishing to pull the plug on me. I gave them eight romances. Eight bestsellers. What happens when the ninth has a little hiccup in sales? Heave-ho! Don't let the door hit you in the—"

Lucy interrupted my tirade. "Look on the bright side. We signed up for a mystery-writing course."

"What's bright about that?" I blotted my face.

"Turn your latest romance into a mystery. Just add a dead body or two and you're all set."

I held up a hand. "Not so loud, Lucy."

"No one's paying attention to us."

She was right. The din of conversations kept us from being overheard. "We've read enough mysteries to know there's more to penning one than dead bodies," I said.

"We'll learn together in class. I don't know how Claudia will be as a teacher, but she can sure turn out a good crime story."

Claudia Marlowe, a bestselling crime writer who'd relocated to

Richmond from Maryland the year before, planned to teach the class the following week. "I looked at one of her webinars and I'd say she's a great teacher. Although her series is far more noirish than what I'd probably write."

Lucy lifted her water glass, making the ice cubes clink. "You could always kill off a publisher."

This time our conversation got someone's attention. Our server almost dropped the soup of the day in my lap.

"We're mystery writers," I rushed to explain.

"Oh. Well, that's good," she said with a nervous giggle as she placed our dishes before us and backed away, nearly colliding with another server.

"Thanks for calling me a writer," Lucy said, picking up her soup spoon.

"You will be a writer. That's what the class is all about."

"Try this," Lucy said. "It's fabulous."

We switched bowls to sample each other's soup.

"Will Sam still be your agent?"

"That's another thing. He's retiring at the end of the year, less than two months away." I sipped Lucy's crab bisque, inhaling the delicate aroma of crab, cream, and spices. "Mmm, heavenly. Tastes as good as it smells."

"Your broccoli cheese is good, too." We swapped bowls again. "Hazel, I know this is hard, but you're a damn good writer, and this is nothing more than a temporary blip in your career. Things will work out."

That was one of many things I loved about my cousin: her faith in me.

"I know they will." I managed a genuine smile. "Publishing's a tough business, no room for slack."

"Have you told Vince?"

"No, I haven't had a chance. I just found out a few hours ago, and he'd already left to do research at the library." My husband, Vince Castelli, was also a published author, writing true crime accounts.

"Didn't you visit a book group this morning?"

"Yes." I told Lucy about the romance readers' group that met at a branch of the Richmond Public Library. "They liked *Aegean Romance*. At least they *said* they did."

"I'm sure they did. Don't let that publisher get you down." Lucy finished her soup and dabbed her mouth with a napkin. "I know how upset you must be because I don't think I've ever seen you cry. Maybe when your parents died."

"That's probably the last time, and it's been years since they passed. I've never been much of a crier. Too shallow, I guess." I shrugged and managed a grin. "Let's talk about something else. I love your suit. Is it new?"

"I got it on sale last spring, but haven't worn it till now."

Even though it was casual Friday at Lucy's business, she always kept current and prospective clients in mind when dressing. Today she paired a hunter green suit with a white silk blouse. Most colors complemented her highlighted brown hair and deep gray eyes.

"Are you going to the signing tomorrow at Richmond Books?" I asked.

"Sure thing. You?"

"Absolutely. After all, Claudia's latest just came out. We have to get in good with the teacher."

Our server appeared with the rest of our order. She seemed to take more time than necessary to replace our empty soup bowls with salads almost too pretty to eat. No doubt she wanted to catch any provocative comments. She looked disappointed when a ding on my phone alerted me to a text, cutting off any promising tidbits to carry back to the kitchen.

I squinted at the screen. "It's Trudy."

Trudy Zimmerman and Sarah Rubottom, friends from our Murder on Tour book group, were at the airport en route to Croatia, a trip they'd anticipated for months.

I read Trudy's text to Lucy: "Flight's about to take off. Guess who else is taking your writing class? Can't guess? Randy! He posted on Facebook."

"Does she mean Randy Zimmerman, her ex?" Lucy asked.

"I guess."

"God help us. Guy's a piece of work."

"You know him?"

"Yes, he's one of my top clients. Always losing staff, which is good business for me."

"Really? I didn't know that." No doubt I was unaware of most of Lucy's client base, but with Randy being the ex-husband of a book group member, his name might have come up in conversation.

"Thankfully, I deal with his office manager, not with him."

"I didn't know Trudy kept in touch with him."

"Didn't he and what's-her-name have an affair?"

"Yes. Carlene Arness." Even after all these years, I still cringed at the thought of Carlene, of how she looked—*dead*—after drinking cyanide-laced tea at book group.

TWO

A large poster in a metal floor stand by the Richmond Books entrance displayed the mystery authors signing inside, including their photos. In the store, a long line snaked in front of Claudia Marlowe's table. Claudia's fans, abuzz with excitement, held her newest tome, *Virginia Menace*, ready for her signature.

The lone figure at the next table wasn't faring as well. Lorraine Popp forced a smile when she saw me. She sat behind a dozen copies of her debut mystery, *Murder at the Quilting Bee*. Lucy, her sole customer, held three copies of the title.

"Lorraine signed these for me," Lucy said. "It's time to think about Christmas."

"Good idea. I'll do that as well." I selected two books from the pile. The colorful cover showed a group of women surrounding a quilt impaled by a knife and covering a body. "Just sign your name. I'm not sure who I'm giving these to, as I'm sure my sisters have already read it." I prayed Lorraine wouldn't notice my adlibbing, but she focused on affixing her signature to her title page. I envied her indecipherable flourish. Even after many signings over the years, my own signature remained unfashionably legible.

"I didn't know you'd be here, Lorraine." I tried for an upbeat tone. "You never said."

Lorraine, our newest book group member, shrugged. "Claudia made me do it. Said it would be a good opportunity for me."

"I'm going to walk around and say hi to some of the other authors," Lucy said. She wandered off, leaving me alone with Lorraine.

Lorraine was a reasonably attractive woman. Chin length smoky gray curls framed a heart-shaped face, devoid of makeup. At our last book group meeting, she had confided that she was fifty. We teased her about being the group's token Gen X member. The rest of us were older, covering the Baby Boomer age continuum.

"Did you do something different with your hair?" Lorraine gazed at a point above my face.

"Yes, I got a trim this morning." I patted the chestnut waves that brushed my shoulders.

"It looks good." Lorraine's eyes often shifted in color from brown to green, the hallmark of the color called hazel. Despite being named Hazel, my own eyes were army-fatigue green, varying in shade but not color.

"What have we over here?" Two men approached Lorraine's table. I recognized Randy Zimmerman from his Facebook picture, but not the taller man with him. Randy held a blue plastic three-ring binder. Both men carried copies of *Virginia Menace*.

"Claudia signed these for us," Randy said, shaking his book at us. "Thank God we got here early. You mark my words, someday these will be collectors' items and anyone with a copy will be sitting on a gold mine." He accompanied this happy prediction with a loud guffaw.

"Yes, Claudia's quite talented," I said. "We're—"

Randy interrupted. "I just met Claudia this past summer and already I've devoured every word she's written." He smacked his forehead. "Oh, pardon my rudeness. Randy Zimmerman, at your service. This here's my buddy, Matt Rowan."

"I'm Hazel Rose and this is Lorraine Popp."

Randy whooped. "Hazel Rose, the *romance* writer. Aren't you the one who found the killer of my good friend, Carlene Arness?" He didn't wait for me to confirm my identity. "Let me shake your hand." He pumped my hand for several seconds before drawing me into a hug. Several people in Claudia's line looked at us, chuckling.

Randy stood no taller than five feet five inches, give or take an inch. His graying mustache lent an incongruous note with his horseshoe fringe of what looked to be dyed black hair. The rest of his head shone like a beacon, like he'd given it a good scrubbing. He wore a gray University of Richmond sweatshirt.

Matt shook our hands while continuing to scroll through his texts. A full head of hair, sandy colored and streaked with gray, crowned his head. Matt also sported a sweatshirt from the U of R, his in navy.

"Lorraine and I are in the same book group as Trudy," I said.

"Great little woman, that Trudy." Randy shook his head, adding, "I shouldn't have let her slip away."

I doubted Trudy felt the same way and knew she wouldn't care for the "little woman" remark. A gold band circled the third finger of Randy's left hand. But his wistful tone about Trudy suggested the marriage with his current wife wasn't going well.

"I hear you're taking the writing class Claudia's teaching," I said. "Lorraine and I are taking it as well."

Randy didn't ask how I knew that. He launched a sales pitch about his thriving personal injury law practice, giving him credentials for writing a legal thriller. "And I mean *thriller*, ladies. I plan to give John Grisham a run for his money." That would be quite a run, considering the bestselling author's financial haul. Randy put his book and blue binder on Lorraine's table, reached into his pocket for his wallet and extracted a leather sleeve full of business cards. He handed one to me and one to Lorraine. "My manuscript's all done, needs a spit and a polish is all. Our friend Claudia graciously offered to critique it for me." He lifted the binder that presumably held the "thrilling" manuscript.

He paused for a second. "And let me tell you about my idea for my second thriller. This rich guy suddenly keels over and dies, leaving everything to his only child, a son. But it turns out the father had another family. What does son number one do? Share the fortune with Daddy's secret family? Or"—here Randy made a throat-slashing gesture with his finger—"Does he eliminate them?"

"How's everything going here?"

Felicia Brimwell, the store's author coordinator, handed Lorraine a paper coffee cup with a plastic lid. Judging from the corrugated sleeve slipped over the cup, it contained a hot beverage. Richmond Books gave authors who were signing complementary drinks.

"Hi, Felicia," I said. "Everything's fine. We're talking about Claudia's mystery writing class and how much we're looking forward to it."

"Oh, wonderful," Felicia started, but several customers drew her away.

I'd heard enough from Randy, so rushed to ask, "What about you, Matt? Are you a writer?"

"Yes, my buddy here's a great writer," Randy said. "He's taking the class as well."

Matt, engrossed by his phone, had said little. As if he suddenly remembered his manners, he dropped the device in his jacket pocket and asked, "Tell us what you ladies write."

"Drivel," Randy proclaimed. "Pure drivel."

Drivel? "Excuse me?"

"Claudia said we should read each other's work, so I read one of yours and one of this one's." He hooked a thumb at Lorraine. "How did you even get published? Or did you publish it yourself? That must be what happened."

"I don't believe you have the gall to stand there and talk to us like that." I leveled a withering look at the man.

"Maybe you should stick with investigating murders." Randy continued with his thumbs-way-down review. "I thought you wrote mysteries. Instead, I had to slog through pages and pages of horny old people trying to get laid. Sheesh!"

A childish urge to stick out my tongue came over me, but I resisted. Instead, I turned to Matt and described my transferring from baby boomer romances to mysteries, rather combining romance with mystery. But Randy interrupted. "You women! Always sticking romance into everything. You'll never get a man to read that crap."

He was right. If we romance writers had to rely on men to read our books we'd go broke. But I didn't give Randy the satisfaction of admitting it.

"Throw in some steamy sex, a few shoot 'em ups, and you have a chance of making some sales."

"Thank you for your input, Randy." I waved a hand at Lorraine. "That's enough about me. Lorraine, tell Matt and Randy about your writing."

She managed an "um" before Randy groaned. "Hers is even worse. It's about *quilting*." He picked up a copy of *Murder at the Quilting Bee*, read the back cover out loud, and flung the book down on the table. He grabbed a Hershey's Kiss from a dish in front of Lorraine, wadded up the wrapper, and tossed it on the table as well.

"Randy, *Murder at the Quilting Bee* is a cozy," I said.

"A *cozy?*" He injected as much derision into the word as possible as he chomped on his chocolate. "What the *hell* is a cozy?"

"A cozy has an amateur sleuth, little or no violence, sex, or profanity."

"No violence! No sex! No profanity! And people buy this crap?" He made an exaggerated point of looking behind him at Lorraine's non-existent line. "Evidently not."

Lorraine sat throughout this exchange, saying nothing in defense of her work or genre. What was her problem? I felt like a mother hen, protecting her young.

Why did Matt stand by while his friend hurled abuse at us? As if he read my mind, he spoke up. "Hey man, take it easy." He picked up one of Lorraine's paperbacks. "I think my sisters and my mom would like this. They're not quilters, but they like to sew."

"It's a great story regardless of whether you're a quilter." I moved to close the sale. "The mystery stands on its own."

"What, is she paying you a commission?"

"Randy, her name is Lorraine Popp, and she's a fine writer." Why wouldn't the woman speak up on her own behalf?

"I'll take three," Matt said.

"What a guy!" Randy clapped a hand on Matt's back. "Matt always was a champ for the underdog."

Matt spelled the names of his mother and sisters as Lorraine signed. When Randy reached for another Hershey's Kiss, I grabbed the dish. "No more candy unless you make a purchase."

"Oh, ho! Feisty one, aren't you? I like my women feisty."

Randy's over-the-top delivery continued to amuse Claudia's fans. My face heated up, making me madder than I already was.

He held up his hands in a surrender pose. "Hazel, I'm sorry." He didn't sound sorry. "I don't have a filter. Maybe one of these days you'll be investigating my murder. I can really piss people off." He sounded happy about this character trait.

It could take years to round up the suspects, I thought. Did I have that many years left?

"Look, I have to go—"

"Don't go, Hazel. Tell us about your playing detective at that redneck bar. You really—Sherry! Sherry baby!"

THREE

Randy couldn't compete with Frankie Valli's falsetto. The trigger for this burst into song, a young woman with a sheet of gleaming waist-length dark hair, laughed in delight. Her snug red sweater left no doubt as to her ample bosom. Now Claudia's fans were getting even more for their entertainment dollars. Hopefully, this woman would divert Randy's attention from me and my second adventure in, as Randy put it, playing detective.

"Sherry, meet my friends." After introducing Matt and me, Randy blanked on Lorraine's name. I held up one of her books as a prompt. "So sorry," he said. "Lorraine Popp."

"Hazel Rose." Sherry looked at me, perhaps searching her memory for a reason my name sounded familiar. "Are you a romance writer?"

"I am." I smiled, ignoring Randy's snort.

"My mom loves your books," Sherry said. "I like mysteries." She picked up Lorraine's book and scanned the back cover. "This looks good."

"If you want to know what's really good, check out Claudia

Marlowe's books." Randy pointed to Claudia, busy signing a copy of *Virginia Menace* and tucking a bookmark between the pages.

Sherry's dark eyes danced. "I may live dangerously and get both."

"Let me take a few pictures for Facebook." I took my phone from my bag. "Hold up your books. It's good promotion for Lorraine and Claudia."

Randy and Matt struck poses, but Sherry didn't join them for the photo opp. "I take terrible pictures," she claimed. Despite Randy's lobbying, and despite her artful draping of her hair over one shoulder, she refused to budge.

"It's okay, Sherry," I said. "This isn't a command performance."

Lorraine stayed seated, a blank expression on her face. The woman tried my patience. "Lorraine, get in the picture. Take one of your books and hold it up in front of you."

With little enthusiasm, she joined the group, and I snapped a few pictures. Matt and Randy wore big grins. Lorraine managed a smile, but in a ghostly Mona Lisa way.

After getting Lorraine's signature, Sherry said it was "fabulous" meeting us. She and Randy moved over to Claudia's queue.

"Nice meeting you both," Matt said as he walked away. "See you in class." He waved to Randy and Sherry before lining up at the register to purchase his books. With Randy dominating the conversation, we hadn't learned about Matt's writing. But the class was only three days away—he could fill us in then.

Lucy appeared, arms laden with more books. "Is that Randy Zimmerman I hear?"

"Yes, he's in Claudia's line." I pointed to Randy, who continued to praise Claudia as the world's greatest crime writer.

"I guess I need to say hello. Keep my clients happy, you know." Lucy left her stack of books on a corner of Lorraine's table. "I'll be back." Randy greeted Lucy in what was apparently his usual effusive manner. After a brief conversation, she returned, eyes rolling.

The two of us hawked Lorraine's book, corralling anyone who entered the store to her table. Lucy could sell anything to anyone. We talked non-cozy readers into buying them for gifts. A surprising number of people knew others who were quilters and welcomed the gift idea. I documented the event in pictures. Felicia Brimwell asked me to tag the store on Instagram.

Lorraine signed and offered watery smiles to her readers, but spoke little. She didn't even have bookmarks or business cards to hand out—only the Hershey's Kisses. A couple of women tried to engage her in conversation. "We're in a quilting group and would love to have you visit us," one of them told her. It soon became apparent that Lorraine knew next to nothing about quilting. The women looked like they regretted buying her book, but, as she'd already signed their copies, they were stuck.

A few of my readers stopped by and asked when my next book was coming out. They liked my idea of crossing over to mysteries and wished me luck. Some wanted to buy Claudia's book, but her long line dampened their enthusiasm. Her lengthy chats with individual readers didn't help.

"I guess that's it," Lorraine said once we sold out the store's copies of her book. She smiled her first genuine smile of the day. "Thanks for your help. I don't think I'm cut out for this sort of thing."

Lorraine needed help if she ever wanted to sell her books on her own. I wasn't sure if she did, and my recent flop didn't qualify me as an expert on book sales—but there were my previous successes.

"Lorraine, would you like to have lunch one day? I have an appointment near where you work next Friday. How about then?"

"Oh. Yeah, okay."

After arranging to meet at the Grapevine at noon, Lorraine put her dish of kisses in a plastic bag, gathered her jacket and purse, and walked toward the back of the store.

"The guy's unbelievable," Lucy said when I ran down my exchange with Randy. "And what's with Lorraine, anyway? You'd think she was at the dentist."

"Signing books isn't easy for everyone. And being next to

someone like Claudia would be ego-deflating. Lorraine needs help. That's why I invited her to lunch."

"Well, I hope she lets you help her. I have to get going. I'm going to buy Claudia's book and get her to sign it at the writing class."

"Good idea," I said. "I'm going to walk around and see how the other authors are doing. See ya."

Four more mystery authors, busy signing their tomes and chatting with readers, sat at tables in the mystery section. Not wanting to interrupt, I smiled, waved, and browsed in the writing reference section before making my way to the front register to pay for my purchases.

A mid-afternoon lull set over the store, making it strangely quiet. Claudia's queue had dwindled to a mere dozen customers. Randy and Sherry were nowhere in sight.

The writing class promised to be a long six weeks with Randy there.

FOUR

Trees ablaze with autumnal reds, golds, and oranges canopied Huguenot Road, but I barely noticed the seasonal display as I drove—the boorish Randy took my mind off my surroundings.

I stopped at the store to pick up a few things for dinner. Before joining the checkout line, I reached in my bag for my phone, planning to call Vince to see if we needed anything else. The phone wasn't there. Not in my jacket pocket, either. Figuring it must be in the car, I paid for the groceries and left.

After searching my car, the phone still didn't show up. I had no choice but to return to Richmond Books. In the store, a stack of Claudia's books sat atop her table, but neither Claudia nor her legions of enthusiastic readers were in sight.

"Hi, Hazel. Back so soon?"

I spun around. Felicia Brimwell, the store's author coordinator, brushed a strand of hair from her face.

"I think I left my phone here. Probably when I paid for my books."

Felicia went behind the counter and retrieved a phone from a shelf under the registers. Holding it up, she asked, "Is this it?"

"That's it." The bright orange case cut down on the number of times I misplaced the phone or left it behind—cut down it did, eliminate it did not.

"How did everything go today?" I asked as I slipped the phone in my purse.

Felicia appeared to be in her mid-thirties. Countless rows of tight braids covered her scalp and cascaded down her back. Long strings of beads swung from her ears.

"Fabulous," Felicia said. "Sales were through the roof. But you missed all the excitement."

"Excitement?"

Felicia lowered her voice. "Claudia Marlowe and this guy were sitting in the café. I started toward them to thank Claudia for being here and selling so many books—I was busy when the signings ended, so didn't have a chance to talk to any of the authors then—but I stopped when I saw the thunderous look on Claudia's face. She was really chewing out this guy."

"Huh. I wonder what that was about. Could you hear what she was saying?"

"No." Felicia sounded aggrieved. "Unfortunately not."

"What was the guy doing?"

"Laughing."

"Laughing?" It took little imagination to come up with Randy Zimmerman as the laughing boy. "What did this guy look like?"

Sure enough, Felicia's description—bald, horseshoe fringe, University of Richmond sweatshirt—matched that of Randy. "In fact, I think you and Lorraine were talking to him earlier."

"Yes, his name is Randy Zimmerman. We're both taking a writing class that Claudia's teaching. It starts on Tuesday."

Felicia gave a half laugh. "Oh yeah, you mentioned that earlier. That should be one interesting class. Anyway, I hid out in the travel section where I could see them, but they couldn't see me. But I still couldn't hear anything. Then, you won't believe this, suddenly Claudia gets up and slaps this Randy."

"You're kidding!"

"I'm not. Then she took her coat and bag and stormed off."

"Then what happened?"

"Not much. Everyone in the café was all aflutter about the whole thing. Let's walk over there and see if anyone can tell us anything."

Felicia didn't need to prod me. I was as aflutter as anyone.

"Rats! Most everyone left. Maybe these folks were here." Felicia went from table to table, surveying the few customers, but they hadn't witnessed the dramatic exchange between Claudia and Randy.

"There was this one woman—" Felicia began as she and I walked toward the main entrance. A couple of harried-looking men buttonholed Felicia, one needing a particular title on Instant Pot cooking, another anything on travel to Antarctica.

"Nice seeing you, Hazel. I want to hear more about that writing class." She winked before turning away to help her customers.

Richmond's Bon Air neighborhood started as a Victorian resort village in the late 19th century. Its name, translated as "good air," explained why the area had attracted Richmond's elite, who sought a respite from the not-so-good air of Richmond's industrial city center. Bon Air's air quality had declined since its auspicious beginnings, but was a significant improvement over Los Angeles, where I'd lived for many years.

Part of Bon Air was designated a National Historic District, with several beautiful and well-maintained Victorian homes. But Bon Air had a second building boom in the 1960s, this time producing split levels, ranch styles, Cape Cods, and the occasional Colonial Revival. Vince and I lived in one of the many split levels that dotted the landscape.

When I pulled into my driveway and parked, Olive, my Norwegian Forest cat, greeted me and followed me into the house. Leaves crunched under our feet and paws as we walked.

"How did the signing go?" Vince asked. He sat in the family room, crossword puzzle in hand.

"Let me put these groceries away and I'll tell you all about it."

"I met Randy Zimmerman," I said, once settled in the family room. "What a jackass." I regaled my husband with an account of my meeting with my soon-to-be classmate. "I can't imagine going through a writing class with him. He thanked me for finding Carlene Arness's killer, but quickly forgot his gratitude. Oh, and then—" I went through Felicia's account of the exchange between Randy and Claudia.

Parts of the *Richmond Times-Dispatch* covered the coffee table. Olive and Morris, an orange and white Manx cat, chased each other through the house. Wood-paneled walls, soft green carpeting, a white brick fireplace, and camel furniture made the room easy on the spirit. We'd used poor judgment in choosing our recliners. The nubby fabric appealed to the cats. Even though they used the several scratching posts stationed around the house, a nice piece of furniture also appealed to them.

"Lots of drama for one afternoon," Vince said when I finally finished. "Sounds like you acquired some ideas for your writing."

"I'll say. I wonder why Claudia slapped Randy. Of course, I felt like slapping him earlier. I bet they had an affair, and things went awry."

"I can see how you came to that conclusion. But there could be other reasons."

"Whatever. I guess Claudia's not as hot on Randy as he is on her." I recalled his rapturous praise of her books. "It was strange meeting him after all these years. I saw him at Carlene's funeral, but never met him till today."

"After you told me about Randy being in your class, I looked up some old news accounts about his involvement with Carlene. Those scenes outside her house were really something. Especially the ones involving your ex-husband."

Vince referred to Evan Arness, my first and long-ago husband, who eventually married Carlene. "Yeah, Randy didn't like being dumped for Evan and came around loudly expressing his feelings on the matter. In a way I can't blame him. From all accounts, he and Carlene had a torrid thing going."

"She sure was one for drama." Vince's blue eyes danced at the memory.

"Her death was dramatic enough. But let's not dredge up all this icky history."

I went to the kitchen and took my phone from my purse, where I'd tossed it on the table. Back in my chair, I brought up Randy's Facebook page. We had a mutual friend, Trudy Zimmerman.

"Randy went to the University of Richmond. He's politically conservative and professes no religion." I continued to scan the information on his "About" page. "He's sixty-four. Partner with Louis P. Treadwell and Associates."

"That's a personal injury practice," Vince said. "They advertise a lot on TV."

I viewed photos of Randy with a blurry-looking blond woman. His wife, perhaps? Most pictures showed him laughing with friends, hoisting beer steins.

Olive jumped in my lap and purred as I stroked her silky fur. Morris dashed around the room, bobbing his abbreviated tail. At last, energy spent, he retreated to a corner for a grooming session. Vince and I found both cats at the Richmond Animal League, a local no-kill shelter. Lucky day for us—and the felines.

"Did Randy ever remarry after he and Trudy split up?" Vince asked.

"According to Trudy he did, and he wears a wedding ring. There's this photo of a blond woman who could be his wife. But he was pretty chummy today with Sherry, the sweater girl. And he mentioned something about Trudy, how he regretted breaking up with her."

"Let me take a look." Vince took his phone from his pocket and set to swiping the small screen. I admired my handsome husband with his shock of white hair and neatly trimmed mustache and beard. While his hairline was receding a bit, he still sported more hair than many men his age. His blue eyes had seen all manner of human depravity and evil during his years as a homicide detective with the Richmond Police Department, yet retained a remarkable gentleness. His Brooklyn accent had also survived decades of living in Virginia.

He retired from the police department to pursue a career writing true crime accounts. As his books required extensive research, it took him an average of three years to publish one. At the moment, he was working on an account of a Virginia couple who'd kidnapped a wealthy man and his mistress and held them captive for a month. He often spoke to writing groups and to criminal justice classes.

Vince said, "From the comments I'd say this was a wedding picture."

I enlarged the picture and viewed the comments offering congratulations and wishes of everlasting happiness to the couple. How everlasting had happiness turned out to be for them? "You're right. That looks like a white gown she's wearing in a vintage style. But the picture's so blurry that it's hard to tell."

Vince put his phone aside. "Who else is going to be in your class? There's Randy, Matt, Lucy, and you so far. You said some of your book group members have joined the ranks of aspiring mystery writers."

"There's Eileen. I'm not sure what she's planning to write."

Eileen Thompson, a librarian and neighbor of Trudy Zimmerman's, was a long-time book group member. "And Lorraine Popp."

"The one from today? The one who knows nothing about quilting?"

I nodded. "First she wrote a traditional mystery, one of those country house murders with lots of suspects. But her editor said country house stories were passé and that craft mysteries were all the rage. She talked Lorraine into revising her story to be about quilting."

"Did she visit any quilting groups for research?" Vince asked. Morris, finished with his toilette, jumped on Vince's lap.

"She says she did and didn't like them. And the people didn't like her. I figure that was what was wrong with her story—no soul, no heart. Wooden characters. Since I'm not a craft person, I've never been in such a group, but I picture the people, likely all women, as being warm and hospitable."

"But she's traditionally published." Vince massaged Morris's back as the cat purred in contentment.

"Yeah, go figure. Still, I think she has potential. That's what Sarah thought when she invited her to the book group as a visiting author and encouraged her to stay on as a group member. She figured that being around mystery readers might help her become a better writer."

"You said Lorraine and Sarah are neighbors?"

"*Were* neighbors. Lorraine's mother's in a retirement home now and Lorraine moved to an apartment. The house got to be too much for them after Mr. Popp died. By the way, I'm having lunch with her, meaning Lorraine, next Friday at the Grapevine."

"Are you going to be her mentor?"

"If that's what she wants."

"Anyone else in the class?" Vince asked.

"Those are the ones I know about. Claudia wants to keep it small, especially for her first teaching gig."

After a back and forth about dinner—eat at home or out?—we settled on our favorite Thai restaurant. I nudged Olive off my lap and stood. "I have things to do upstairs," I said. Vince reached for his crossword puzzle.

Short flights of steps accessed each level of our split-level house. Vince and I constantly went up and down the steps, giving us bonus exercise. The felines benefitted as well, making our household a heart-healthy one.

In my den, I emptied the tote bag of the books I'd purchased, wondering who on my gift list would enjoy Lorraine's book. The blue notebook I pulled out puzzled me. Where did that come from? When I opened the cover, I was stunned. *Murder Most Legal* by Randall Zimmerman.

How did Randy's manuscript end up in my bag? It must have happened during the picture-taking. Likely, Randy put his notebook on Lorraine's table while he posed with his copy of Claudia's book. Then he'd walked away without the notebook. I must have taken it by accident, thinking it was mine. As I owned several of these plastic binders, my absent-mindedness didn't surprise me.

The pages bled with red-inked notes in the margins and between the lines. Claudia's notes, I bet. I found Randy's business card in the side pocket of my purse and shot him an email, letting him know I had his manuscript.

"Hazel, my love," he wrote back. "I'm so glad you have it. Are you at home? Can I come around and pick it up?"

I wasn't keen on Randy knowing where I lived. He probably didn't moonlight as a burglar and he could certainly find out my address, but something told me to guard that information.

"No, I'm not home right now," I wrote. "Where do you live? Vince and I can come by tomorrow. Early afternoon." That fit in with our plans to go out for Sunday brunch.

"Sure, whatever works for you guys. I'd love to meet your hubby. Maybe we can chat over a beer or two. If I don't answer the front door, come around back to the patio and knock on the French doors." He gave me his address in the Westover Hills area of Richmond, not far from Bon Air.

I didn't relish another conversation with the man. But his accommodating tone made me think he regretted his earlier obnoxiousness. Plus, I might find out about his row with Claudia if I talked to him.

The writer in me was always curious about conflicts.

FIVE

The Richmond district of Carytown featured an eclectic assortment of stores and restaurants. Storefronts showcased trendy fashion, home décor, a couple of chocolatiers, crafts, hobbies, and one-of-a-kind gifts. Health and wellness practices abounded.

The ninety-year-old Byrd Theatre, a restored movie palace and Carytown's jewel, was a Virginia Historic Landmark. The theatre showed second-run movies and hosted an annual French Film Festival. As a bonus, customers could enjoy a lavish interior and a Wurlitzer organ.

Carytown was the place to be—at least it was on that Saturday evening, as Vince and I ran into several friends and acquaintances on the street as well as in Thai Garden.

Over Pad Thai and chicken curry, we continued to discuss Randy and Claudia, focusing on Claudia's assaulting Randy in the Richmond Books café. "Do you think they're lovers? Or were lovers?"

"I couldn't say. It's all speculation." Vince had a cop's aversion to speculation. As a writer, I relished it. "She hasn't confided in you about any of this? Since you two reconnected, you get together often."

"No, she doesn't talk much about her personal life, certainly not any clandestine aspects of it."

Claudia Brown and I were neighbors decades before in New Jersey. She was a bit younger, so we weren't close. But one summer day my sister Madeline wandered into the deep end of a community pool and Claudia rescued her. My family felt they owed an enormous debt to this "brave, selfless" girl.

Soon after that event, I went away to college, Claudia's father died, and her mother relocated the family to Baltimore. Our families fell out of touch—until my saved-from-drowning sister Madeline informed me that Claudia Brown was now Baltimore-based best-selling crime novelist Claudia Marlowe.

I spooned more Pad Thai on my plate. "When she moved to Richmond last year, I expected that we'd become good friends. That hasn't happened, not yet anyway. Oh, we have lunch occasionally, but we mostly talk about writing. Since she's been so successful, I encouraged her to teach this writing class."

"And she and her family came here one day over the summer for a barbeque," Vince said. "But they haven't reciprocated."

"I know. And I still haven't met her husband. I thought he'd be at the barbeque, but Claudia only brought her daughter, son-in-law, and grandson."

Claudia and her husband moved to Richmond when he retired to be near their grandson. When I met Claudia at a writing conference, the two of us were delighted to reunite after so many years, and started meeting for lunch. I invited her to speak to our book group— one of our best author visits.

"Every so often I think about that debt my family owes her for rescuing Madeline. I can't imagine how I could repay it."

"Something may come up. You can't force these things." After a pause, Vince asked, "What's the book group planning for the coming year?"

"I don't know. We have to start thinking about that. Probably books set in the countries Trudy and Sarah are visiting. Croatia, Slovenia, Italy. I'd love to set up Zoom sessions with the authors."

The Murder on Tour book group had launched several years before. It differed from other groups in that we each read a book of our choosing based on a travel theme and met to discuss our selections. For the past year we'd strayed from a travel theme and chose stories written by Virginia mystery authors. The authors often visited with us in person.

"And when do Trudy and Sarah get back from their trip?"

"Sometime in December. Before Christmas."

"Sarah's becoming quite the globetrotter since Den died."

"Yes, she's always wanted to travel." Sarah's husband, Den Rubottom, had died the year before. As he was a paraplegic, Sarah had traveled little. Now she was making up for lost time, frequently on a jaunt somewhere in the world. Since Trudy's retirement after a career as a librarian, the two often traveled together.

"I guess Trudy's glad she took this trip," I said. "Else she would have taken this class and been stuck with Randy."

What we didn't know then was that Trudy wouldn't have been stuck with him for long.

Chain establishments were rare in Carytown, making it a fun place to spend an evening. After dinner, Vince and I walked around, visiting some of the shops.

On Sunday, we met friends for brunch at Joe's Inn, a local eatery. Dennis Mulligan, Vince's former partner in the Richmond PD, and his wife Paula waved to us from a table in the spacious and bustling restaurant. I ordered my usual Greek omelette. Dennis and Paula were interested in my move from romance to mysteries and in the class Claudia Marlowe was to teach.

"I've talked with Claudia," Dennis said. "She interviewed me for a story she wrote. Smart woman. But she doesn't get police procedure quite right, sorry to say." He and Vince grumbled about the mistakes crime writers made. They segued to TV, which they deemed worse. Paula and I smiled—we'd heard this ranting before.

"I'm sure I can count on you and Vince to make sure I get it right," I said.

We fell to talking about people we knew in common—so and so was getting divorced; someone else planned to retire and move to Phoenix. A Billy Ruffalo left the police force after being shot in the leg during a chase and bought Café Sweetbrew, a local independent coffee house.

Vince and I said our goodbyes and drove to Westover Hills to return Randy's manuscript. Located along the James River, Westover Hills was one of Richmond's most established neighborhoods and a favorite of mine. Most of the homes in this eclectic area were built during the 1920-1940 period. The styles included Cape Cod, Spanish Colonial, Tudor Revival, with an occasional farmhouse or Arts and Crafts bungalow.

We drove up Westover Hills Boulevard, turned left, and cruised down Randy's street, checking the numbers as we went. The man lived in a white colonial style house with black shutters. A fan window crowned the front door. Evergreen and magnolia trees presided over a small yard.

"Randy strikes me as the sort who would live a life of conspicuous consumption," I said. "This neighborhood, charming as it is, wouldn't be likely to appeal to someone like that."

"Maybe he inherited his home," Vince said.

"You know, I vaguely recall Trudy saying that he *had* inherited the family home, and that he liked having money, but not necessarily spending it. I admire that trait. Some people are way too flashy."

Vince parked in front of Randy's house. We walked up a flagstone walkway bordered with Monkey Grass. After climbing a set of wooden steps, I smacked the front door a few times with a brass knocker personalized with the name "Zimmerman." A real estate agent once told me it was best to knock before ringing a bell, because often bells didn't work. When my knocks went unanswered, I pressed the button for the bell. Still no response.

"He said if he didn't answer the front door to go around back. Oh, look—someone left flowers." A bouquet of white carnations, wrapped in a cellophane cone, leaned against the house by the door. "I'll take them with me."

We followed a brick path to the back of the house, where bushes formed a thick border around the yard. Randy and his wife sure valued their privacy—unless it was his parents who created the virtual fortress around the property.

Several planters in the Grecian urn style, filled with Sky Pencil hollies, stood like sentries on a small brick-paved patio. A folded umbrella pierced a round metal table. A thick coating of dirt covered the table top and cushions of the four chairs surrounding it.

I approached the French doors and was about to knock when I shrieked.

A kaleidoscope of images on the other side of the door met my eyes—images I'd never forget: a man's body sprawled face down on the floor; an overturned wine glass; congealed blood that matted the back of the man's skull; a red stain—wine? blood?—on the white area rug.

Vince looked through the door. He took a handkerchief from his pocket and used it to try the doorknob. Finding it locked, he took out his phone and punched 9-1-1. I trembled.

Vince's voice sounded far away as he barked orders to the dispatcher. "Send an ambulance. And the police."

SIX

"**I**s it really Randy? Is he dead?" I didn't wait for Vince to weigh in. "It must be Randy. He wore that gray sweatshirt yesterday. I'll bet my last dollar it has the U of R logo on the front. And that horseshoe fringe—" Using my free hand, I made circling hand gestures around the bottom of my scalp to suggest a ring of hair and declared with finality, "It's Randy, all right."

Vince put his arm around my shoulders and pulled me close. "Come on, sweetheart. Let's go out front and wait."

We walked back to the front of the house and stood on the sidewalk.

I couldn't stop my flow of words. "Did he fall and hit his head on the coffee table? Something like a brass statue lay on the floor near him. Did someone swing it at him?"

Vince pulled me closer and didn't even attempt to respond to my unanswerable questions. It didn't take long for sirens to pierce the silence of a deceptively peaceful Sunday afternoon. First the ambulance and then the squad car.

A cloud of blue-tinted black hair framed the female EMT's heart-shaped face. Copious amounts of makeup readied her for an impromptu appearance before TV cameras. In contrast, her middle-aged male partner's longish gray hair and wire-rimmed glasses would attract little notice from the media.

The two uniformed officers from the Richmond PD were both male, with buzz cuts and physiques that said they spent their off-duty time at the gym. The taller of the two wore an ID tag identifying him as "Coulter." His shorter partner's tag read "Fitzpatrick."

Vince and I led the two EMTs to the back patio. The officers followed.

"We tried the door," Vince said as the young woman jiggled the doorknob. "But it's locked."

"No problem." She lifted a foot, shod in a combat-style boot. With a couple of powerful kicks, the door swung open.

The EMTs knelt beside Randy and tried to find some sign of life. It took only seconds for them to turn to the officers and say, "No pulse." Officer Coulter called their division and asked for a detective and medical examiner to be dispatched to Randy's address. Officer Fitzpatrick left to make a cursory check of the house and secure it until the investigative team arrived.

Officer Coulter turned to Vince and me, still standing on the patio, and asked for our identification. He took down our names and contact information. When he didn't recognize Vince as a long time detective in the Richmond PD, I pegged him as a new recruit.

Between the two of us, we relayed why we were there and how we came to find Randy's body.

"What's the full name of the deceased?" Officer Coulter asked.

"Randall Zimmerman," I said.

"Is this his house?"

"Yes. I believe his wife lives here as well."

"Her name?"

"I'm sorry, but I don't know."

"What's your relationship to the deceased? Was, rather."

"He was an acquaintance. I met him yesterday at Richmond Books. Like I said, I was bringing him this notebook that I picked up by accident." I indicated the notebook cradled in my arm along with the now-crushed carnations. "Oh, and these flowers—"

Detective Thomas Fischella's grand entrance cut off my words. He came around a corner of the house, accompanied by a tall woman who was a stranger to me.

"Why hello, Ms. Rose." The detective sounded like he'd arrived at a garden party. "Nice to see you again, Detective Castelli." The three of us shook hands. Officer Coulter looked up at the mention of *Detective* Castelli.

I had dealt with Detective Fischella, a.k.a. Fish, before and had mixed feelings about him. The man was charming, a teddy bear type, someone to cuddle up with. But he was a shrewd detective, his goofy manner as deceptive as that of Columbo, the TV detective played by the late Peter Falk. Fish was in his mid-to-late forties and as stylish as I remembered him in a well-cut navy suit.

He gestured toward the tall woman. "Do you know my new partner, Detective Stephanie Garcia?" We went through another round of hand shaking.

Detective Garcia was in her early thirties, with short dark hair that fell like a curtain over one eye. She'd paired a tailored tan pantsuit with a black shirt.

Introductions over, Fish focused on Vince and me. "What brings you two here?"

Ten words into my account, Fish held up a hand. "Excuse me, Ms. Rose." Turning to Officer Coulter, he asked, "Where's your partner?"

"He's checking the house and property."

"Okay, good. Where's the victim?"

Officer Coulter pointed to the French doors. "On the other side of those doors."

Officer Fitzgerald appeared. "Building's secured, Detective. No one's in there. I haven't checked all these bushes out here."

"For now, the two of you canvas the neighborhood. Maybe someone saw something useful." The two officers left.

Fish said to Vince and me, "Please wait out here, we need to talk to you."

Fish and Detective Garcia opened the door and approached Randy. They squatted on either side of his body. Vince and I stayed on the patio, keeping the detectives in our sight.

A woman in her fifties with short blond-going-gray hair, large black-framed glasses that tilted to one side, and beat up black sneakers arrived. The medical bag she carried indicated she was the medical examiner.

"Don't touch anything!" she warned Fish and Garcia when she spotted them on the other side of the door.

The two detectives stood to greet her.

"Hi, Margot," Fish said. "You know my new partner, Stephanie Garcia?"

"Yes, we've met." The two women exchanged cordial, but businesslike, nods.

Vince lowered his voice. "That's Dr. Margot Rothenberg, the new medical examiner."

"So I gathered," I said.

"Okay, Fish, what's the story?" Dr. Rothenberg knelt beside Randy and opened the medical bag. "Not nice," she said, shaking her head. "Not nice at all."

Two forensic technicians, one male and one female, appeared. After greeting the detectives and Dr. Rothenberg, they took out their cameras and started documenting the scene.

Fish and Garcia came out to the patio. Fish said, "Let's get out of their way and find a place to chat. I'm sure you told your stories to the responding officers, but we'd appreciate your going through them again."

The detectives chose their vehicles as the perfect places for chatting. Vince went with Detective Garcia, while Fish shepherded me into his Ford Explorer. Boy-girl, boy-girl. I hoped I didn't slip and call him "Fish." That was fine for his colleagues, but I wasn't one.

"Ms. Rose." He took a pen and a small notebook from his pocket. "Please tell me what happened. From the beginning."

I described meeting Randy Zimmerman at Richmond Books, the upcoming writing class with Claudia Marlowe, how I happened to have Randy's manuscript, and the arrangements I'd made with him to come to his house to deliver said manuscript.

"You say Claudia Marlowe is to be your teacher?"

"Yes."

"She's well-regarded in the department." Echoing Dennis Mulligan's earlier statement, he added, "But sometimes she doesn't get things right."

When I didn't weigh in on the accuracy of Claudia's writing, Fish said, "So Mr. Zimmerman criticized your writing. I bet you didn't like that."

"No."

"And he was raving about Claudia's writing."

"Yes."

"Criticism would prompt some people to murder. Did you feel like murdering Mr. Zimmerman?"

"No."

When Fish didn't follow up with another provocative question, I willed myself not to fall for the silent treatment. Most people felt compelled to fill silence with words, any words, and the police used this need to their advantage.

He finally spoke. "It seems odd that you'd pick up his manuscript by accident."

Did Fish think I'd picked up the blue notebook to have an excuse to come to Randy's house and swing a statue at him? Assuming the brass statue was the weapon. "I wasn't thinking." I held up the plastic notebook. "You can find these anywhere. I have at least a dozen of them and must have assumed it was mine. These flowers—"

Fish's phone rang, and he stopped to answer it. "Okay. Okay. Okay. Thanks, Doctor." He ended the call and gave me a long look. I forced myself to maintain my cool and not squirm under his scrutiny.

"Ms. Rose, where were you last night between six and eight p.m.?"

"At Thai Garden in Carytown, eating dinner."

"Can anyone verify that?"

"My husband can. Plus we saw several people we knew."

"Names?" Fish jotted down the names I gave him. "How about a restaurant receipt?"

"Vince has it." I hoped my husband's sterling reputation in the department gave me an edge. Somehow I doubted it would.

"Why was Vince with you today? If you were just dropping off the manuscript?"

"Randy said he wanted to meet Vince, maybe have a beer or two. It's in the emails. I haven't deleted them." Even if I had, Fish could get hold of them.

"I'm surprised you wanted to spend time with him after he criticized you."

"Writers get used to criticism. I don't hold grudges."

Fish pushed back a lock of dark hair and gave me an "oh sure" look.

When he asked about other conversations I remembered from Richmond Books, I mentioned Matt, Lorraine Popp, and Sherry, including anything I recalled about what they said or did. "Oh, and Felicia Brimwell from the store. She's the author coordinator."

"Last names for Matt and Sherry?"

"I don't remember. I'm not sure Randy even mentioned their last names when he introduced them."

"How do you spell Sherry? Women spell it different ways."

"I don't know. Maybe she signed Claudia Marlowe's mailing list."

"What about Lorraine Popp? Did she have a mailing list? You said Sherry bought one of her books."

"No, she didn't have one." I could have added my thoughts about Lorraine and her substandard marketing efforts but Fish hadn't asked about that. "You could check the store receipts. Though there wouldn't be a record if someone paid cash."

"Why thank you, Ms. Rose. What a great suggestion."

"Sorry." I smiled at his sarcasm. "Naturally, you'll be checking receipts."

"Anything else you care to share about the victim?"

Should I tell Fish about Claudia and Randy's row in the café? Granted, slapping someone didn't necessarily lead to killing. Still, it was pertinent information. "I heard that Claudia and Randy had some kind of altercation in the café. After the signing."

Fish's right eyebrow shot up. "Oh? What kind of altercation?"

"I understand that she slapped him."

"Slapped? Who told you this?"

"Felicia Brimwell, the author coordinator I mentioned. She witnessed it." Fish made a note of this information.

"Does Ms. Brimwell know what prompted this slapping?"

"No."

Fish finally ran out of questions and we climbed out of the SUV. Vince stood in the street along with a crowd of onlookers who awaited any tidbits of news. Crime scene tape formed a perimeter around Randy's property.

Before I moved away to join my husband, Fish asked me to come down to headquarters the next day to sign my statement.

"At your convenience, of course." He didn't exactly bow, but somehow gave the impression of making a gallant gesture.

"Of course."

"One more thing, Ms. Rose." Again, Columbo came to mind. The TV detective had made the "One more thing" catchphrase famous. "We'll need that manuscript." Fish pointed to the blue notebook I still held in front of me like a shield. "If you don't mind."

It would hold no sway if I did mind. Besides, I had no proprietary interest in the thing and handed the notebook to the detective without comment.

"How about these flowers? I found them by the front door." I explained how I'd planned to give them to Randy—a plan that went awry.

Fish looked at the crushed bouquet like he'd never seen a flower before. "Any reason you didn't mention these before, Ms. Rose? Now we'll need your prints for elimination."

"Sorry." I didn't add that both he and Officer Coulter had cut off my attempts to mention the flowers. "But my prints should be on file. You've had to eliminate them before."

"Oh, right. Thank you so much for your help, Ms. Rose." Fish flashed white teeth as he pulled on a pair of latex gloves. The cellophane cone crinkled when I handed him the flowers.

"I just met the guy yesterday, and today I find his body. Finding a dead body is very, well . . . *intimate*."

"You're right, sweetheart. Death is intimate. Especially foul play. But we don't know that it is foul play yet. Dr. Rothenberg will let us know."

"But it probably is, don't you think?"

"Yes, *probably*. But he could have fallen and hit his head on the table."

The police let us go at five o'clock. Vince and I sat in our recliners, reviewing the harrowing events of the afternoon, the soothing sounds of *Music Choice* in the background. The aroma of my steaming herbal tea was pleasant, but it would take many mugs to relax me.

While I wasn't heartbroken over Randy's demise, I did have a mix of curiosity, plus compassion for his wife—providing she was still in the picture—and his family.

"What about Randy's wife? What's her name, anyway? Where was she today? Does she know what happened?"

"Yes, Joyce Zimmerman. She didn't have her phone on and it

took a while to run her down, but Detective Garcia found a neighbor who said Joyce had gone to a spa for the weekend. But she didn't know the name of the place, only that it was on the Northern Neck. Garcia called all the spas up there until she reached the right one. Joyce is on her way home now."

The Northern Neck was the northernmost of three Virginia peninsulas on the Chesapeake Bay. "Which spa?" I asked.

"The Inn by the Bay in Irvington."

"Nice getaway, about a two-hour drive." I sipped my tea and pictured Joyce interrupting a spa weekend to come home, kill her husband, and dash back in time for a massage or soak in a hot tub. "What will happen now? Will they question people?"

"Yes. Tomorrow—maybe tonight—they'll question Randy's friends and business associates."

"What about that restaurant receipt? Did you give it to Fish?"

"Yes, I emailed it."

"He sure acted like he suspected me. *Me.* Randy and I had a civil conversation. Okay, not that civil, but it's a far cry from being annoyed with someone to killing him."

"I know, I know, but the police have to consider all possibilities. They're not accusing you of anything, they just want to know what you observed, any information you can give them."

"Hmmph. And another thing—they haven't even determined that it was murder."

At six o'clock, Vince turned on the news.

Today the body of local attorney Randall Zimmerman, 64, was found in his home in the Westover Hills neighborhood of Richmond.

The newscast cut to a photo of the victim. It was Randy, all right, looking spiffy in a jacket and tie with the now-familiar mischievous smile. Footage of his house displayed on the screen, along with police cars and a covered stretcher being carried to a waiting ambulance.

The well-coiffed news anchor continued:

Vincent Castelli, a retired homicide detective with the Richmond Police Department, and his wife, romance author Hazel Rose, found Mr. Zimmerman when they arrived at the house for a visit. The police haven't ruled out foul play.

The anchor urged anyone with information about the incident to call the Richmond Police Tip Line or Metro Richmond Crime Stoppers. She ran off the contact information for the law enforcement agencies before segueing to a report of a robbery elsewhere in Richmond.

Vince called Dennis Mulligan, hoping to get the latest information. After ten minutes of mostly "uh huhs" and "hmms," Vince stabbed the end button and turned to me. "Randy's death is ruled as blunt force trauma to the back of the head, a brass sculpture, wiped clean of prints, the likely weapon."

"So it was murder."

"Yes."

"And didn't the medical examiner say Randy died last night, between six and eight p.m.?"

When Vince nodded, I said, "That makes sense because Randy was wearing the same clothes he had on yesterday at the book store."

I gazed at the knots in the pine wall and tried to marshal my thoughts. "What about the neighbors?" I asked. "Did they see anything?"

"Someone heard Randy laughing last night, about six-thirty."

"So sure about the time?"

"Yes. This couple lives two doors from Randy. They were going out, so yes, they were sure about the time."

"Was anyone with Randy?"

Morris and Olive appeared at the top of the steps, each taking a meatloaf position, eyes fixed on us. I fancied they hoped to hypnotize us into feeding them.

"They heard someone, they thought it was a woman, but she wasn't as loud as Randy."

"That's it for the neighbors?"

"The ones directly behind Randy were away on a cruise. And there's something else." Vince stroked his beard as he thought. "Got it. Another neighbor was out for a walk and saw a vehicle with a small child in the back seat, alone. A woman came along and got in the car. This neighbor started yelling at her about leaving the child unattended, but the woman ignored the rants and drove away."

"Was the car in front of Randy's house?"

"No, it was several houses down. It can be hard to park on some of those Westover Hills streets. Since there aren't many garages, the residents have to park on the street, leaving little space for visitors."

"That either means something . . . or it doesn't. Did this neighbor get a plate number?"

"No. She was too mad to think of it at the time."

Morris and Olive remained at the top of the steps with the same expectant expressions. Their built-in clocks told them, and me, that it was past their feeding time.

"Surely these guys will starve if I don't feed them immediately." I stood and walked up the steps to the kitchen. "Any word on Joyce? Did she show up?"

"Yes. Fish is talking to her."

Upstairs in my den, I found a couple of voicemail messages: one from Lucy and one from Eileen. They had seen the news and wanted to make sure I was all right. I called Lucy.

After assuring my cousin that, while still in shock, I had survived the ordeal of finding Randy, I ran down the events of the past twenty-four hours, including the slapping incident, finding Randy's manuscript in my tote bag, and finding his body.

"I hate to ask, but do you think Claudia killed him?" Lucy asked.

"I sure hope not, but it's possible."

"I guess Fish will call Felicia about the slapping incident."

Next, I called Eileen and repeated what I'd told Lucy. As Eileen didn't know what had transpired at Richmond Books, I had to include those details.

"Oh, my! That's awful," she said when I finished. "Does Trudy know?"

"I'm about to email her, but it's the middle of the night in Croatia or wherever she is right now. I'm not telling her about Randy. Hopefully we can set up a Skype call and I'll tell her then."

"I wonder if he laughed at the wrong person," Eileen said. "People don't like being laughed at."

We ended the conversation. Lorraine hadn't touched base, and I didn't feel up to multiple phone conversations, so I gave her the news in an email.

I switched off the light and sat in the recliner I had in my den. Morris jumped on my lap and curled up. I mused on Eileen's last words.

Did Randy die laughing? Can laughing kill you?

EIGHT

The Thin Blue Line sculpture greeted Vince and me on Monday morning. The oversized stainless steel sculpture of a police officer's head was attached to the gray wall of the police headquarters building in downtown Richmond, making a striking contrast to the blank expanse of the wall. A thin blue line draped over the officer's cap and down his face, bisecting the sculpture.

When we left the building after signing our statements, we ran into Claudia Marlowe. After exchanging greetings and expressions of shock and dismay about Randy Zimmerman's fate, Claudia said, "I heard you two found him."

"Yes." I gave a bare-bones account of picking up Randy's notebook by accident, leading to the grim discovery of his body. The front page of the day's *Richmond Times-Dispatch* featured an article about the murder. Like on the news broadcast, the writer named Vince and me discoverers of the victim. "How come you're here?" I asked.

"Oh, I don't know." Claudia flapped a hand. A tall, large-framed woman, she wore a loose-fitting beige sweater, black jeans, and black suede boots. Her reddish-brown hair, cut in a swingy style, brushed her collar. "Detective Fischella thinks I have information about Randy. I don't, of course. But it's always good to stay on the right side of these law enforcement types." She shot a playful look at Vince.

Most likely, Felicia Brimwell had told Fish about the slapping incident in the Richmond Books café and now Fish wanted Claudia's account. I didn't let on that I had such information, and neither did Vince.

"It'll be interesting to hear what she says about her little assault," I said to Vince once we left Claudia and walked down Grace Street to the car.

—

"It's a wonder someone didn't kill him before now. He was so obnoxious." Trudy's voice took on a wistful quality. "Still, it's hard to believe someone actually did it."

"I know." I stretched out on the sofa in the family room, wishing I could come up with the right words for the ex-wife of a murder victim.

After seeing the email I sent the night before, Trudy had checked the Richmond news online. "I figured something must have happened for you to get in touch and want to Skype." Despite having to deal with distressing news, Trudy looked rested. She piled her long white hair on top of her head. Metal earrings of an intricate design dangled from her ears and a rose tattoo decorated the side of her neck. "Go ahead, tell me what you know," she said.

I started with finding Randy's body and included the bits and pieces of information from Vince's conversation with Dennis. Then I described meeting Randy and Matt at Richmond Books.

"That was Randy," Trudy said. "No filter."

The "no filter" reminded me of Randy's cheerful prediction that someday I might be investigating his murder. "I don't have a filter" and "I can really piss people off" were two statements he'd made with a note of braggadocio. I didn't imagine he expected "someday" to be that very day.

"You're kidding! Claudia slapped Randy? Did you tell Fish about it?"

"Yes, and I guess he called Felicia Brimwell for a firsthand account. Vince and I met Claudia going into headquarters this morning. She was cagey about why Fish had called her in, but I'm guessing he wanted to question her about the assault."

"You say Joyce was away at a spa?"

"Yeah, she got home sometime last night after we left. I don't know where she is now. How was their marriage going?"

"I have no idea. I haven't seen or talked to Randy in a few years, not since he married. We're friends on Facebook, but he didn't post that much." Trudy sighed. "I can't believe he's dead."

"I know. It's hard to take in."

"I'm flashing back to this bus trip Randy and I took. I guess because I'm on one now and have buses on the brain. Anyway, let me tell you about it." Trudy paused for a moment before starting. "We were in Germany—no, Belgium. The bus came upon this guy lying in the middle of the road. The driver stopped, and he and the tour guide moved the guy to the side of the road and called the Belgian version of EMTs. Apparently, the guy was drunk and destitute. Randy started ranting about how we should just leave him in the road, why should we care, etc.

"People had been steering clear of us, but it got worse after that performance. He'd always embarrassed me and I spent a lot of energy trying to change him."

"Yes, lots of us have done that." Had I? The introspection of my five marriages and numerous relationships would have to wait. Hubby number five appeared, mouthing that he'd be on a conference call for a while.

Trudy continued. "I knew then that I should leave. He was such a jerk. But I didn't want to be alone. I finally did leave and I've been alone for going on twenty years. It's been fine."

Trudy rarely ventured into the world of dating. Some people didn't, especially after a bad marriage. She came close to a second marriage on a cruise, but her intended dumped her for another passenger.

"Do the rest of the book group know what happened?" Trudy asked.

"Oh, yes."

"Well, keep me posted. I suppose I should get in touch with Matt. I've already talked to Randy's sister."

"How is she doing?"

"In shock."

"I can imagine. Any word yet on funeral plans?"

"The funeral will be private, family only. There will be a memorial service, but it isn't scheduled yet."

"Are you coming back for that?"

"No."

When Trudy didn't expand on her "no," I changed the subject. "How's Sarah? And tell me about your trip. Are you in Croatia now?"

"Sarah's doing great and yes, we're in Croatia. We just finished touring the Diocletian's Palace in Split and we start for Dubrovnik in about fifteen minutes." She described the sights of Croatia, a country on my bucket list.

After we ended the call, I reflected on the brevity of life. Briefer for some than for others.

NINE

The hilly streets of Bon Air always gave me a good workout, and I wanted to enjoy autumn while the trees still blazed with color. Once outside, I inhaled the scent I associated with the season, something woodsy, flinty.

What I didn't expect, but probably should have, was the excitement my appearance on the street caused. Neighbors who hibernated in all seasons emerged from their homes, eager for the gory details about Randy. Their expressions of compassion for my ordeal— "I simply can't imagine finding a dead body" —were sincere, but clearly a necessary prelude to getting the lowdown. The word "vulture" came to mind more than once.

After telling and retelling my tale many times over, I got smart and started walking away. Since not everyone was a fan of walking hills, they left me on my own and didn't follow.

Leaves crunched under my feet as I walked and snapped pictures of the fiery foliage. It was hard to believe the reds, golds, and oranges of fall symbolized death. Death. Randy. My thoughts refused to stray from the man or his dead body. A search through his social media accounts might yield hints about who ended his life.

I arrived home without being waylaid by neighbors and uploaded my foliage pictures to Instagram and Facebook. Friends and followers on social media always clicked "like" on postings of outdoor images.

When Vince came downstairs and joined me at the kitchen table, I said, "Wait'll you hear about this bus trip."

He listened as I repeated Trudy's account of Randy's boorish behavior. Shaking his head, he said, "That verifies Randy's insensitivity. She was married to the guy for how long?"

"A while. Fifteen years or so."

"Too long to stick with such a jackass."

"Well, she did leave him. Better late than never." We laughed at my lack of originality. One might think being a writer made me more eloquent in conversation. Not so.

I sipped my coffee, an Arabica brew Vince had discovered at a local Big Lots store. "God only knows how he treated his clients. Maybe one of them killed him."

Vince raked his fingers through his snowy white hair. "It's more likely that defendants would seek revenge."

"Yeah, I guess the person being sued would have a stronger motive. Are the police looking into those folks?"

Vince smiled. "They are. There are many people to question: Richmond Books customers, Randy's neighbors, his office staff. Probably your friend Lorraine."

"Lorraine. Hmm. She has as good a motive as anyone—including me. Randy was really nasty about her writing." I rummaged through the refrigerator for lunch possibilities. "How about some of this mushroom barley soup? We need to eat it before it goes bad."

Vince snickered. "You make it sound so appetizing. Sure, I'll have some."

I put the soup in the microwave and set the timer for four minutes. "I got an email from Lorraine. She didn't read the message I sent last night and didn't watch the news. So Fish pretty much startled her when he called, wanting to interview her about her conversation with Randy on Saturday. Not that they had much of one."

"Hmm" served as Vince's shorthand response.

"She said she'd let me know how the interview goes." I set spoons and napkins on the table and sat. "How will the police know who all the Richmond Books customers are?"

"They have a copy of Claudia's sign-in sheet for her mailing list, and—"

"Yes, but most of the people in line were probably already on her list."

"If you'd let me finish, I'd tell you they can get names from credit and debit card statements."

"That's true. The book titles show on the receipts. But what if the customers paid cash?"

"That could be a problem."

"What about Sherry as a possible culprit?"

"The sweater girl?" Vince smiled. "Did you tell Fish about her?"

"Yes. I didn't know her last name, though. Maybe she signed up for Claudia's list." We fell silent for a moment. "I hope Fish doesn't still think I went over to Randy's house and did him in because he dissed my writing. Do people kill over stuff like that?"

"You yourself said Lorraine had a motive because Randy laughed at her writing."

"Yeah, I did say that. I don't know Lorraine well enough to judge her mental state. I mean, she's a bit scatty, but seems mentally healthy enough. But people don't like to be ridiculed, especially in public. As for me, I'm not unhinged enough to kill."

"I'm only telling you the way my former colleagues think. They can't make assumptions about your mental health. If they find out you're upset about being dropped by your publisher and then having to endure Randy's ribbing, they might look at you. And you could have had prior knowledge that his wife would be away. He might have mentioned it at the store."

I threw up my hands in frustration. "But I have an alibi. We were at Thai Garden. You gave Fish the receipt."

"My word wouldn't mean much to Fish in this case. I'm your husband before I'm a colleague." Vince reached across the table and covered my hand with his. "But we saw quite a few people on Saturday night who can verify your alibi."

"It would help if we knew what happened with Claudia and Randy. Specifically: why did she slap him?"

The microwave chimed. I dished the soup into small bowls and set them on the table. We suspended talk of murder, taking time to enjoy the savory mixture of barley, mushrooms, carrots, and onions. My recipe closely matched the famous one from Langer's Delicatessen in Los Angeles—so closely, that one wouldn't be able to tell them apart in a blind taste test. When we finished, Vince took the dishes to the sink.

"Fish needs proof, right?" I asked.

"Right."

"Then I'll have to come up with some."

"Hazel . . ."

I ignored his warning tone. "I'm not going to sit back and let innocent people be murder suspects. I'll get the book group in on this. Trudy would like to know who killed her ex."

"Remember what happened the other times you played detective."

I groaned. "I remember."

TEN

My scouring the Internet for clues about Randy's killer yielded nothing. Facebook had been it as far as his social media activity, and he had only posted sporadically, mostly about football and get-togethers in bars. His personal Facebook messages could reveal something helpful, but as personal messages were, well, *personal*, I didn't have access. That was a job for Fish. My job was converting my romance into a mystery. Detective work was a hard-to-resist temptation, but I gave resistance my best effort and, over the next three hours, buckled down and made progress on my writing.

I kept the Costa Rica setting from my original story and changed my fictional couple to one modeled after Nick and Nora Charles of *Thin Man* fame. My sleuths would solve the murder of a tourist from Argentina.

Vince and I had married in Costa Rica and revisited earlier this year. The trip was part research for me, part second honeymoon for us. The Central Valley town of Grecia featured a unique red metal church. I could murder one of the many tourists who traipse through such churches—namely, the man from Argentina.

My thoughts continued to drift to the subject of Randy and who ended his life. When I heard Vince talking to Dennis, I abandoned my literary attempts for the latest on the investigation. Standing in the doorway of my husband's den, I listened to the one-sided conversation.

Vince said, "Talk to you later," pressed the end button, and shook his head. "Randy threatened her. Claudia."

"He threatened her? How? Details, please."

"When Claudia told him his book still needed a lot of work, he said, 'How 'bout if you write it, Claudia?' "

"You mean ghostwrite?"

"Yes. She refused, said she didn't have time, and that she wasn't a ghostwriter. He offered to top the going rate, but she still said no. That's when he threatened her."

"With what?"

"Said he was going to ruin her life, mainly by telling her husband they'd had an affair. He'd tell her mother, too."

"That would strike fear into her. I don't know about her husband, but she's terrified of her mother. She's always threatening to write her kids out of her will if they step out of line. There's a fortune at stake, so Claudia is kind of tied to her mother's purse strings."

When Claudia's father died and her mother whisked the family away to Baltimore, the mother launched a line of health and beauty products. The business became a huge success.

"Anyway," Vince said, "That's when she slapped him, after the threat."

"That means she has a motive. Does she have an alibi for Saturday evening?"

"Says she was babysitting for her two-year-old grandson."

"Can anyone verify that?"

"Yes and no. Her daughter and son-in-law left the kid with her, but they can't say what she did after they left."

"I'm sure she didn't take the kid with her on a killing mission." Then I remembered something Vince said a moment before. "You said Claudia *still* thought Randy's book needed a lot of work. Had she critiqued an earlier version?"

"Yes, sorry. I guess I should have started at the beginning. She met Randy last summer at a James River Writers event. When he told her he was an attorney, she asked if she could interview him for a story she was writing."

Morris jumped on Vince's lap and perched on his knee.

Vince continued. "They met for coffee and she interviewed him. When he said he'd written a legal thriller, he asked her to critique it. She read it and thought it was terrible."

"And I'm guessing he didn't take her critique too well."

"No. He laughed, said she was afraid of a little competition. Then he left."

"Left where?"

"She couldn't remember, but thinks it was a Starbucks." Vince stroked Morris's back. The cat didn't object. "But later he apologized for leaving. They met a few more times and went over the story, discussing ways to improve it.

"She didn't hear from him for a few months until he signed up for her class. He emailed her his latest manuscript, saying he'd rewritten it. Said he'd see her at her signing, the one at Richmond Books from the other day. He was anxious to know what she thought of his latest version."

"And that brings us to the threats?"

"Right."

"Now for your friend Lorraine. She told Fish pretty much what you told him about Randy—he was rude and disrespectful to both of you. As for her alibi, she was visiting her mother at her retirement place. She signed in at the reception desk at six and signed out at nine."

"And Randy was killed between six and eight," I said. "But those hours have a margin of error. She still could have done it. But it's like with Claudia fitting in a murder around babysitting. Do you murder someone right before, or after, visiting your mom?"

"Many criminals lead pretty ordinary lives. Especially the amateur ones."

"I guess. Do you suppose Randy and Claudia *did* have an affair?"

"She says no."

"Well, she would, wouldn't she?"

"Unless an eyewitness comes forth with evidence, we may never know for sure. It was a 'he said, she said' sort of thing."

"And he's no longer saying *anything*."

While waiting for dinner to cook, I called Lucy to catch up on the news of the day.

"Rich and controlling, not a good combination," she said when I told her about Randy threatening to tell Claudia's mother about their affair—an affair that may, or may not, have happened. "Our mothers had their faults, but I don't think they'd have got up in arms about us having affairs. Especially in our fifties and sixties."

I laughed, remembering Lucy's mother and mine, who had been sisters. "They would have been green with envy."

"I'm guessing that at some point Claudia shared her feelings about her mother with Randy."

"And he used the knowledge to his advantage." I took plates from the cabinet and started setting the kitchen table. "Essentially, he blackmailed her. Let's face it, Claudia had plenty of motive. But it doesn't mean she did it."

"I stopped at headquarters on my way home—just a minute, Hazel." After a muffled conversation between Lucy and someone else—presumably her husband, Dave—she was back.

"Sorry. Where was I? Oh yeah, I stopped at headquarters on my way home to give Detective Garcia a statement about my business relationship with Randy. Believe me, it was a short statement. I was in and out of there in fifteen minutes. Like I told you, I dealt with his office manager, and rarely saw Randy himself."

Vince came into the kitchen to check on the turkey burgers that sizzled under the broiler. The aroma of onions, peppers, and garlic filled not only the air, but me with anticipation.

"Before I forget—let's not mention my publisher dropping me during the writing class tomorrow." I set knives, forks, and napkins beside the plates. "It gives me a motive for killing Randy and I don't need anyone telling Fish about it. As it is, I'm a minor suspect. I hope minor, anyway."

"Person of interest is more likely," Lucy said. "Don't worry about me saying anything. Mum's the word."

ELEVEN

On Election Day, Vince and I walked to our polling precinct through an on-again, off-again drizzle. Our civic duty fulfilled, I posted a selfie of us sporting "I Voted" stickers on Instagram and Facebook.

Vince left for the Library of Virginia, planning to spend the day researching for his work in progress. I made headway on transitioning my romance into a mystery. When my body demanded a break, I put on my athletic shoes and headed outdoors for another walk. As most of my neighbors had buttonholed me the day before about Randy and his untimely death, I only had to go over the account twice before being allowed to walk in peace.

The cats enjoyed tidbits of the turkey sandwich I fixed for lunch. Did Randy and Joyce have pets? If they were the talking kind, we could bribe them with a piece of turkey into revealing the killer.

Creative investigating. I liked the sound of it.

The writing class met in one of Richmond's newest libraries, a building composed mostly of glass. When Lucy quoted the expression "those who live in glass houses shouldn't throw stones," I said, "I sure hope no one throws a stone through one of these glass walls, especially not with our class in session."

We passed the circulation desk and took the long, curving staircase to the lower level. The place was hushed. Surprising, as many libraries served as community hubs and were anything but quiet.

In a conference room, three tables were arranged in a standard horseshoe pattern. Lorraine and Matt huddled together, talking quietly. Lucy and I took seats at the table across from them. Claudia set up her PowerPoint presentation.

"Will you sign our books?" Lucy asked as she pulled Claudia's tome from her messenger bag. "Your line was so long the other day."

"Of course." Claudia assumed the role of gracious author and autographed Lucy's copy of *Virginia Menace*, as well as mine. "Sorry about the line."

"Don't be," I said. "It's a good problem to have."

Eileen Thompson breezed in and plopped down next to Lucy and me. "I thought I'd be late," she said breathlessly.

Lucy smiled. "You made it with seconds to spare."

Claudia, clad in a sage green pants suit and low-heeled pumps, took roll call. As soon as she said "Matt Rowan," I remembered Randy using that last name when he introduced us at Richmond Books.

"And now . . ." Claudia took a deep breath. "I'm sure you've all heard the news about Randy Zimmerman. He would have been the sixth student in this class. I think some of you knew him."

Matt looked up from his phone. "Randy and I were friends since first grade. We were neighbors. We—" His voice caught, but he finished his thought. "We went to grade school, high school, college, and law school together."

"I'm sorry for your loss," Claudia said. We echoed her condolences. "We don't need to discuss this further."

"No, it's fine to talk about him. I'd love for the police to find the scum who did it."

"How about the rest of you?" Claudia asked. "Any of you knew Randy?"

"I met him and Matt on Saturday at Richmond Books," I said. "And I had the misfortune . . ." I trailed off, unable to finish my sentence. Matt stared at me and I felt my face flush under his scrutiny.

"Oh dear, I'm so sorry, Hazel," Claudia said. "For a minute, I forgot about you and Vince finding Randy. We won't go into that. Lorraine?"

"I met them the same time Hazel did," Lorraine said, nodding toward Matt.

"Randy was one of my clients," Lucy said. For Matt's benefit, she explained that she managed the staffing firm that kept Randy's office up and running.

"I met him a few times, years ago," Eileen said. "I worked with Trudy Zimmerman, his ex."

"Is that the Trudy in your book group?" Claudia asked.

"It is," Eileen said.

"Funny, I didn't know she was his ex. I met Randy a while back at a writing event. He told me he was one of my biggest fans. We met a few times to discuss his manuscript and last week he sent me the finished version. I hope someone publishes it posthumously. It's a legal thriller, quite interesting—"

I nudged Lucy. Claudia had told the police that Randy's writing efforts were "terrible." Now she found them "interesting." Perhaps she used interesting as a euphemism for terrible? I think Claudia caught the nudge, because she faltered, said, "I sure hope they find his killer," and left the subject of Randy.

"And now I'd like for each of you to tell us what brings you here. Hazel, let's start with you."

"Most fiction has elements of mystery and romance," Claudia said when I stated my intention of switching from romances into mysteries. "Hazel's been in a long-running mystery book group, so she's more than qualified to turn out a mystery."

"Yes, I'm excited about it," I said. "I've been thinking of doing that for a while. Broaden my scope, so to speak."

"Hazel, tell us about your story idea," Eileen said, twirling a lock of curly brown hair around her finger.

"It's along the lines of *The Thin Man*. Lots of humor, lots of romance, but not as much alcohol."

"It's hard to imagine *The Thin Man* without alcohol," Matt said.

"I loved *The Thin Man*," Claudia said. "William Powell and Myrna Loy were perfect in that."

"I watched an episode of the TV series on YouTube," I said.

"There was a TV series?" Lorraine asked.

"Yes, in the late fifties. It starred Peter Lawford and Phyllis Kirk. Oh, and Asta the dog."

Claudia checked her watch. "Okay, we need to move on. How about you, Lorraine? Tell us what brings you here."

One by one, we described our writing experience and what we hoped to gain from the class. Lorraine wanted to write "something terrific." She mentioned publishing the quilting mystery, but planned to abandon the series that really wasn't a series at all. Lucy described her idea of a client being murdered in a corporate setting.

"Will you use your experience as a placement expert?" Claudia asked.

"Yes," Lucy said. "I figure I'll follow the 'write what you know' advice, at least for my first attempt."

Eileen had a manuscript she'd worked on for so long that it had originally been on a floppy disk. "I have a first draft of a noirish story about a Richmond-area private investigator," she said. "She's clean-living and chases down types who aren't at all clean-living." As Eileen was clean-living, I guessed her PI took after her.

Matt said he was a trademark lawyer. Like Randy, he'd turned out a legal thriller, this one set in the late nineteenth century. Matt slid his finger up and down the screen of his phone while he talked. Teenagers weren't as riveted to their phones as he was.

Claudia smiled. "Thank you for sharing your plans and for taking this class. Full disclosure: Hazel and I were neighbors many years ago in New Jersey, before my mother whisked our family away to Baltimore."

This wasn't news to those of us in the book group, but it was to Matt, who appeared somewhat surprised, but not especially interested in the "full disclosure."

Claudia went on with a synopsis of her career and writing credentials. "I lived in Baltimore for many years and was a stay-at-home mom. I devoured mysteries, especially police procedurals. Then in the early nineties, I took a writing class. The rest is history. To date, I've written twenty-three books in the Astrid Gordon series. Astrid is a Baltimore-based homicide detective and solves cold cases at an impressive rate. Much more impressive than her real-life counterparts." We joined Claudia in a laugh over the high success rate of fictional crime solving.

Would Randy's murder become a cold case? Perhaps someone in this class should pen a fictional account of his murder, complete with the killer being led away in handcuffs.

Sometimes we have to take justice anyway we can.

TWELVE

When Claudia announced a break, Lucy and I walked upstairs to the library's lobby and sat on an upholstered bench.

"I like those boots," Lucy said. "Are they new?"

"New to me." I extended my leg and flexed a foot in my black leather ankle boot. "I found them at Luxor's the other night when Vince and I went out for dinner in Carytown. Twenty-four dollars."

"Oh, is Luxor that vintage clothing place?" Lucy wrapped her hunter green shawl closer around her as the sliding glass doors opened and closed, letting in the chill evening air.

"Yes. Vince calls these squared-off toes roach killers."

Lucy laughed. "Roach killer boots are pointier. Still, a roach wouldn't stand a chance with yours. You could give a person a good swift kick you know where."

Eileen joined us. "Tell me what's going on. Any news about Randy?"

"Things don't sound good for Claudia," Eileen said once Lucy and I filled her in.

"I know, but I sure hope it isn't her." I explained to Eileen about my family's debt to Claudia. "I need to prove her guilt or innocence. Preferably innocence."

Lucy fiddled with a diamond earring. "Did you notice she said Randy's story was interesting, but she told Fish it was terrible?"

"Yeah, she hopes it gets published posthumously," Eileen said, adding, "Maybe she doesn't want to speak ill of the dead."

I laughed. "Yeah, that must be it."

Eileen took off her tortoise shell-framed glasses and cleaned the lenses with a corner of her skirt. "We're kind of an old group here, everyone in the fifty to seventy age range," she said. "No Millennials. Don't young people write?"

Lucy grinned. "Apparently not in this town."

The sliding doors opened again, this time admitting Claudia and Matt. "Time to go back," Claudia said, heels clicking as she passed us.

"Let's get started," Claudia said once we reassembled in the conference room. "But first, I must ask you to silence your phones—or put them on vibrate mode. If you have an emergency, you may excuse yourselves and go upstairs to the lobby."

Matt looked pained, but he complied with Claudia's wishes and dropped his phone in his pocket.

Claudia summarized her syllabus. "We have a lot to cover in six weeks: setting, dialogue, character development, plotting, editing, publishing. I also cover these topics in my webinars. You can find information about them on my website."

"You should take a look at her webinars," I said. "They're quite good. Thorough."

Claudia beamed at my testimonial. "Thank you, Hazel." She launched PowerPoint to present her lecture on setting. A slide listing bulleted items appeared on a screen.

"Setting is an important part of your story, especially if you're planning a series. Your setting could be anywhere—ocean, mountains, desert, a city or a small town. It could be in the United States or in another country altogether."

"But don't most authors set their stories where they live?" Lorraine asked.

"Most do, but not all. The setting could also be a place an author knows well."

"The writing team of Sparkle Abbey sets their mysteries in Southern California, but they live in Iowa," Lucy said.

"And you're free to do the same, but be sure to keep up with current events and try to visit your chosen settings often."

Claudia continued. "Settings offer distinctive aspects you can work into your plot, such as climate, economics, politics, religion, food, transportation, entertainment, education . . ." She went on with a litany of features that we could work into our stories to make them come alive and be authentic.

"You mentioned politics and religion," Eileen said. "Shouldn't we avoid those subjects?"

"You need to be careful when writing about politics. If you sound at all partisan, you risk alienating half your readers. People are sensitive, especially in this day and age. The same holds true for religion and for social issues in general. I'm not telling you to stay away from those topics, but be careful."

Claudia proceeded to the next slide. "You'll often hear the advice to make your setting a character in your novel. One way to do that is to find something unique in the setting." After expounding on this idea, Claudia gave us fifteen minutes to write a setting description.

"Remember to bring in the five senses. Let the reader see, smell, taste, feel, and hear the place where your characters are at any point in the story. Can they 'hear' the roar of the ocean? Can they 'smell' the hot dogs from the vendor carts in Manhattan?"

Settings weren't my strong suit, and neither were writing exercises. Mine could best be described as stream of consciousness, a writing device that gave readers a glimpse of the thoughts and feelings of a character as they occurred. I associated stream of consciousness with authors like Virginia Woolf and James Joyce. I held no illusions that my ramblings would topple either of those literary giants.

But, since I'd set my romance-turned-mystery in Costa Rica and had worked on it recently, coming up with a decent description of a bird-watching cruise was easy enough.

Except for Lorraine, we all made decent attempts. Although she chose a Richmond coffee shop for her setting, not one of my five senses perked up as she read her short effort. Taking this class was a good decision on her part, a start in improving her craft.

At nine-thirty, Claudia gave us our assignments for the following week: write a scene with two strangers talking at a bus stop.

"Hazel, aren't you giving a workshop on writing soon?" Eileen asked.

"Yes, on romance writing. I forget the exact date, but it's the Wednesday after Thanksgiving at one o'clock, at the downtown branch of the Richmond Public Library. I've taught it before and always have a good turnout."

After fielding a couple of questions about the workshop, I stood to leave. I stopped Lorraine on her way out of the room and asked, "Lorraine, are you still up for lunch on Friday at the Grapevine?"

"Sure, Hazel. See you there at noon."

"Oh, Lorraine—" I remembered my promise to send her the photos from Richmond Books and was about to tell her I'd email them when I got home. Although with Randy dead, it seemed in poor taste. Besides, Lorraine had displayed no interest in mementos of the occasion.

"What is it, Hazel?"

"Oh—never mind. Nothing important. See you on Friday."

Lorraine knitted her brow. After a beat, she said "Okay," drawing out the "Okay."

Claudia, busy packing up her messenger bag, said, "Hazel and Lucy, do you have a minute?"

"Sure," I said. "What's up?"

"You have to help me! I think they're going to arrest me."

The door to the conference room stood open. No doubt Claudia's voice carried to anyone standing outside or passing by. "Claudia, you need to keep your voice down," I cautioned.

"Can we meet somewhere to talk? Tomorrow morning?"

"I don't know how we can help you, Claudia."

"Please." Her pleading look made me think of the cats, lobbying for treats.

"Fine with me. How about you, Lucy?"

Lucy nodded. "I have to be at the office by nine-thirty. How about eight at Café Sweetbrew on Forest Hill?"

Claudia hesitated. I imagined she was hoping to meet closer to her home in Short Pump. But as Lucy was the one with a business schedule, we needed to cater to her.

Claudia nodded. "Thanks so much. See you then."

On the way to the car, Lucy said, "I bet she wants us to find Randy's killer."

"That's my guess." I pulled my keys from my purse. "I noticed she didn't mention the little tiff with Randy in the café. But I guess we can't blame her for omitting incriminating details, especially to a class she's teaching."

"True."

"I do want to help her. Now that I have this opportunity to pay off this family debt . . ."

"I understand, Hazel. But just because she rescued Madeline decades ago doesn't mean she didn't kill Randy."

"Yeah, you're right. We need to be careful with her. So let's not let on that we know anything beyond what's been in the news. Play dumb."

"No problem," Lucy said with a laugh. "I can play dumb."

THIRTEEN

"Hazel, are you going to investigate Randy's murder?" Matt Rowan came around a behemoth SUV parked next to my car.

"Excuse me?"

"I couldn't help overhearing your conversation with Claudia. And your conversation just now. You're meeting her tomorrow at Café Sweetbrew."

And I thought the man only had eyes, and ears, for his iPhone.

"Claudia's a friend. Lucy and I are going to see what's up with her and offer our support. That doesn't mean we're investigating."

"It's not every day that you run into someone, an ordinary citizen, who solves murders. You should be proud of your accomplishments."

I laughed, but said nothing.

"Randy said you solved Carlene Arness's murder. Why not solve his as well?"

"Once is more than enough." The mere memory of that scene when I faced the business end of a gun made me shudder. "And that was a long time ago."

Matt's eyes narrowed. "Why were you at Randy's the other day? I didn't think you two hit it off on Saturday."

After explaining about picking up Randy's notebook by accident, I added, "I took my husband with me." No need for Matt to think I was visiting Randy for a rendezvous.

"Yes, he was mentioned in the article." Looking like he suddenly remembered something, Matt said, "The other day, Randy mentioned a murder you investigated at a redneck bar. So that makes two."

"Okay, there were two. Flukes, both of them." Matt alluded to my second crime-solving adventure when I also found myself in a harrowing situation.

Lucy intervened. "Hazel was motivated in those cases. Carlene Arness was a friend and she died at a meeting of our book group. *Years* later, Roxanne Howard was murdered in the parking lot of the Moonshine Inn. She was married to Hazel's cousin, and he was the prime suspect. Friendship drove the first case, family drove the second."

The Moonshine Inn, on Richmond's Southside, attracted an unruly crowd—one that had included my cousin's wife, a top-level executive who visited the place in business attire.

"Lucy's right," I said. "I *knew* those victims. I just met Randy three days ago at Richmond Books."

"And he ripped your writing to shreds. Lorraine's as well. That makes both of you suspects, and I'm sure you want to clear your own name, if not Lorraine's. And it sounds like you owe a debt to Claudia."

First Fish suspecting me, now Matt. "You think *I* killed Randy?" My voice rose. "If I killed everyone who ripped my writing to shreds—"

"But this wasn't on Amazon. It was in Richmond Books, a public place."

Matt moved closer, his hard-as-marble dark eyes focused on me. Despite feeling unsettled, I stared back, willing myself not to flinch.

Lucy took out her phone.

"If I find out that you killed my friend—"

"You'll what? Are you threatening me, Matt?" What was I doing, facing down a man his size?

"Calm down, both of you," Lucy ordered.

Matt took a few steps back and held up his hands. "Look, I'm sorry. It's just that . . ."

"I know," I said. "You lost a dear friend in a horrific way. I can't imagine what that must be like. But you know, I've found myself in some tough spots and I don't care for replays. I repeat—I'm *not* investigating. I have full confidence in the police. And I did *not* kill Randy."

"How about Lorraine?" Matt asked. "Could she have done it?"

"I can't speak for Lorraine. But I can't see her killing anyone. Can you, Lucy?"

"Not hardly."

"Anyone has the capacity to kill, given the right motivation," Matt said. "And there's Claudia. You must think she had a motive if you suspect her. What's this about a tiff in the café?"

"Nothing. It's hearsay." Maybe tossing out a legal term could redirect the conversation.

"Why do you owe a debt to Claudia?"

"That's none of your business," I said. "I'm not sure any of what you're asking is."

Lucy jumped into the fray. "Do you think there might be others who could have done it?"

"Oh, sure. Defendants in lawsuits come to mind. Randy seldom lost a case. He was a damn good lawyer, one of the best."

"And your specialty is trademark law, you said?"

I looked at Lucy. Was she fishing for a new client or diverting Matt's attention?

"Yes, I'm with Hannan and Hannan. Let me give you my card." The three of us swapped business cards. I dropped Matt's in a side pocket of my purse.

"Do you think it's okay if we go to the memorial service?" Lucy asked. "Trudy's out of the country. She talked to Randy's sister, but she won't be able to attend the service."

"Oh, sure. You're more than welcome. I don't think it's an invitation affair. If it is, I'll make sure you two get on the list. It should be a great place to troll for suspects."

"Let us know when it is," I said, ignoring the trolling comment.

Matt's gaze lingered on me. "If you're so great at solving murders, let's see you solve Randy's." With that, he climbed into his SUV and started the engine.

Lucy gave a short laugh. "No matter what you say, he's convinced you're going to investigate."

"He sure is. He's also convinced that I killed Randy. Or that Lorraine or Claudia did."

"I don't think he's convinced of anything. Just spouting off."

In my car, Lucy said, "I didn't like the way he looked at you. Or spoke to you. Kind of menacing."

"Yeah, but he backed off. I bet your taking out your phone mitigated the situation."

"I think we should give Matt a wide berth. He may be overly emotional at the moment, but that could make him dangerous."

"Maybe he killed Randy."

"Maybe. But why would he?"

"Beats me."

Election returns wracked my nerves. I preferred waiting for the ultimate results. Knowing this, Vince switched to *Music Choice* when I came home and joined him in the family room.

"Tell me about your class," he said.

I ran down the details of the evening. "I think that's everything. Matt—you know, Randy's friend—he gave us all copies of his manuscript."

I omitted the parking lot conversation with Matt. I'd see what happened the next time the two of us met. No sense getting Vince riled.

"Funny thing," I said. "No one mentioned the election. But a few of us had these *I Voted* stickers."

Vince stood. "Do you want something to eat? Coconut gelato?"

"I shouldn't. It's getting late. But . . . okay."

"Don't let me twist your arm."

Minutes later, I savored my creamy coconut concoction, enjoying the soothing sounds of the Easy Listening channel on *Music Choice*.

"Vince . . . I have to tell you something."

"Yes?" My husband sounded wary.

"It's Claudia. She wants to meet Lucy and me tomorrow at Café Sweetbrew. She's afraid she's going to be arrested for Randy's murder and she wants our help."

"And you want to help her because of this decades-old obligation?"

"Yes, there's that. But I'm curious about what she has to say. After all, she might not have told the police everything. Lucy will be with me and we already talked about playing dumb, not admitting that we know anything. Remember, I'm also concerned about myself. We talked about that yesterday, about my being a suspect."

"Let the police do their jobs. Just because Claudia saved your sister's life doesn't mean she didn't take Randy's."

"Do I hear an echo? Lucy said the same thing earlier." I finished my dessert and scraped the sides of the dish. "You know, this might be good for my writing."

Vince sighed. "Can't you use your imagination? How many mystery writers solve actual murders?"

At least one, I thought with a smile.

FOURTEEN

In this day and age, there was no good reason to die from a lack of coffee. Virtually every neighborhood boasted an establishment dedicated to the fragrant brew. Café Sweetbrew served hand-crafted beverages to the coffee fanatics of Westover Hills, and was no more than two minutes from Randy's house.

Did Joyce Zimmerman frequent the place? Would I even recognize her from the fuzzy wedding picture on Randy's Facebook page? Couldn't he have come up with a better picture to showcase their wedding day? Or found someone with Photoshop skills?

The place was jumping as customers prepared for the rigors of the day with copious amounts of caffeine. I joined the line at the counter.

Besides coffee drinks, Café Sweetbrew offered sandwiches, pastries, ice cream, and even deli meats by the pound. How did they fare with the deli meats? How many latte addicts suddenly realized they were fresh out of cold cuts?

As I picked up my latte and bagel, Lucy and Claudia came through the door. I headed for a window table, narrowly avoiding a collision with another customer.

A few minutes later, Lucy and Claudia joined me. Claudia was in a dither, going back and forth for napkins and cinnamon for her latte. Then she toppled the latte, sending Lucy and me scurrying for more napkins. Once we wiped up the spill, Claudia went to collect her replacement latte.

She finally settled at the table. "Sorry about all that," she said with a laugh. "Thanks so much for meeting with me."

A woman with light brown hair and oversized tinted glasses took a seat at the next table, hitting Claudia's chair in the process. "Sorry," she said in a gruff voice as she sat, her back to us. I admired the deep rose pashmina draped around her shoulders, but not her matted hair, done up in a messy bun. Bed hair from a night of passion?

Claudia drew my attention from the disheveled woman to the matter at hand. "Hazel, tell me what you know about Randy's murder. Vince must still have his contacts in the police department."

I laughed. "You think he tells me anything? All I know is that they haven't arrested anyone. Yet."

"Have you talked to the police?"

"Why, yes, I did. After all, Vince and I found Randy's body."

"Oh, of course. I saw you two at police headquarters." Claudia went on with her probing. "What about you, Lucy? Did you talk to the police?"

"Yes. I talked to Randy at Richmond Books. I mentioned last night that he was one of my clients. I made a statement but I'm sure it wasn't helpful."

"I didn't kill him," Claudia announced.

"Did someone, like the police, say you did?" I spread a layer of cream cheese on my bagel.

"Well . . ." She hesitated, smiled, looked out the window. After another smile, she took the plunge. "On Saturday, after the signing, Randy and I had coffee in the Richmond Books café. Things got heated between us."

"How so?" Lucy asked.

"Let me give you a little background. During the summer, Randy and I met every week or so to critique his story. Suddenly we stopped meeting. He wouldn't answer my emails. Then two weeks ago he registers for my class. Last week he sends me his manuscript, wanting me to critique it. After ignoring me since August. Really fried me. Saturday was the first time I'd seen him since August. I let him have it."

"What did he say?"

"He laughed at me."

There was that laughing motive again. Had Claudia killed Randy because he laughed at her?

"And?" I asked.

"And what?" Claudia gripped her cheese Danish so hard it crumbled through her fingers.

"What else happened?"

Claudia shot me a shrewd look as she wiped her fingers. Did she guess I knew more about what had gone down in the café than she'd revealed? "Okay, he wanted me to rescue his dreary story."

She told an account that squared with what she'd told the police. "He said he'd tell my husband and mother *everything* if I didn't agree to be his ghostwriter. I don't know what he even meant by *everything*. There's nothing to tell. That's when I hit him."

"You hit him?" Lucy's pewter eyes opened wide. My cousin wasn't kidding when she said she knew how to play dumb.

"Yes. I so regretted it."

"Did you apologize?"

"No." A wistful note crept into Claudia's voice. "I never had the chance."

"Did you tell the police about the argument?"

"Of *course*. But I didn't kill him."

"Someone sure did," I said. "And believe me, it wasn't a pretty sight."

"Yes, I'm so sorry you had to be the one to find him." Claudia knit her brow, looking like she wrestled with a weighty question. "When I met you and Vince at headquarters the other day, you said you'd picked up Randy's notebook by accident and that's why you were at his house."

"Yes, it was the story you critiqued for him. Speaking of the notebook, why did you take it to the signing? Why not to the writing class?"

"I figured if I gave it to him in class, he might have caused a scene." After a beat, Claudia said, "I'm guessing that the police have the notebook. Fish wouldn't say."

"I had to give it to them," I said.

"What was wrong with the book?" Lucy asked.

"Lots of gratuitous sex and violence. Plus treating women like sex objects." After a pause, Claudia added, "Not much of a plot."

"Did he ever tell you anything about his work or personal life that hinted someone wanted to kill him?" Lucy asked.

"Well, no. Unless . . . his wife? Did you see her at the house the other day?"

No, because she was at a spa, getting pampered, while her husband lay dead in their living room. Aloud, I said, "No."

"I don't know if she ever came back from the west coast," Claudia said.

"What was she doing out there?" Lucy asked.

"Taking care of her mother, then settling her mother's estate when she died. She was there the whole time we were critiquing his work."

"And you don't know if she came back?" I added a dollop of cream cheese to my bagel.

"No."

"If she's still out there, she didn't kill him," I said. Lucy's eyes met mine for a split second, signaling that she would play along with me in feigning ignorance of Joyce's current whereabouts.

"No," Claudia allowed. "Not on her own, anyway."

"Where on the west coast?" I asked.

"Randy didn't know."

"He didn't *know*?" Lucy looked incredulous.

"Somehow I think California. But I'm not sure."

Since California took up a good portion of the west coast, it was a good guess.

"Randy knew nothing of her family," Claudia said.

"And it sounds like he couldn't have cared less," I said.

Claudia sniffed. "Yes, well. Randy only cared about Randy."

I expected her to add a cliché like "Not to speak ill of the dead," but she made no further comment.

"Why do you think Randy's wife killed him?" I asked.

"I said she *might* have killed him."

"Okay, *might*. Why?"

"Isn't the spouse always the first, and most likely, suspect?"

For a mystery writer, Claudia lacked imagination. "Is there any other reason you think she killed her husband?"

"Randy said the marriage had problems and that his wife couldn't stand him. He wasn't specific about the problems."

"If she couldn't stand him, she could have divorced him. Unless there were money issues that made his demise preferable to divorce."

"He never mentioned anything about money." Claudia finished her crumbled Danish and dabbed her lips with a napkin.

"Well, if it isn't the mother of the year. Or should I say grandmother of the year?"

FIFTEEN

Awoman of imposing size and an abundance of hair the color of falling snow loomed before us. Her eyes, irises an almost colorless ice blue, were at the same time beautiful, creepy, and unsettling. I'd once read that Lizzie Borden, the infamous nineteenth century axe murderer, had eyes of the same pale color.

At that moment, those spooky eyes blazed as she fixed them on Claudia. Stabbing the air with her finger, she said, "You left that kid in your car the other night. I should have called the cops on you."

Customers looked up from their phones and devices. Newspapers lowered.

Claudia flushed. "It was only for a minute."

"What were you doing on our street anyway?"

"Dropping something off for a friend. If it's any of your business."

"I bet you're the one who killed Randy Zimmerman."

"Why, you—" Claudia stood, shaking. She had a height advantage, but lacked the woman's body mass.

At the mention of Randy Zimmerman, all conversation stopped as customers and employees waited to see what happened next.

"Ladies—" I held up a hand. "This isn't the place for this kind of talk." The woman stood with shoulders hunched and hands fisted, ready for battle. "You can't go around accusing people of murder," I told her.

After another scowl at Claudia, the woman stormed away. She joined a young man at a table across the room, positioning herself so she had us in her sights. Normal activity and conversation resumed.

My mind flashed to Dennis's report that one of Randy's neighbors saw a child left unattended in a vehicle.

"Claudia, what was that all about? Who is that woman?" No doubt my own eyes blazed, but their deep green shade lacked the eerie effect of the woman's icy blue one.

"I don't know who she is."

"Why would she say you killed Randy? And what's this about leaving a kid in the car?"

"Oh—" Claudia trembled. "I went to his house. I wanted to apologize for hitting him, and try to talk him out of carrying out his threats. I took flowers."

That explained the carnations on Randy's doorstep.

Claudia continued. "I didn't think Randy was a person to cross. I gave some thought to the ghostwriting offer and decided to do it."

"What about his wife? If she had been there, wouldn't it have been an awkward situation?"

"I didn't think about her. For all I knew, she was still on the west coast."

"But you didn't know that."

"No." Tears spilled down Claudia's cheeks. Lucy handed her a tissue.

"What about the kid in the car?" I asked.

"My grandson. I was babysitting. I was only going to be a minute. When I got back to the car, that *woman*—" Claudia scowled at her accuser across the room— "she was there, screaming her head off. Zachary was fine."

"You were going to apologize and try to negotiate with Randy," Lucy said. "Seems like that would take more than a minute."

Claudia bit her lip and said nothing. She mopped her tears and blew her nose.

Lucy continued. "Especially after traveling all the way from Short Pump to Westover Hills, a distance of roughly fifteen miles. With a kid in the car, no less."

Short Pump was an affluent suburb in a section of Richmond the locals nicknamed the "Far West End." In the early nineteenth century, a tavern and stagecoach stop in the area had a well in its yard with an unusually short pump handle—hence the unique name.

"I worried that he'd carry out his threats. If my mother knew . . ." She shook her head and pressed her lips into a thin line.

"What did he say when you arrived with flowers?" I asked.

"Nothing. No one answered the door, so I left them on the steps."

After a full minute of silence, I asked, "Did you tell this to the police? About going to Randy's place that night?"

"Um, no."

"Then you lied to them."

"I did not lie." Claudia assumed an air of indignation. "They asked what I was doing Saturday night, and I said I was babysitting. I was."

"You'd better call Fish and tell him the whole story."

"Okay, *okay*. I'll tell him." She blew her nose again on her now damp and twisted tissue. Lucy passed her a fresh one. "But I didn't kill Randy. I may be a bad babysitter, but that doesn't make me a murderer."

Claudia's rising volume attracted more attention. I held up my hand to stop her flow of words. "Okay, let's relax, take a few deep breaths."

Claudia maintained silence for several seconds before continuing her claim of innocence. "If I planned to kill someone, I wouldn't take my grandchild with me."

"Tell us about meeting Randy for the first time," I said.

"We met last summer." She described their meeting at a James River Writers event when she was conducting research for her next novel. They continued to meet to discuss his own work in progress. Her version matched the one she'd told the police.

"How long did you two meet?"

"Oh, a couple of months or so."

"You never mentioned him when we had lunch," I said.

"I didn't think of it. I critique lots of people. It's not a big deal."

Claudia looked from me to Lucy. "Will you help me?"

Here was my opportunity to make good on the debt my family owed Claudia. But I resisted saying "yes."

"How?" I asked. "We didn't know Randy or anyone associated with him. Except Matt, and we just met him." I gave Lucy a don't-mention-the-incident-with-Matt look. Her slight nod told me she got the message.

"Hmm." Claudia pondered the roadblock of not knowing anyone who could help nail Randy's killer. Brightening, she said, "I know. You can go to his memorial service. Won't Trudy be there? You can keep her company."

I was about to say that Trudy was out of the country, but thought better of it. Apparently Lucy had the same thought, as she said nothing.

"You'll probably find Randy's staff there," Claudia added.

I sighed. "All right, we'll go to the service. Okay with you, Lucy?"

She nodded. "But that's all we'll commit to. Once we know when and where it is."

"Claudia, why don't you investigate? Go to the service. You knew Randy a lot better than Lucy and I did."

"Oh, I can't go to the service. I'd feel so uncomfortable. I'm a suspect."

So am I, I thought. Although Claudia was higher on the suspect list. Had she even considered me as a suspect? Aloud, I said, "If you're a suspect, you need to clear your name."

Claudia made a face. "I don't have time. I'm on a deadline."

I heaved a mighty sigh.

"Did you find any clues in Randy's manuscript?" Lucy asked.

"Can't think of anything," Claudia said after a moment's thought. "Do you two want to read it?"

"Yes," we said in unison. "Send it to us."

Claudia picked up her phone from the table and spent some time swiping and tapping. "Done. Oh, here's an email from Matt about the memorial service."

I picked up my phone and checked my mail. "I got it, too. It's on Sunday at one."

"Yes, he sent it to all of us," Lucy said as she scrolled through her messages.

I asked, "Claudia, what does your husband think about all this?"

"Well, naturally he's concerned. He's away on a gig. Coming back tomorrow." She avoided eye contact when she said this. I was no expert on body language, but I had decent instincts and suspected something was up with her musician husband that she didn't want us to know.

Before leaving the café, we discussed the election results. Women had claimed victories countrywide, an outcome that pleased the three of us.

As we gathered our belongings and bussed our table, I looked for the scary woman, but didn't see her. Her young male companion sat alone, thumbing through his phone. I thought of Matt and smiled.

"I'll call you after the memorial service," Claudia said as we spilled out into the parking lot.

"If you find out anything, let us know," I said. "Better yet, let the police know."

Claudia hugged each of us before disappearing around the corner of the café. Lucy and I lingered by my car.

"I feel so terrible. I want to help her, but . . ."

Lucy finished my sentence. "She may be guilty."

"Yeah."

"Then again, she may not be. But you two were out of touch for years, decades. You have no idea what she's capable of."

"I know. And I'm not keen on helping a killer escape justice." I took a deep breath. "What do you think? Did she kill Randy?"

Lucy considered my question and shrugged. "Hard to say—"

Shouts cut off Lucy's words.

"I'll sue your ass."

"You'll be suing my ass from prison."

At Lucy's "That sounds like Claudia," we ran around the corner of the building Claudia had rounded a moment before. She stood by the open door of her SUV, arm shielding her face, shrieking a litany of curse words. The scary woman held up her phone, clicking away. After capturing digital images of Claudia, she added pictures of the vehicle and license plate to her phone's photo gallery.

"I'm sure these pictures will thrill the detectives," she said, cackling.

"Amazing," Lucy said. "Why doesn't Claudia just leave?"

We had kept our distance from the two women, so I doubted that Claudia heard Lucy. But she climbed in the SUV, started the engine, and backed up, missing the self-appointed *paparazzi* by an inch. We watched her drive out of the parking lot, execute a u-turn, and disappear from view.

"Enjoy the show, ladies?" The scary woman flashed a broad smile and held up her hand, fingers making the V for victory sign. She got in her own vehicle and took off, heading toward the street where Randy lived.

"That was quite a show," Lucy said as we walked back to our cars. "Too bad the customers inside missed it."

"Yeah." I shook my head in wonderment. "I'm guessing that woman will lose no time sending those pictures to Fish."

"I take it this woman is the neighbor who spoke to the police about the kid?"

"That's my guess."

SIXTEEN

"**B**ut back to what we were talking about before being so rudely, but interestingly, interrupted: did Claudia kill Randy?"

"I don't know," Lucy said. "Leaving a kid in a car isn't good, but it's not the same as killing someone."

"And you wouldn't leave a kid in a car and go kill someone. Would you?"

"No, I can't see bringing the kid along—it wouldn't be the usual thing. Maybe she hadn't planned on killing Randy, but things got out of hand. Crime of passion."

"If she needed to talk to Randy that badly, she could have done it the next day."

"But I imagine she was pretty overwrought about the incident in the café and needed to get things settled between them, one way or the other."

The two of us stood by my car, posing questions that had no answers. Yet.

"Was Claudia the same woman another neighbor heard at six-thirty?" Lucy asked. "If she was, she left the kid alone for an hour."

"We don't know how long Claudia was at Randy's house, and we don't know how truthful she is. It doesn't take long to leave flowers."

"I wonder if she'll tell Fish her whereabouts on Saturday night. For sure, that woman who just confronted her will."

"At the last investigation we had the full book group to help," I said. "Trudy and Sarah picked a bad time to be out of the country."

"Or Randy picked a bad time to get himself killed," Lucy said with a half laugh. She took her keys from her purse.

"I suppose we can ask Eileen to research Joyce. She's not the most dependable person, but she does have access to those library databases."

"Eileen might be better now," Lucy said. "When we were investigating before, she was having all those problems with her mother at the assisted living place. But her mother's much more settled now."

"Vince might help. He says he needs a break from his current project."

"That way he wouldn't be so worried about you."

"But he can't go with me to question people. He gets into cop mode, gets that look on his face. He can't help it."

"But at least he can tell us what the police are doing. If we're lucky, they'll arrest someone soon and we can drop the whole thing."

The unkempt woman who had been sitting by our table left the café and walked toward the alley that ran behind the building.

After a pause, I asked, "What about Lorraine? Do we want to include her?"

"Hell, no. We don't know her that well. And to be honest, I'm not sure how bright she is. Although I guess you can be ditzy *and* bright." Lucy shook her keys. "I have to get going."

"Okay, I'll let you go. Let's kick things off with the memorial service. It's only a few days away. And I'm having lunch with Lorraine on Friday. She didn't seem to know Randy, but she might know someone who knew him."

"If anyone from Randy's office is at the memorial service, I can get some information from them. His lawyer buddies, too." Lucy unlocked her door with her remote key fob. Turning to me, she said, "You know, Hazel, I'm feeling the pull."

I sighed. "So am I. Kind of. Still, we do have other things to do. Like writing."

"Yes. And I have a business to run."

"By the way, how's Dave doing?"

"Fine."

I thought Lucy and her husband, Dave Considine, enjoyed a happy marriage. Or did they? Her terse "fine" and the set of her jaw told me otherwise. "Lucy, is everything okay?"

"No. Dave and I are . . . we're having problems." After a deep sigh, she said, "He's been acting strange. Distant. I thought he might be having problems at work. But I've asked him a few times if anything's wrong, and he says no, everything's fine, he's working on a new song that's giving him problems."

Dave worked as a lawyer by day and moonlighted as a musician and songwriter. "Does he have writer's block?"

"Maybe." Lucy didn't sound convinced about the writer's block. "Let me tell you what I found the other day when he was in the shower. I snuck a look at his phone and saw this text with a picture of a scantily clad young woman. Very scantily clad."

"Sexting? Dave? Are you sure it wasn't one of his male buddies passing on a picture?"

"Not unless his male buddy's name is Arianna."

"Do you know who Arianna is?"

"Yes, she's a temp in his office. Answers the phone. Sounds like she's about sixteen. Looks like it, too. Has one of those perfect bodies reserved for the young, elastic boobs and all." Lucy's eyes filled with tears. "Damn it, I can't cry now."

I pulled a tissue from my purse and she caught the tears before they streamed down her face.

"At least I didn't place her there," Lucy said. "I don't do business with his law firm. Conflict of interest."

"Did you say anything to him?"

"Not yet."

"Well . . ." I trailed off. What was the appropriate response to such shocking news? The words I chose were heartfelt, if inadequate. "I'm so sorry, Lucy." We hugged. "Let me know if I can help in any way."

My heart ached for my dear cousin. Perhaps a murder investigation would distract her from her marital troubles. I needed my own distraction from her distressing news and it didn't take me long to come up with one: a detour by Randy's house.

Crime scene tape still festooned his property. I saw no sign of activity, police or otherwise, as I cruised along his street.

I imagined myself walking around the property, clipboard in hand, looking officious, finding valuable clues the police overlooked. I could gain insight into how the killer killed, crack the case wide open.

But there was that dang crime scene tape. And me without a clipboard.

There had to be another way.

I drove around the block, counting the houses as I went, and parked in front of the one behind Randy's. Vince had said these neighbors were away on a cruise. I prayed they hadn't yet arrived home. Without a driveway, I couldn't tell which of the cars parked on the street belonged to them.

Did I need a weapon? I opened my trunk, hoping to find something to defend myself, should the need arise. I grabbed an ice scraper and held it at my side, feeling pretty silly.

The brick house before me would benefit from a power washing. A long crack ran across a picture window framed by shutters in need of paint. If the owners thought taking a cruise took priority over sprucing up their property, I could relate. In my view, travel was the better choice.

I waded through a two inch accumulation of leaves on the right side of the house. More leaves dominated the back yard. I caught something white in the leaves gathered around an empty bird bath and moved closer to see what it was. Probably a scrap of paper. Not wanting to touch anything, I used the ice scraper to separate it from the leaves.

A receipt from Starbucks, the one on Forest Hill Avenue, near Target. It was dated four days before, at one o'clock in the afternoon. One caffe mocha, paid for in cash. Did this discovery mean anything? In case it did, I took out my phone and snapped a picture, feeling like a contemporary version of Nancy Drew.

I pictured the silhouette of Nancy holding a magnifying glass that graced the covers of the earlier books in the series. These days she'd do her detective work armed with a cell phone that could resize and enhance her digital images. I found a quarter in my pocket and placed it over the receipt. Makeshift paperweight.

A wall of boxwoods separated the property from Randy's. Had his killer cut through these bushes? They looked impregnable. I understood why none of the neighbors saw anyone go in and out of Randy's house—with all the greenery, one could do all kinds of nefarious deeds without being seen. I found a narrow opening at the far end where the leafy barrier stopped. The opening allowed me a view of the patio scene from three days before, with the French doors that opened to the room where Vince and I had found Randy's body. A chill ran through me when I realized someone could have accessed Randy's property through this gap in the bushes. Was I in the same spot where the killer stood?

"What are you doing here?"

SEVENTEEN

"Oh, my God!" I held a hand over my pounding heart. The imposing figure of the scary woman from Sweetbrew appeared seemingly out of nowhere. "You almost scared me to death!"

"What are you doing here?" she repeated, unmoved by my attempts to restore my circulatory system to normal. Her spooky blue eyes bored into mine.

"Oh! We just saw you at Sweetbrew," I said.

There were no bushes or other barriers between the yard where I stood and the one to the right. Neither was access barred to the yard next to Randy's. The woman before me stood at the point where the four properties met. She folded her arms under an impressive bosom and waited for me to explain my actions.

Why wasn't I prepared for this eventuality? My first instinct was to refuse to answer and bolt. But she might have seen someone the other night, or have other useful information—if I could coax it out of her.

Deciding to tell the truth, I said, "My husband and I were here the other day, and—"

"What day?"

"Sunday."

"Oh, you must be the ones who found Randy. Are you Hazel Rose?"

When I admitted to being me, the woman said, "I read one of your books."

She didn't offer an opinion and her tone suggested it wouldn't be a favorable one. Still, I murmured a "Thank you" to display my stellar manners. "And you are?"

It took her a moment, but at last she said, "Ruby Landis." She emphasized each syllable of her name like it had particular importance.

"So, Ruby, did—"

"And you're a detective as well. I've heard about your exploits. So, why were you here the other day?"

"My husband and I were here at Randy's invitation."

"Ah, yes, your husband, a *real* detective." Ruby fixed a flinty look on me. "Hmm. Maybe one of you killed Randy on Saturday night and came over the next day and put on a big act of being surprised."

"Why would we kill Randy?"

Not having a ready answer for that, she asked, "Are you working for that woman you were with at Sweetbrew? The one who left a kid in her car?"

"Um, no."

"Who is she, anyway?"

"She's an author as well. Writes mysteries."

"Name?"

"Claudia Marlowe."

"Why was she here the other night?"

"I don't know," I lied. "What I'm wondering is—"

"Why are you here today? You still haven't said. Looking for something your friend Claudia dropped when she killed Randy?" Ruby curled her lip and added, "I'm sure you authors stick together. Not that Randy's any big loss."

"Really? Know anyone who might have a motive for killing him?"

An *uh-oh* look crossed Ruby's face. Did she realize too late that she shouldn't be expressing negative opinions about Randy? Recovering her aplomb, she said, "Certainly not. I don't know murderers. And now, for the *third* time, what are you doing here?"

"I was curious, thought maybe someone accessed Randy's yard through here, and I wanted to check it out. So," I hurried on, hoping to complete my question before Ruby interrupted me. "Did you see anyone approach Randy's house on Saturday night?"

Ruby shook her head, making her mass of white hair shimmer. "No. When I saw Claudia, she was walking toward her SUV, which was parked down the street." She pointed in a direction to the right of Randy's house. "*But*—she was coming from Randy's house."

"How do you know where she was coming from?"

Ruby didn't have an answer for that question either.

"Did you see anyone approach from back here?" I waved the arm holding the ice scraper to include "back here."

"How would I see anyone with all these bushes?"

"Well, you just saw me back here. So you could have seen someone on Saturday night."

A smirk played at the corners of Ruby's lips. "It's daytime now, easier to see trespassers."

"You know, it's not good to leave a kid alone in a car, but it doesn't mean that Claudia—"

Ruby broke off my attempt to defend Claudia. "Want to see the pictures I took at Sweetbrew?" Ruby started to pass me her phone when she looked at a point behind me. "Uh, oh. Here are the cops. You're busted, Hazel."

I spun around to see Officers Coulter and Fitzgerald, first responders to Vince's call after discovering Randy's body.

"Thank you, officers. I'm Ruby Landis. Here's the trespasser I called about."

"Officer Coulter. Officer Fitzgerald. So nice to see you again." I smiled, satisfied when Ruby appeared taken aback by my familiarity with the two.

"Thank you, Mrs. Landis. We'll take it from here."

Mrs. Landis wanted the last word. "I guess that with her husband being a retired hot shot with the department, you'll let her off with a slap on the wrist."

A slap on the wrist is pretty much what I got. Figuratively speaking.

"Why were you trespassing, Ms. Rose?" Officer Coulter asked as he and his partner escorted me to my car.

"I was curious. Wanted to see if the person who killed Mr. Zimmerman cut through those bushes."

The officers gave me the usual warnings about staying away from crime scenes and not interfering with an investigation.

"Detectives Fischella and Garcia know what they're doing," Officer Fitzgerald said. "And we discovered the rear entry to the yard the other day."

By this time, we stood next to my car. "Oh! I didn't show you the receipt."

We traipsed back to the bird bath where each officer crouched down and studied the receipt. I didn't look over to where Ruby Landis had been, but felt her presence.

Officer Fitzgerald stood and reached for his phone. "I'll call this in."

This time, only Officer Coulter accompanied me to my car. "Detective Fischella will want to talk to you," he said.

No doubt. I'm sure he'll have plenty to say. Aloud, I said, "Okay."

"What's with the ice scraper?"

I looked at the item in my hand. "In case I needed to defend myself."

We laughed. I hoped the sound carried back to Ruby.

EIGHTEEN

"Hazel!" George Monahan always greeted me like he hadn't seen me in years. In reality, it had been two days. He was one of the neighbors who'd gathered around me, spellbound, listening to me describe finding Randy.

"How are you, George?" I laughed as I petted Opa, George's dog of an indeterminate mix of breeds.

"Never better."

George was a hale and hearty eighty-five. The widower had moved next door to Vince and me a year before, along with his daughter and family, including two boys, aged eight and ten. George shopped and cooked for the family, and took care of his grandsons while their parents worked.

"So tell me about your writing class. Didn't you say that Randy Zimmerman was supposed to be in it?"

"Yes, we talked about setting. I hate to say it, but I was dreading having Randy in the class." I grimaced. "Speaking ill of the dead, I know."

George made a dismissive gesture. "Some of the dead deserve it.

Whoever murdered him obviously thought so. Do the police have any leads yet?"

"No, not according to Vince."

"Do you think it was someone from the signing? Or from your class?"

"I have no idea. It could have been a client, a defendant . . . or just about anyone."

"So are you going to investigate?"

"Investigate? I don't plan to. Why do you ask?"

"According to the neighbors, you've investigated two murders."

"Yes, I did." I repeated what I'd told Matt about my previous investigations being motivated by knowing the victims. "I just met Randy the other day. I've had some scary moments—really close calls. I value my life much too much."

"Tell me about those murders," George said, adding, "If you want to."

I offered brief accounts of Carlene Arness's long-ago murder and the more recent one involving my newfound relatives. "I was lucky in both cases. I had no expertise, and a lot of people helped me. I'm no lone ranger."

"They could help you with this one as well."

Going for a change of subject, I asked, "How's your memoir coming along?"

George reported on his progress, sharing anecdotes from his career as a theology professor at a New Jersey college. "Speaking of memoirs, you should write your own. It's not everyone who solves one murder, much less two. Plus, you're a bestselling author."

"A memoir? What would I say? Write about my four failed marriages before my current successful one? My ho-hum childhood spent reading Nancy Drew books? I didn't even take music or dancing lessons. I spent a lot of time trying to learn to swim and ice skate, only to fail dismally. There's my career in IT. Who wants to read about that? Besides, I'm not—" I'd been about to tell George about being dropped by my publisher, but caught myself in time. I didn't need him telling the neighbors my tale of woe. "But enough about me. What's going on in the volunteering world?"

"Tomorrow I'm going to a birthday lunch with some folks from the Infinity Center."

The Infinity Center, an adult day care center, was one of the volunteer gigs that occupied George. He also devoted his time to the American Heart Association and Friends of the Library.

I didn't expect to hear his next words: "Speaking of the Infinity Center, I recently found out that Randy Zimmerman was a generous donor. His aunt is one of the program participants."

"Really? Randy?"

Obnoxious frat boy on one hand, compassionate benefactor on the other?

In the house, I traced the sound of inharmonious meowing to the kitchen. Vince was dispensing treats to the felines.

After greeting my husband with a kiss, I poured coffee for both of us and put the mugs on the table. We sat.

"So, tell me about your conversation with Claudia," Vince said.

I smiled. "I've had an interesting morning."

"Go on."

"I'll start with finding the receipt. If I don't tell you, someone else will." I ran down my adventure with finding the receipt, followed by the confrontation with Ruby. That required backtracking to the Ruby-Claudia face-off at Café Sweetbrew. My summary ended with Officers Coulter and Fitzgerald escorting me to my car.

Vince didn't speak for a full minute. I sipped my coffee and waited him out. Finally, he said, "Why? Why would you do that? You were trespassing. Plus, the killer might have been there, looking for the receipt."

"The people in that house were away on a cruise. And no one was around, except for Ruby. I thought I might find a clue. And I did!

I'm guessing that the killer dropped the receipt when he or she went through that opening I mentioned. I'm sure Fish will thank me."

"He'll be calling you, and soon. Be prepared." Vince sipped his coffee and glowered at me. "You don't know that the killer was the one with the receipt."

"Well, no. But it *was* the same date. Isn't that awfully coincidental?"

"It probably points to the killer. But, unless a Brad Pitt or Jennifer Lopez lookalike paid cash for a caffe mocha that day, it will be hard to get positive IDs from the Starbucks staff. Anyway, it's Fish's headache."

"And Garcia's." I didn't want Detective Garcia sidelined.

"And Garcia's." A smile brightened Vince's face before it clouded again.

"The timestamp on the receipt is one o'clock in the afternoon. Here, let me show you." I accessed my pictures and passed the phone to Vince. "That leaves out Randy and the possible suspects in his murder: Claudia, Lorraine, Matt. They were all at Richmond Books at that time. Joyce was at Inn by the Bay, but who's to say she didn't come back to Richmond and stop at Starbucks?"

"The receipt on its own doesn't point to a killer," Vince repeated.

"Maybe the wind blew it into the yard. Or we're dealing with a different killer altogether. Like one of those defendants in Randy's lawsuits."

"Let Fish deal with the receipt," Vince said. "As for this Ruby, I don't like the sound of her. Have you even agreed to investigate? You're supposed to investigate in pairs."

"True." That was my policy, but sometimes it didn't work out. "It was a spur of the moment thing. And no, I haven't agreed to investigate, but I want to."

"Sounds to me like you've started." Vince's smile was rueful. "What about Claudia? How did things go with her?"

He listened, interrupting with an occasional "hmm" or a clarifying question. "Promise me you won't poke around on your own, like you did today. And I hope you'll include your book group in this, like the last time—except for the end when you went off by yourself."

I sniffed. "I thought it was safe."

"Of course, you don't have much of a book group right now." Vince finished his coffee and set the mug on the table.

"I know. It will be Lucy. We can ask Eileen—we need a librarian on the team. We're not asking Lorraine." I described Lucy's and my reservations about Lorraine.

"Good idea, we're not sure about her. But you said you haven't committed to investigating."

"No. Lucy and I agreed to go to the memorial service on Sunday —Matt emailed us about the day—and see how we felt about things. Who knows, the case may be solved by then."

"I sure hope so. But the memorial service should be safe. I'm sure Fish will be there. Maybe Garcia as well."

"What about you?"

"I can't make it on Sunday. I have that talk to give in Charlottesville. But I can help you with research. As I recall, Eileen isn't dependable."

"Yes, but we should ask her."

"In fact, you can count on me to help you with anything you need. I may be writing about this case one day."

"Thanks, sweetheart. We may need your help."

"Don't tell anyone you're investigating. Especially anyone who's a suspect. And be careful what you share with Claudia."

"Will do, rather won't do. By the way, did anyone, like Fish or Garcia, read Randy's manuscript?"

"Yes, but they didn't find anything helpful."

"Do they have any leads?"

"No."

"And the forty-eight hour window is closed now." I referred to the commonly held belief that the ideal time to solve a murder was in the first forty-eight hours after a murder took place.

"That's the best-case scenario, but many murders take days, months, even years to solve. Sometimes being in a rush results in arresting the wrong person."

"True. Well, I have work to do. Oh—I was talking to George before I came in and he told me something surprising. Randy was a generous donor to the Infinity Center. His aunt is a program participant there."

"That puts him in a different light," Vince said.

"I'll say. But if Randy had personal qualities that seemed at odds with each other, he wouldn't be the first."

"No, he wouldn't be."

"I have some bad news," I said.

"You're kidding!" Vince exclaimed when I finished my account of Lucy's discovery of Dave's sexting.

"I wish."

"I'm sorry to hear that. What's she going to do?"

"I don't know. I think she needs time to figure things out."

We didn't speak for several minutes.

"I hope things work out for Lucy and Dave," Vince said.

"Me too."

My husband's blue eyes filled with love. "I hope you never feel that you can't trust me."

"I'm confident we'll always trust each other."

We stood and hugged. It was a long hug.

It was all we could think of to do.

NINETEEN

As Vince predicted, Fish called. After admonishing me for trespassing, interfering in an investigation, and putting myself in harm's way, he grudgingly thanked me for finding the receipt.

"Look, Ms. Rose, if you *happen* to learn anything, let us know. But leave the investigating to us. We know what we're doing."

But you didn't find the receipt. I bit back that retort and expressed my sincere hope that Randy's killer would soon be behind bars.

After such an adventurous morning, writing held little appeal. Facebook beckoned. With Matt and Ruby being such prominent figures in the past twenty-four hours, I might as well see what they were up to on social media.

I forced myself to stay focused and not get distracted by personal messages, friend requests, and post notifications. For all the time Matt spent on his phone, little of it was on Facebook. Unless he was a lurker, preferring to read other people's posts while guarding his own thoughts. I could think of some friends who would do well to follow that course. I reviewed his likes and concluded that we were politically incompatible. He belonged to a number of groups devoted to football.

Ruby was much more social online, posting about books—probably not mine—and knitting.

As for other social media sites, Facebook was it for Ruby. Matt's skimpy profile on LinkedIn included his education and long tenure with Hannan and Hannan. If the man was a cold-blooded killer, I found no sign of it online. Vince or Eileen could find more information, but I'd wait before asking them.

Later that day, Vince heard from Dennis. True to her word, Claudia did contact Fish about her presence on Randy's street around the time of his murder. Ruby Landis lost no time telling Fish about Claudia's actions on Saturday night. She supplied pictures of Claudia's SUV and her license plate in Sweetbrew's parking lot.

When Fish called Claudia in for another round of questioning, she arrived with her attorney in tow. Her explanation for not telling Fish where she was on Saturday night: he didn't ask. She had said she was babysitting and that's what she had been doing.

"But Claudia still has that iffy alibi," I said to Vince. "Her daughter and son-in-law can't know what happened once they left for their date night. I'm sure they wouldn't be happy if they knew about their kid being left in the car."

Aside from talking to Lucy a couple of times, I hunkered down and caught up on my romance-turned-mystery over the next couple of days. The Murder on Tour book group needed to start planning next year's program. First we had to establish our theme, or themes, for the year. To that end, I emailed the members for ideas.

I read Randy's story. Like he'd said, it was a legal thriller. Despite Claudia's thumbs down opinion, I didn't find it a bad effort—but not a story I'd read on my own or recommend to the book group. Kind of a mishmash of politics, law, jewelry theft, mob involvement, and murder, with plenty of gratuitous sex and violence thrown in for good measure. The main character was a lawyer who directed a posse of gorgeous women to do the investigating. They were willing bed partners as well. A bit too Charlie's Angels for my taste—although I wasn't sure if the angels had slept with their boss.

But the main character had another side: he donated vast sums to cancer research and formed a platonic relationship with a patient. Remembering Randy's philanthropy to the Infinity Center, I noted that he gave his sleuth a similar practice.

Was there any foreshadowing of Randy's death in his debut effort? How many other people had read his manuscript? If someone objected to his treatment of women as sex objects, had she, or he, sought revenge? An overreaction in my view, but I had to allow for people being irrational.

TWENTY

The Grapevine was a Greek-Italian eatery in Richmond's Far West End, not far from where Claudia lived. A reproduction of Michelangelo's David presided over the parking lot. The sculpture had caused a stir when the Grapevine's owners first placed it in the middle of their lot. But once it was deemed "art" the controversy died down. A high wall hid the well-endowed David from the view of passing drivers and their small charges. I always smiled when I thought of, or relayed, this story.

When I walked into the restaurant on Friday for my lunch date with Lorraine Popp, a stone-faced Venus de Milo greeted me from a corner. Dark red booths and strings of white lights created a year-round holiday atmosphere. Lorraine sat by a window that offered a stellar view of David's backside. She waved.

We went through the usual pleasantries— "How are you?" and "How was traffic?" —while perusing the menu. I ordered egg lemon soup and a Greek salad with anchovies. Lorraine hemmed and hawed before deciding on moussaka with a side Greek salad.

Once the perky wait person bounced away, I turned my attention to Lorraine. A black beret covered her gray curls. That, along with the black turtleneck she paired with a blue denim jacket, made me think of the beatniks of the early sixties. I tried to picture Lorraine as a true beatnik, hanging out in coffee houses. But weren't beatniks a serious bunch, insisting on artistic self-expression and rejecting the values conventional society held dear? Lorraine, with her ditzy ways, didn't fit the image.

My original purpose in asking Lorraine to lunch was to coach her on social media. The problem was that she hadn't asked for my help, and it seemed presumptuous to assume she wanted it. But now I had a second purpose—seeing how she fit into this investigation. I tackled the social media subject first, trying for an oblique approach.

"You said you don't like Facebook much. How about Twitter or Instagram?"

She shook her head. "No. It takes too much time. When am I supposed to write?"

"I know. It all takes time. Still, you might want to rethink your position on Facebook. It's a must for authors these days."

She made a sound between a sigh and a laugh. "Why?"

"It's how you get your name out and get a following." I tried to explain the concept of social media and its importance. "Plus you can join quilting groups on Facebook. On Twitter as well."

"I'm not writing any more quilting mysteries."

"Oh, right. You said that the other night in class." Remembering her saying she planned to write "something terrific," I asked, "So what are you going to write about?"

Lorraine gazed into the middle distance as if imagining what she *would* write. Shrugging, she said, "I'm not sure."

"What are your interests?"

It took her a full minute to come up with one. "I've helped my mom with our family tree. We found some interesting stuff. I had a great, great uncle who was a bank robber, and a great aunt who embezzled a fortune from her employer. I found news accounts of their crimes. Another ancestor was a midwife." As she spoke, Lorraine grew more animated.

"Genealogy is a great interest to work into a mystery," I said. "You can write about financial crime, either in the present day with links to the past. Or something historical."

"I'll think about it." The momentary spark faded.

"My sister is the genealogist in our family," I said. "She found some relatives we never knew about. One of them lives right here in Richmond."

Lorraine's tepid "Really?" didn't invite elaboration.

"Whatever you decide to write, you'll still need to be active on Facebook."

Again, that laughing sigh—or was it a sighing laugh? "I can't get away from Facebook, can I?"

The wait person delivered a basket of bread. Lorraine took great care breaking and buttering her roll before taking a dainty bite.

I went on. "And you need a website—with a blog."

"Isn't my publisher supposed to take care of all that?"

The woman was getting overwhelmed, but I couldn't seem to quiet my inner mother hen. "How about Sisters in Crime? Do you belong to that?"

"What's Sisters in Crime?"

Lorraine's ignorance of Sisters in Crime shouldn't have surprised me, but somehow it did. I held back a sigh and explained the organization's mission of supporting women crime writers, adding, "Many men belong as well, they're called *misters*."

Lorraine continued to nibble on her roll, saying nothing. I concluded my spiel on the organization. "I'll find out about the meetings. We can go together." Maybe Sisters in Crime could drum some sense into this woman who didn't want my advice. "But they might not be doing much until after the holidays."

"You know, I have carpal tunnel syndrome. Really bad." A black wrist brace peeked out from her sleeve.

"Oh. I'm sorry. I didn't know."

"So I can't be messing around on the computer. I have to use it enough at work."

Our soup and salad arrived, and we took a moment to tuck in to our food. I savored the creamy egg lemon soup. We watched a group of high-spirited women taking selfies with David in the parking lot. No doubt they planned to post the pictures on social media. Lorraine and I laughed.

"So Hazel, what do you think about self-publishing?"

"It's become a respectable option, provided an author invests in a decent editor, formatter, and cover designer."

"I'm thinking of trying it. Once I write my new book, that is."

"If you self-publish, you'll definitely need to do your own promotion."

An oh-no-I-didn't-think-of-that look crossed Lorraine's face. "Can't I hire someone to do my promotion?"

"Sure. You can hire a publicist. But they can be pretty pricey."

She fell silent. When I asked about her work, she said, "Last week I got a permanent position with the Board of Nursing."

"Permanent? Haven't you been there for a while?"

"A couple of years, but first as a contractor."

"Well, congratulations." After asking a few questions about the job, I dived in to the Randy subject. "So what do you think about Randy getting killed?" I asked.

"What am I supposed to think? It's awful."

"Did the police talk to you? They talked to me."

"Yeah. I guess because we were talking to him at Richmond Books. I couldn't help them, though. All I said was that he wasn't very nice."

"He sure wasn't. Did they ask you for an alibi? They asked me for one."

"Yes, they did. I was visiting my mother at her retirement place. I'm sure they checked the sign out form. What was your alibi, Hazel?"

"I was at a restaurant in Carytown with my husband. Then we went home and watched TV. We have a receipt for the restaurant, and we saw several people we knew."

"When was Randy killed?"

"Between six and eight. But those times have a margin of error."

"Isn't your husband a retired detective? The police should believe him."

"Yes. But first and foremost he's my husband. The police don't trust spouses corroborating alibis."

The rest of our food arrived. In my opinion the Grapevine served the best Greek salad in Richmond. That was saying something because the region abounded with Greek eating spots with excellent menus.

After a few bites, I continued my Randy probe. "I take it you never met Randy before?"

"No. But, funny thing, when I met him I thought his name sounded familiar. Last night I finally realized why.

"I was waiting in line at the post office. It was a week before Christmas, but I don't think it was last year. Maybe two or three years ago. The woman in front of me was going on and on about this lawyer, Randy Zimmerman, how horrible he was to work for. She said she had to stay because she needed a paycheck, but he was horrible."

"Do you remember her name? The police might want to talk to her."

"No, I don't think she said." Lorraine gave her moussaka a suspicious look. "Does this have eggplant in it?"

"It usually does."

"I hate eggplant."

But Lorraine dismissed my suggestion that she order something else and absently pushed the moussaka around on her plate.

"What did the woman look like?" I asked.

"Tall. Hispanic-looking. Or Italian. Not sure. She wore big glasses. You think she might have killed him?"

"If she was that unhappy she might have. You never know."

"I wish I could remember more, but I wasn't paying close

attention to her. The line was slow, even for Christmas, and I was running late. I just wanted to get out of there."

"Are you ladies interested in dessert?" The bubbly wait person asked as she cleared our dishes.

"I'd love some galaktoboureko," I said, butchering the pronunciation. "I'll take two, one to go." I planned to take a serving home to Vince.

"What's that?" Lorraine asked.

When the wait person described the custard and phyllo dough confection, Lorraine said, "Sounds good to me." This from a woman who'd barely touched her food. *Stop it!* This time I listened to my own advice and quelled my maternal itch to chide her.

"It's truly heaven on earth," the wait person raved as she left to put in our orders.

Lorraine picked up the conversation. "Hazel, thinking this woman from the post office is a suspect is a bit far-fetched. She could have quit if she was that unhappy. God knows there're plenty of lawyers around to work for."

"I'm sure." Laughing, I said, "Sometimes my imagination takes off. Occupational hazard of being a writer, I suppose."

"Oh, my. I have more to learn about writing than I realized."

When the galaktoboureko arrived, the server asked, "Separate checks?"

"No," I said. "Bring the check to me."

"Enjoy your desserts, ladies."

"Hazel, I didn't know you were treating. You really shouldn't." This last lacked a ring of conviction.

"Sure, I should," I said with a flap of my hand.

We put off talk of murder and social media to focus on the galaktoboureko. A hint of lemon merged with creamy custard and honey. Lorraine agreed it was "to die for" and all but licked the plate.

As I signed my credit card receipt I asked Lorraine, "How does your mother like her new retirement place?"

"Oh, she likes it."

"What's the name of the place?"

"River Edge."

"I think River Edge is where my friend lives. Do you know Marjorie Adams?"

"I don't know Marjorie. Is she a recluse? The recluses eat dinner together."

They sounded like a fun group. "Well, she is kind of a loner."

"My mother's quite social." We stepped out into the parking lot. Lorraine unlocked the door of a Subaru that might have been a few decades old. "Thanks for lunch, Hazel. And for the idea about genealogy."

"I'm always happy to help."

Driving home, I crossed the James River via the Willey Bridge. As I followed the curves of the bridge's unique serpentine design, I planned my reconnaissance to River Edge to check on Lorraine's alibi.

TWENTY-ONE

"I hope we don't run into Lorraine tonight. Although I can always say we're visiting the non-existent Marjorie Adams. Wouldn't it be funny if a Marjorie Adams actually lives at River Edge?"

"How did you come up with that name?" Vince asked as he turned right on Westover Hills Boulevard.

"I thought it might have been popular back in the twenties and thirties, which is when my fictional Marjorie was born. The Social Security Administration has an index of baby names and I use it for naming my characters. I can see if a name was popular during a certain time period. After all, my baby boomer characters can hardly be Brittanys or Caitlins. I checked the index before we left and verified that Marjorie was a popular name between the world wars."

Vince pulled into the parking lot for River Edge Retirement Villa. While the James River wasn't far away, the "edge" designation was a misnomer.

A soft shade of yellow covered the walls in the lobby. A large brick fireplace provided a focal point for the space. An arrangement of chairs facing each other over a shared coffee table encouraged easy conversation. But no fire glowed in the hearth and no one conversed. The lobby was deserted.

Perhaps the middle-aged woman sitting behind a glass window discouraged after-dinner lingering. She pursed her lips together in an almost invisible line. *American Gothic* came to mind. The famous painting depicted a farmer, pitchfork in hand, standing beside a woman who bore an uncanny resemblance to the woman before me. The painting had been lampooned time and again. In fact, I'd recently seen a parody of it in a magazine, and that probably accounted for my comparing the two women.

"How may I be of assistance?" She asked with no smile.

"I'm here to pick up a book that my friend left for me. *Murder at the Quilting Bee.*"

After another disapproving look, the woman stood and cast a sharp eye on what were probably shelves under her desk. Did a recent weight loss explain the loose fit of her gray business suit? Or did she prefer to hide her figure under copious amounts of cloth? The latter was my guess. "I do not see a book," she announced.

She turned and scanned an area filled with more shelves and mail slots for the apparently large number of employees on River Edge's payroll. A multi-function machine that copied, printed, faxed, and who-knew-what-else dominated a corner. "No. No book."

"Oh, dear. She said she left it at the front desk. This is the front desk, isn't it?"

"It is." Her expression suggested I was quite dim to ask such a question. "When did your friend leave the book here?"

"Last week. Last Saturday night, I'm pretty sure. Were you working then?"

"No, that irresponsible young woman was stationed here."

"Oh, dear," I repeated. "When will she be here again?"

"She is no longer with us."

I sensed that this prim and proper woman wanted to dish.

"Yeah, some of these young people . . ." I trailed off, shaking my head in commiseration.

"This one was worse than most. She actually signed in and out for someone, making it look like this person, probably a friend of hers, was visiting her grandfather. This friend was probably at one of those nightclubs the young people rave about. The family is furious and may decide to sue us."

"Oh, that's just awful."

"Such carryings on, not like in my day."

"I agree. You're well rid of that employee. She probably misbehaved in other ways as well."

"Don't get me started." Then she started. "Always leaving greasy food wrappings around. Another time she spilled soda all over the keyboard. And she spent a *great* deal of time carrying on with the assistant manager in the back office. *He's* still here." Her eyes flashed.

"That's so unfair!" I cried, mirroring her indignation. "He should be let go as well."

The ringing of the phone interrupted our grumbling about today's youth. The woman greeted the caller in the same lofty tone she had used with me, adding, "Please hold."

She pushed a pen and pad of white paper decorated with the River Edge logo under the window, instructing me to leave my name and number. "If we locate your book, we will contact you." She returned to the caller.

Spying a notebook open to the guest sign-in sheet, I placed the pad of paper on the sheet so I could surreptitiously peruse the names. As I scribbled the name "Marjorie Adams" and made up a number, I checked the names on the sign-in sheet. Lorraine had signed in at six o'clock and out at seven, visiting Greta Popp. Short visit tonight. I wanted to check back to the previous Saturday to see for myself when Lorraine had signed in and out. Ms. Congeniality was still on the phone. Did I dare?

When she said "Please hold" to the caller, I figured my window of opportunity had come and gone in the proverbial blink of an eye. "Is there anything else I can help you with, Miss?"

"Oh, no," I said with a flutter. "Thanks *so* much for checking on my book." I added the title of the book I was pretending to need before passing pen and paper back under the window.

Vince put down the magazine he'd been flipping through and we left. The receptionist kept her caller on hold while she tracked our exit with a flinty stare.

Once outside, we burst out laughing. "One thing I liked about her is that she called me 'Miss.' I don't remember the last time someone called me that. Only Ma'am." At the time I turned thirty I lived in Los Angeles and teenagers took to addressing me as Ma'am. Those with military affiliations followed suit. But it wasn't until I moved to Virginia in 2000 that the general population preferred the moniker reserved for addressing a woman of a "certain age."

Vince pulled me close and whispered in my ear. "You're one sexy ma'am. How 'bout we go home and you show me just how sexy you can be?"

"Thought you'd never ask."

TWENTY-TWO

The Hermitage Road Historic District on Richmond's Northside started life as a streetcar suburb in the late 19th century. Developing the area north of the city to solve the housing problems caused by a rapidly growing city population became possible with the invention of the electric streetcar. The trolley line ran down the middle of Hermitage Road. At some point, a wide, grassy median replaced the line.

As I drove along the historic stretch lined with trees and architecturally significant houses, I told Lucy about Vince's and my visit to River Edge.

"So do you think this irresponsible young woman signed in and out for Lorraine?" she asked.

"I don't know. Vince says the police compared Lorraine's signature on River Edge's sign-in sheet with the one on the statement she gave the police and they match. Last night she signed out at seven, shortly before we arrived."

"How was your lunch with her the other day?"

When I got to the part about Lorraine's carpal tunnel problem, she said, "So I guess she couldn't swing a statue."

"Guess not. Unless she's making up the carpal tunnel. Anyone can wear a wrist brace. She was unenthused about any suggestions I made about her writing. I mean, she has *criminals* in her family tree. How could she not want to write about them?"

"You're right," Lucy said when I described Lorraine's ancestors and my mentoring attempts. "Even if they weren't criminals, genealogy is a minefield of possibilities."

Randy's sister, Gail Bayer, lived in one of the many Colonial Revival houses in the historic district. I learned about the various architectural styles on a long-ago walking tour of the area. Parking was at a premium and required hunting for a space. I found one two blocks from the house and we hiked back.

"I wonder if Ruby Landis will be here," I said as we approached Gail's brick-with-white-trim treasure and climbed the steps to a wraparound porch.

"She might be. Although you said she didn't think Randy was a great loss."

We walked into an entrance hall where a small group of people surrounded an elderly woman in a wheel chair. The kitchen overflowed with a cheerful crowd garbed in everything from suits to jeans. Lucy and I had chosen slacks with blazers and silk blouses, always a safe bet when unsure of the dress code. A man sporting a neatly trimmed goatee raised his beer stein in a toast to Randy's memory. So far, we hadn't spotted a familiar face.

"Look at that chandelier." Lucy said. A glass light fixture in the shape of a ship hung over a food-laden table in the dining room. We heaped various salads on paper plates, avoiding the fried chicken that looked too cumbersome to eat with any appearance of manners. I couldn't resist the meatballs and marinara sauce.

As we ate, we listened to the eulogies, most given by Randy's fellow lawyers and University of Richmond classmates, including Matt Rowan. Like he had at the writing class, Matt talked about how he and Randy were neighbors and classmates while growing up, continuing their friendship into adulthood.

While Matt's eulogy was quite emotional, the others bordered on the raucous. The raucous Randy would have been pleased with his service.

Finished with my plate but still feeling peckish, I turned to see what else I could find to nibble on under the crystal ship chandelier. The haunting melody and lyrics of "The Crystal Ship," recorded by The Doors, came to me. Had anyone in this conservative-appearing crowd been Jim Morrison fans? A table in front of the window overlooking the front porch grabbed my attention, and I walked over, plate in hand. Two women stood by the table, talking quietly. A glob of red sauce oozed down the back of the beige sleeve of one of the women.

Guessing she was unaware of her sleeve decoration, I said, "Excuse me for interrupting, but you have some sauce on your sleeve."

Her companion looked and verified my statement. The woman took off her jacket and surveyed the damage.

"Damn." She glared at me, like I had flung sauce at her.

"It probably came from the meatballs and marinara," I said.

"You need to get some cold water on that before the stain sets," the other woman advised. And away they went, presumably to a powder room, without so much as thanking me. I stifled an urge to yell, "That beige is not your color," but decided that a memorial service was not the place for snarkiness.

The table that had attracted my attention in the first place held a display of framed pictures and albums, a silent tribute to Randy's memory. A geeky-looking Randy and an equally geeky girl posed for their prom picture. A few decades later, a blond bride posed with him —the same woman I'd sent off to the powder room. Randy's widow. I offered up a silent thank you that I'd held back any rude comments.

Circling back to childhood, Randy stood outside a church with a young girl—Gail?—and two adults I assumed were their parents. Randy took after his father, sly smile and all; mother, a statuesque redhead with a long-suffering expression. Perhaps her husband and son wore her out. No pictures of Randy with Trudy.

I moved back to the kitchen. The eulogies ended, and Randy's well-wishers descended on the food table like starving vultures.

"I'm going to mingle." Lucy dropped her empty plate in a garbage can. I followed suit.

"Yes, we both need to do that," I said. "We'll touch base later."

I wound my way through the crowd in the kitchen, decorated by a deft and talented artist with a bent for whimsy and every color in the spectrum. No boring pastels and beiges for Gail Bayer.

Ruby Landis leaned against the wall by a window, her cloud of white hair pulled into a bun that perched on top of her head. Our eyes met.

"Why, Ms. Rose. Fancy seeing you here."

I'd know that boyish voice anywhere. I turned my gaze from Ruby to Detective Tom Fischella.

"Detective." For good measure, I added a smile to my greeting.

"What brings you here today? I thought you didn't know Mr. Zimmerman."

"Mr. Zimmerman was a client of my cousin Lucy, and she wanted to pay her respects. You know she runs a staffing firm."

"Oh, yes. That slipped my mind." The golly-gee tone didn't fool me for a minute. Nothing slipped the detective's mind. A bespoke tailor might have designed his well-cut sage suit. Not a hair on his head moved, indicating a recent trip to a hair stylist or a liberal amount of hair product. I recalled him tossing his floppy locks about during our interview the week before.

"So, how's the investigation going?" I asked.

Fish held up a hand, perhaps waving to someone behind me. "Oh, Ms. Rose, I think we're closing in on our culprit. Any time now. Any time."

When a Joe Namath lookalike loomed next to me, he and Fish greeted each other with hail-fellow-well-met handshakes and slaps on the back. When they launched a conversation that obviously didn't include me, I drifted away. Did Fish's holding up his hand the moment before signal to his friend that he needed rescuing from me and my pesky questions?

Ruby had moved away from her spot by the window. I chatted with Randy's neighbors, friends, and fellow lawyers. Matt, giving no indication that our previous encounter after the writing class was less than cordial, introduced me to his wife. Susan Rowan, a petite woman in her forties, favored lavish amounts of makeup and sported a chin length hairstyle. Straight bangs hid her eyebrows. Her short sleeves displayed well-toned arms, much like Michelle Obama's.

Lucy appeared at my side. "Matt, that was a lovely tribute you made for Randy," she said.

"Thanks, Lucy. Have you met my wife?"

After going through the usual courtesies, Lucy said, "Would you excuse us? I want Hazel to meet a friend of mine in the other room."

Permission granted, my cousin whisked me away to a room at the back of the house, a sun porch with comfortable-looking furniture. French doors offered a glimpse of a walled garden.

"Here's one of your fans, Hazel. Rhea Hewitt was Randy's office manager. This is my cousin, Hazel Rose. We're in a book group with Trudy Zimmerman."

Rhea's cropped salt and pepper curls framed her heart-shaped face. Her simple navy suit and matching low-heeled pumps told me she was a woman with a practical approach to life. Next to her, my teal blouse and multi-colored boucle jacket struck a frivolous note.

"Hazel Rose, the romance writer," Rhea said. "I *love* your books."

"I do *not* read your books." This came from a man with a sour lemon expression. Why did he deem it important to voice his opinion? Did he think I'd produce a book from my sleeve and force him to purchase it?

Keeping my voice even, I asked, "What do you read?"

"Non-fiction," he pronounced. "I'm going outside."

"Please excuse my husband," Rhea said as the man walked away. "His ulcer's acting up."

I smiled, but her husband and his ulcers didn't interest me. "Like Lucy said, I've known Trudy for a long time. But I only met Randy once." I didn't specify that our meeting turned out to be on his last day on earth. "I sort of met Randy's wife in the front room, but I haven't met his sister. Is she in the kitchen?"

Rhea went to the kitchen doorway and scanned the crowd. "No," she reported. "She might be in the front hall. Foyer, I think they call it in these houses."

"We saw some people there when we came in," Lucy said. "There was a woman in a wheel chair."

"That's Randy's Aunt Starla," Rhea said.

"Any other relatives?" I asked.

"I don't think so," Rhea said. "His parents are deceased and I don't think he had other family. Cousins, maybe. Most of the people here are lawyers and neighbors."

"Excuse me, but there's someone I need to see," Lucy said. She disappeared into the kitchen crowd.

"Joyce isn't very friendly today," Rhea said. "I guess that's understandable. She's always quiet, but you'd think she'd look sad or bereaved—but she just looks, well . . . *stoic*."

"Did Randy and Joyce have a happy marriage?" I asked.

"I've never been sure. Randy always acted like everything was hunky dory, but he acted that way about everything."

"So what was he like to work with?"

Rhea laughed. "Hard-driving. Fought like a terrier for his clients. And he paid his staff well. But he was rough around the edges, not polite or cultured."

Trying for an offhand tone, I said, "I wonder who could have killed him."

"Defendants in any number of lawsuits."

"Any one in particular?"

"Oh, no, but it's always a risk in the legal profession. That detective over there"—Rhea pointed to Fish, standing in the kitchen, high-fiving with a tall man—"came to the office and asked us if we had any ideas about who killed Randy. We didn't."

"I don't imagine anyone on your staff would do such a thing."

Rhea gave me a sharp look before responding. "No, I can't think of anyone who would resort to murder. Not staff or attorneys. Randy didn't like temps much. There was one in particular. I'll never forget that scene he made. He blasted the poor woman."

"Why did he blast her?"

"She made a mistake on a letter," Rhea said. "He had a fit. Fired her on the spot."

"Huh. When was this?"

"Oh, two years ago or so. The man had no patience, none at all. I always try to give people a chance."

"I wonder—you know, a while back I was at the post office . . ." I told Lorraine's story about the woman in the post office line complaining about Randy as if it was my own. "She said the man's name was Randy but I don't recall his last name. Was this woman he fired tall and Hispanic? With thick black hair?"

"No, this woman wasn't that tall, and she had reddish hair. She colored it at home and did a really bad job. You could always see her roots."

Despite Rhea's belief that Randy's law firm harbored no killers, she could be mistaken. Questioning lawyers was the logical next step, a task beyond my skill set. Lucy was adept in working a room, but I didn't know if even she had what it took to get information from a legal professional. I glimpsed her in the kitchen, exchanging business cards with a group of suited men.

An attractive woman with hair the color of red wine had cornered Fish. While enchanted by her charms, the detective kept one eye on the crowd, probably hoping to find a sign of a killer in the midst.

"If you ask me, a woman's involved," Rhea said. "*Cherchez la femme* as they say."

Cherchez la femme. My French was far from fluent, but I recognized that idiom.

Look for the woman.

TWENTY-THREE

"Any women in his life?" I asked Rhea. "Besides his wife."

Rhea shrugged. "A while back, I heard him on his cell phone. He was laughing but the woman on the other end yelled. Probably Joyce. Or someone else."

"But you don't know if there actually *was* someone else?"

Rhea dismissed my probe with a wave of her hand. "I can't say there was or there wasn't. Speaking of Randy and women, where's Trudy? Was she still in touch with Randy? I *liked* her." Rhea's emphasis on "liked" told me she didn't feel the same toward Randy's current wife. Widow, rather.

"Trudy's traveling," I said. "She knows about Randy, and—"

Rhea's husband appeared at her side, looking as sour as before and sounding pained as he asked his wife: "Can we go now?"

"Yes, dear." She patted his arm. "Let me say goodbye to Gail."

"Oh, would you introduce me to Gail?" I asked.

"Certainly." The three of us made our way through the kitchen.

In the front hall—a.k.a. foyer—Aunt Starla accepted condolences from the people who continued to pile into the house. Next to her stood a female version of Randy, although far more attractive with her Rubenesque figure and thick, dark mane.

Rhea spoke to Gail for a moment, but her ailing husband pulled on her sleeve, like a little kid. Turning to me, she introduced me to Gail before leaving with hubby in tow.

"Randy and I were going to be in the same writing class," I said to Gail.

"Oh, yes. He was so excited about his first novel." A pale shade of lipstick covered Gail's full lips that she'd outlined in a darker color.

"I understand he was a benefactor to the Infinity Center. Does your aunt participate in the program there?" I gestured toward the woman in the wheel chair.

"She does. It's a wonderful program."

I started to mention Trudy, but Aunt Starla cried, "I'm tired. I want to go to bed!"

"Excuse me, Hazel," Gail said. "I need to get my aunt upstairs."

That left me looking around for more information sources. Joyce lingered near the dining table, talking to Matt's wife, Susan. I couldn't see if Joyce had succeeded in removing the stain from her jacket, and didn't dare ask.

She paired the beige suit with a white blouse and beige low-heeled pumps, a color choice that washed out her blond, Germanic coloring. The bland outfit didn't square with the piercings lining her ears. Her hair, secured with a gold clip, trailed down her back. I assessed her age at forty, making her much younger than her late husband. From her height, I guessed she had towered over him.

Susan smiled at my approach. Joyce didn't. Rhea was right, Randy's widow looked stoic.

"Hello, Joyce. I'm Hazel Rose. I'm so sorry for your loss."

A ghost of a smile crossed Joyce's face. "Are you the one who's playing detective? Trying to find my husband's killer?"

"Um, no. I met Randy last week at Richmond Books. We were to be in the same writing class."

"So you barely knew him. Then why are you here?"

I repeated what I'd told Fish, using Lucy's ties to Randy's firm as credentials to justify my presence. I should claim a longer acquaintance with Randy. Make up something.

Joyce gave me an "Oh, sure" look before saying, "Thank you for coming." She turned back to Susan, dismissing me.

A man heaped deviled eggs and ham biscuits on a plate. One of the eggs slid off and landed an inch from Joyce's foot. He scooped up the egg, dropping a ham biscuit on her shoe. Joyce was fighting a losing battle between her wardrobe and food. Amid her peevish cries and the man's profuse apologies, I coughed to suppress my laughter and moved on to the kitchen, where the crowd was thinning out. I fell into conversation with a group of Randy's lawyer friends.

One of them pointed to Matt and Susan, standing in the dining room. When Susan stood on her toes and kissed her husband, the lawyer said, "Last I heard, Matt wanted to divorce her. I guess he changed his mind."

"Didn't she come into money when her old man croaked?" Another lawyer asked. "That probably changed his mind, and fast." A chorus of guffaws followed.

Normally I'd have walked away from such a conversation, but didn't want to miss an opportunity to ferret information about Randy. But, despite my questions about their departed colleague, nothing these lawyers said made "Killer!" flash in lights before my eyes.

I walked through the kitchen heading for a restroom I'd noticed earlier. A streak of red went by so quickly it could have been a bird in flight. The restroom was tucked in an alcove where five women chatted while waiting to use the facilities. None of them wore red. A set of steps on the other side of the alcove ascended to the second floor. Had the person in red gone up there?

Curious, and unwilling to wait in line, I ran up the steps that came out to a hall with thick carpeting featuring a fussy floral pattern. Dried flower arrangements filled vases set on tables before mirrors with gold leaf frames. No red color in sight. No one waited in line to use the facilities and it was hard to tell which door to try.

Was that a faint cry I heard? The din from downstairs drowned it out, but I heard it again. Thinking that Aunt Starla might need help, I opened the nearest door.

The light from the hall let me make out a collage of images in the darkened room: a tumble of shoes took up space in the middle of the room—a pair of men's athletic shoes and a pair of low-heeled shoes in a pale shade—beige would be my guess. But what drew my attention was the activity on the king-sized canopied bed: a man wearing a red plaid shirt with his pants pulled down, exposing a derriere worthy of a scene in an R-rated movie, shared a vigorous moment with a woman who cried out in pleasure.

It didn't take a genius to conclude that the woman was *not* Aunt Starla—likely she was Joyce Zimmerman, stealing away for a quickie at her husband's memorial service.

The two were too involved in their passion to notice me. I started to leave, only to run into Ruby Landis. Literally.

"You again!" the woman glared at me.

"I'm not thrilled to see you again, either," I shot back, returning her glare. The door swung wide when I took my hand off the knob, letting more light in the room, revealing the couple on the bed, confirming my guess that the woman was Joyce Zimmerman.

"What the hell is going on here?" Joyce shrieked. She pushed her partner off of her and quickly pulled down her skirt.

"What's going on in here? Is everything all right?" I swung around to find Gail Bayer and Susan Rowan. Gail carried a cup of a steaming beverage that smelled like strong tea. She balanced the dainty-looking porcelain cup on a matching saucer.

Joyce, now off the bed, smoothed her skirt and slipped into her pumps. She stood, crossing her arms, saying nothing. Her partner swung his legs over the side of the bed and stood, treating us to a view of his private parts. He took his time pulling up his underwear and jeans, a reverse striptease.

Gail's eyes widened at the scene before her and her initial tone of concern turned to one of steel. "*What* is going on here?"

When neither Joyce nor her partner spoke up, I said, "I'll go first. I came up here to use the restroom, but I heard cries and thought your aunt might need some help, so I tried this door. When I saw that your aunt wasn't in here"—I waved a hand at the misbehaving couple —"I turned to leave, only to run into Ms. Landis here." Ruby maintained her glare. "Then you and Susan arrived. That's all I know."

"What I want to know is why my sister-in-law is screwing someone at her husband's, my brother's, memorial service."

Joyce stayed silent, looking defiant and, as already described, stoic. The man, pants now zipped, sat on the bed, tugging on his shoes, regarding us like we were actors on a stage.

I had no doubt his red plaid shirt was the streak of red I'd seen earlier.

"Hey, ladies, chill," he said. "Come join us. We can start over."

"Out! Get out of my house now! Both of you!" The cup and saucer Gail still held shook and Susan took both from her.

A disheveled Joyce held her head high as she left the room, her only words addressed to Ruby: "You were supposed to guard the room."

"Sorry. I had to go to the bathroom."

The man swaggered out, winking at Ruby and me. His rumpled brown hair enhanced his sexiness. A two-day growth didn't hide a nasty scar that ran down the side of his face. Ruby followed him down the hall.

Susan and I looked at each other, then quickly away to avoid laughing.

In soothing tones, Susan said to Gail, "I'll take this tea to your aunt. Which room?"

Gail gestured behind her. "Second door on the left."

Susan moved away, leaving me alone with Gail. Feeling awkward, I said, "Can I get you anything?"

"No." Gail looked dazed for a moment before asking, "Who was he?"

"I don't know."

"How did he get in the house?"

"I think he came in the back way and went up the back stairs."

"Nervy. Both of them."

I nodded my agreement.

"Well, I need to make sure they left." With that, Gail returned by the main staircase to the front hall below and I finally got to use the facilities.

Downstairs, people were leaving and Lucy and I started the lengthy process of saying goodbye—a process I expedited as I itched to tell Lucy of the goings-on upstairs. When we got to Gail, she hugged both of us, whispering a "Thanks" to me.

Susan stood nearby. She waved to us, adding a wink. She chatted with a handsome man roughly her age. Between them, they flashed enough white teeth to make them candidates for a toothpaste commercial. Something about the quick furtive looks Susan cast at the man intrigued me—like she savored his handsomeness while hoping no one caught her doing so. As always, my writer's imagination went into overdrive, picturing a dalliance between the two. But maybe Susan just appreciated a handsome man.

Didn't we all?

TWENTY-FOUR

Matt and Joyce stood on the sidewalk in front of the house. They embraced. No sign of a red plaid shirt. Joyce still looked rumpled.

Lucy and I made it to the corner before I grabbed my cousin's arm. "I can't wait a second longer. I have so much to tell you."

"You're kidding!" Lucy raised an arched brow once I shared my news. "At her husband's memorial service? In her sister-in-law's house?"

"If I hadn't been there, I wouldn't believe it myself. Such nerve! This guy flaunting his family jewels."

"I bet you enjoyed that." Lucy's eyes danced.

"Maybe I should stick with writing romances. I got quite inspired today."

"I need to hang around you more," Lucy said. "You catch all the good stuff. And Ruby guarding the room? Aren't you supposed to hang a necktie on the doorknob if you don't want to be disturbed?"

We laughed. We laughed till our sides ached. People leaving the memorial service walked by, some amused, others puzzled.

"Did you see anyone in a red plaid shirt? Probably flannel."

"No," Lucy said. "A shirt like that would have been pretty noticeable in that group."

We started walking. "So did Joyce want Randy out of the way so she could carry on with this guy?"

"He doesn't sound like the kind of guy you kill your husband over. From what you've said, I get the idea she wanted sex, free and clear. Maybe it's her way of handling her grief."

"You think she's grieving?"

"You never know how people feel. I remember when my Charlie died. It was so hard, all the strange feelings."

Lucy referred to her long marriage to her first husband, who had left her a widow. "But you and Charlie had a great marriage. You loved each other. And I'm sure you didn't rendezvous with some ne'er-do-well during Charlie's service."

Or did she? I slanted my eyes at Lucy. Maybe grief sex was a thing and I could use it in my writing.

"I saw that look!" Lucy pointed at me. "You're wondering about me."

Again, we erupted in laughter. "Well, in the interest of thoroughness, I'm going to tell Fish about the incident," I said as we reached my car. "Let's go to Sweetbrew and talk."

"How about The Beanery? We haven't been there in a while." Lucy referred to a coffee spot on Richmond's Southside, near downtown.

"Fine with me."

Hermitage Road turned into Arthur Ashe Boulevard. As I drove, we passed The Diamond, a baseball stadium and home of the Richmond Flying Squirrels. At the Nickel Bridge toll booth, I tossed coins into the drop bin. At some point in the past, drivers paid a mere nickel to cross the James River. While the toll now cost thirty-five cents, the Nickel moniker endured.

The Beanery had been a gas station in another life. Oversized purple sofas and mosaic-topped bistro tables created a funky and comfortable atmosphere. An array of pastries in the glass display case might have tempted me, but I'd over-indulged at the memorial service so kept my order to a latte—decaf at this time of day. Lucy echoed my choice. In a nod to our environmental leanings, we specified ceramic mugs.

We carried our drinks to a sofa pushed up against what was once a service bay door and set them on a table covered with discarded newspapers.

"Let me put one of my cards on the bulletin board before I forget."

I pinned my business card to the board, adding it to the collection of flyers alerting the community about lost pets, music lessons, Bible study groups, and the like. That accomplished, I settled next to Lucy on the sofa. We rehashed the conversations of the afternoon.

"Rhea thinks the culprit is a woman, but she's not sure *which* woman." I blew on my latte, making the foam quiver. "As for the woman in the post office line, Rhea didn't have a clue who that could be."

Lucy's brows drew together. "What are you talking about?"

"Oh, didn't I tell you? Lorraine was waiting in line at the post office . . ." I repeated what Lorraine had shared about a woman ranting about Randy, adding, "It might not mean anything."

Lucy picked up her drink and sipped. "I met a young woman named Christina Bigelow. She's a librarian at the Chesterfield County Library and met Randy there when he was doing research for his next book."

"Oh, I saw Christina, but didn't get to talk to her. I know her from Virginia Romance Writers."

"Yes, she said she was a romance writer."

"So what's this about a next book?"

"Randy wanted to write a biography of this guy, some multimillionaire. I can't remember his name now. It meant nothing to me, so it didn't stick. Randy had wanted to interview him, but the guy died before he got a chance. That's when he, meaning Randy, started researching. Christina often answered questions for him and thought his subject fascinating."

"Sounds like the same one he talked about last week at the store. Had he finished his research?"

"I didn't think to ask about that."

"Anyway," I said. "Vince said the police are going through Randy's cases, but it'll take a while. Rhea said something vague about unhappy defendants."

"There will always be unhappy defendants."

We lapsed into silence, concentrating on our lattes. But not for long.

"Let me tell you about my other interactions with Joyce today." I described the marinara sauce incident and the moment when I actually met the woman.

"You were smart to deny that you were investigating," Lucy said. "She could be the killer. She wasn't friendly to me, either. Gave me a dead-fish handshake and a thanks for coming."

"She sure was friendly up in the bedroom—that is, till I barged in. Anyway, I think we should focus on her for the time being. The police can concentrate on Randy's cases. The boring stuff."

"I'll Google her." Lucy tapped and swiped on her phone before announcing, "Here's a LinkedIn profile. She worked for Kellogg Publishing downtown. I know the office manager there, she's a client."

Lucy scrolled through the page. "Joyce worked there till two years ago, and nowhere since."

"So she quit working?"

"She might have. Either she didn't like the job, and no longer needed the income, or she didn't bother updating her LinkedIn account." Lucy continued to scan Joyce's LinkedIn profile. "She went to the University of California Santa Barbara."

"UCSB," I said. "I wonder what brought her to Richmond."

"Family? Job prospects?"

"Is she on Facebook?" I picked up my own phone and accessed

the Facebook app. A few Joyce Zimmermans came up in my search but none resembled the woman from the memorial service. "There's a sultry-looking young woman with boobs up to her chin. But she isn't Joyce. But Joyce could be using her maiden name. We need to find out what it is."

"So we're going to take this on?" Lucy said.

"I guess. We can at least look into Joyce's possible culpability. But first I want to talk to Vince and see if he heard something today. Then I'll contact Eileen and ask her to do some research."

"Vince could do research."

"Yeah, he already offered, but Eileen might be hurt if we don't ask her. And you'll contact the woman from the publishing company?"

"Yes, I will."

"What about Sherry?" Lucy asked. "I didn't see her today."

"Me, neither. And she'd be hard to miss. So who else did you talk to?"

"A few neighbors. Nothing much there. They called the police more than once when Randy's parties went into the wee hours."

"I heard that too, and it could provide motive. Loss of sleep over loud parties could put some people over the edge. I know the police questioned the neighbors. Another reason to check in with Vince."

"Have you read Randy's manuscript?" Lucy asked.

"Yes."

"That yes tells me you share my opinion of the story."

"Not my cup of tea, but I'm sure men would like it. And judging from his comments last week at Richmond Books, men were his target market."

"The question is, did something in the story prompt someone to kill him?"

"Hard to tell, especially since we don't really know anyone who knew him. I'm thinking he was writing about someone and that someone objected—"

"You mean like a roman à clef?"

"Could be. Or, maybe he plagiarized someone's work."

Lucy drained her latte and set the mug on the table. "But wouldn't you sue someone for plagiarizing?"

"Well, *I* would. But then, my homicidal tendencies aren't that well-honed."

"By the way, Matt seemed okay today," Lucy said. "Charming, actually."

"Yes, he was. And I've been thinking—he did apologize the other night, so maybe we should give him the benefit of the doubt and attribute his surliness to grief."

"I guess. But I'd still be wary of him."

"We should be doing more," I said. "This is a slow start. We have a bunch of suspects—Joyce, her lover, unhappy defendants, sleep-deprived neighbors. And"—I winced—"Claudia. All we're doing is speculating."

"Speculating's okay as long as we don't drown in it. Don't worry, Hazel. Things will get rolling once we get some information."

"There must be another way of settling my family's debt to Claudia. I could treat her to a nice dinner at Lemaire, or one of Richmond's other upscale restaurants. Maybe two dinners would do it."

TWENTY-FIVE

"So, Ms. Rose—you just *happened* to walk into this room at random and catch Mrs. Zimmerman and an unidentified male in the act?"

"It wasn't at random. Like I said, I heard a cry and thought Randy's aunt needed help."

Fish's skepticism was understandable—somewhat—but he did take note of the details I provided about my surprise encounter with Joyce and her lover. I pictured his goofy grin as he said, "Thank you so much, Ms. Rose." With that, we wrapped up our brief conversation.

Vince came through the door with Olive in tow. Once settled in our recliners, with Morris curled up on my lap and Olive on Vince's, we exchanged accounts of our days. He'd been the featured speaker at a Charlottesville writing group, sharing his knowledge of researching true crime. My own afternoon adventures, while less scholarly, were more exciting.

"I don't know if Fish believes me," I said after describing Joyce's breach of memorial service etiquette.

"He has no reason not to. Although it does sound like a French farce."

"It does, doesn't it? Anything new on the case?"

"Nothing today. Unless Fish came up with something at the service. I'll check with Dennis tomorrow."

"Do you know if Randy and Joyce had a pre-nup?"

"There's no record of one."

"That's too bad. It would give Joyce a motive. According to Claudia, Joyce loathed Randy."

"Claudia may be trying to deflect suspicion from herself."

"She may be, but that doesn't mean Joyce didn't have a motive."

"True." Vince petted Olive. She stretched one paw, then the other, before resuming her nap. "Does Claudia know you're trying to prove her innocence in order to settle your family's debt for her saving your sister's life?"

"No, and it's best she doesn't know. If it turns out she's guilty, things would be awkward between us."

Vince laughed. "If she's guilty, things would *certainly* be awkward between you."

"That woman from Randy's office seemed unsure about his relationship with Joyce. What did Fish find out about Joyce's alibi?"

"Several people at the spa saw her during the time frame when Randy was killed. And even a few hours before and after, to allow for a margin of error."

"Lucy and I are going to focus on Joyce. Will you try to find her mom's obit?"

"Will do."

In cat fashion, Morris jumped off my lap and raced upstairs like he had a train to catch. I took advantage of my catless state and started up to my den.

I caught up on my emails and was about to see about dinner when Trudy called.

"Hi, Trudy. Where are you?"

"In Bled, Slovenia. It's a small, quaint town, teeming with tourists. But so is every place we visit."

Trudy spent a few minutes on the trip before saying, "But I can tell you more when I see you. What's the latest on my ex?"

I described meeting Joyce and catching her having an afternoon delight at her husband's memorial service.

"Oh, my God!" Trudy exclaimed. "I can't believe it! Gail must have been beside herself."

"She wasn't too happy, I can tell you that. Trudy, do you know *anything* about Joyce? Anything at all?"

"Very little. I never even met her, but I know what she looks like from LinkedIn. I ran into Randy at the library a few years ago, shortly before they married. According to him, Joyce worked as an editor for a local publishing company. The name escapes me."

"Kellogg Publishing in downtown Richmond," I said. "Lucy found Joyce on LinkedIn. She left that company a few years back."

"With Randy raking in the bucks, I guess she decided to ditch her day job. Maybe she wanted to write. Many editors do."

"Do you know anything about her background?"

"Not much. Randy said she was from somewhere on the west coast." Again, I wondered why Randy didn't know his wife's hometown.

"Why did she come to Richmond if she's an editor? Why not New York? Or Los Angeles?"

"She had a boyfriend who had moved to Richmond, so she followed him. Apparently the relationship didn't last."

"I'm going to ask Eileen to do some research on Joyce."

"Eileen has her hands full right now. The library director is on family leave and one of the head librarians is recovering from a car accident. I'd help you out but I don't have access to the databases like I used to have."

"And you're on vacation. No problem, Vince will help. I'll ask Eileen anyway, give her the chance to say no. I don't want her to feel left out."

"Yeah, you're right," Trudy said. "Did everyone respond when you asked for suggestions about our reading list?"

"Yes, but I haven't had a chance to look at anything. Hopefully tomorrow. I'd like to read mysteries set in European countries from the Communist regime, like the ones you've visited."

"Sarah and I have been to some bookstores, looking for mysteries written by locals and translated into English."

I chuckled. "I certainly hope they're translated. Else we'll need a really good dictionary. Have you found any mysteries?"

"Yes, I found one in a bookstore in Pula." She described the Croatian town and their tour of a Roman arena. "The title of the book is *The Return of Philip Latinowicz*. Not a mystery per se, but it sounds dark enough for book group."

We already had a dark mystery on our hands. And not the fictional kind.

TWENTY-SIX

Were my arms too flabby? The question occupied my thoughts during my Monday morning walk. I'd let my gym membership expire, thinking that walking was good enough exercise. I pictured myself fighting off Randy's killer with saggy arms. Time to make room on my calendar for upper body strength.

I expected a call from Lucy, reporting on Joyce Zimmerman's former job at the publishing house. Vince was unearthing Joyce's mother's obit. Waiting could be brutal and patience wasn't my strong suit.

Lucy called at eleven. Without preamble, she said, "Bernie Underwood, the office manager from Kellogg Publishing, says Joyce worked for her as an editor. Her name was Joyce Bennett before—"

"Joyce Bennett?" I broke in. "That name rings a bell. Not that Joyce or Bennett are unusual."

Lucy went on. "She was quiet as a mouse. Not long after marrying Randy, she beat it out of Kellogg's. No one missed her, although they sent her off in style at a goodbye party at the Tobacco Company."

"Never pass up an opportunity for a party," I quipped. "I've never been to the Tobacco Company. Name always put me off."

"They have a no smoking policy, like all restaurants these days. And the food is excellent. You should try it."

"Still. The name."

"Whatever." Lucy sighed. "Anyway, Bernie said she and her husband had dinner once with Joyce and Randy. Randy was giving Joyce a hard time about the pronunciation of Handel."

"What?"

"Handel. Randy claimed it was *Handle*, like a door handle. Joyce preferred *Hondel*."

"Are you talking about the composer?"

"Yes. What did you think I was talking about?"

"Door handles, I guess. I wondered why they were fighting about door handles." I laughed. "But that's the kind of minor thing that gets couples up in arms. I had a fight with one of my exes about how to pronounce 'orange.' "

"Which ex was that?"

"Bobby Dee. But he's my least favorite ex so let's not get started on him. Go on with the dinner story."

"Randy wouldn't let the Handel thing go. Joyce started shrieking at him, calling him a boorish jackass, among other things. Then she stormed out of the house, slamming the door."

"Wow."

"Bernie says Joyce never apologized or even got in touch again. Of course, she had already left Kellogg's."

"What did Randy do when Joyce left? Don't tell me—he laughed."

"Yes, that's what he did do. And he insisted that Bernie and her husband stay. So they finished dinner, including dessert. Randy was unfazed. They were very fazed."

"Interesting. And it says volumes about Randy and Joyce's marriage. But it doesn't move us forward in our investigation."

"Not so fast, Hazel dear." After a dramatic pause, Lucy said, "At the time Joyce worked at Kellogg's she was seeing someone. Bernie thought he was a lawyer who worked nearby. This was before Randy."

"Is that it? Did she say anything else about the guy?"

"She'd see them walking around downtown, getting lunch from the food trucks."

"So?"

"There's more." After another stagy pause, Lucy said, "Bernie saw them recently, at Zelda's in Church Hill." Zelda's Café was an independent coffee shop in one of Richmond's most historic areas.

"Hmm. I wonder what that could mean."

"The two met and conspired to kill Randy?"

"But why?"

"Bernie thinks Joyce ditched the other guy when the high-spirited and boisterous Randy came on the scene. Joyce married Randy because he was so much fun."

"The theory of opposites attracting at play there," I said. "Still, I guess the fun wore off. So, this Zelda's sighting . . . did Bernie meet this guy?"

"Yeah, but she was in a rush—Bernie's always in a rush—and doesn't remember his name. Thinks it was Rob or Ron, something like that. They were hunched over something that might have been a manuscript, making Bernie think Joyce could be doing some freelance editing. Or writing a story of her own. Oh, and she said this guy was at the memorial service the other day."

"Bernie was at the service?"

"Yes, but she left before we got there. She had to go to a baby shower."

"You know something? This could be a good lead. Maybe he's the one Joyce was with in the bedroom. Did Bernie say what he looked like?"

"Tall, brownish hair, fiftyish."

"Hmm. Could be the same one. Did we meet anyone with a name like Ron or Rob?"

"I don't remember a Ron or a Rob. And I don't remember anyone in a red plaid shirt. I'll go through these cards I collected. Some of these people put their photos on the cards."

"We have these bits and pieces of information, sightings, and such. How do we put them together to answer the burning question—who killed Randy Zimmerman?"

"We need to find out more about Joyce. Find people who knew her."

"Vince is looking for her mother's obit. Hopefully that will give us some information on Joyce. He's also researching Claudia—just to be thorough."

"Have you started your homework assignment?" Lucy asked.

"Homework assignment? Oh, the one on dialogue, two strangers talking at a bus stop? No, I'm planning to do that this afternoon."

"You forgot all about it, didn't you?" I couldn't fool my cousin.

"Well, yes. But I'm sure I *would* have remembered. Although I'm glad you reminded me."

"You're good with dialogue."

"Thanks. But in mysteries the dialogue has to move the plot along. That reminds me—Claudia called last night, asking about the memorial service. I was vague, and only said we had some interesting conversations."

"Good."

"She *tsked* at me, but apparently thought it best to let us deal with things in our own way. She has the option of hiring a professional. Although—"

Lucy finished my thought. "You'd have to find another way to pay that debt."

"Exactly. Oh well, there's always the upscale restaurant idea."

We ended the call with a laugh.

"Joyce Bennett," I yelled to Vince.

When he didn't respond, I walked down the hall to his den and found him with his headset cutting off communication with the household. Namely me. Plus his noisy, and slow, printer was spitting out sheets of paper.

When he removed the headset, I repeated, "Joyce Bennett. That was her name before she married."

"Thanks, but I already found that on her marriage certificate." He picked up the papers from the printer tray and handed them to me.

"You need a faster printer."

"Yeah, yeah, I know."

"Thanks for finding these." I started back to my den before stopping. "Oh, let me tell you what Lucy found out about Joyce."

I ran down Lucy's accounts of Joyce's job at Kellogg Publishing and her storming out of the house during a dinner she hosted. "Oh, and wait'll you hear this."

"The sighting at Zelda's may be significant," Vince said when I finished Bernie Underwood's report on the guy Joyce had palled around with pre-Randy. And post-Randy.

"Bernie told Lucy the guy's name is Ron or Rob. *Maybe*. But Lucy's going to check the business cards she got yesterday."

"Okay, now I'll see what I can find on Claudia," Vince said.

I read as I walked back to my den. Not a good practice for someone my age with iffy bones and cats given to lounging at the top of the steps—an accident waiting to happen.

Randy and Joyce's marriage certificate provided the usual details of such documents: the marriage took place three years before in a non-denominational ceremony in Richmond. The bride was born in Ventura, California forty-two years before.

The obit for Joyce's mother skimped on information:

Mrs. Martha Sage Bennett Hirsch, 69, of Ventura, California, retired from 30 years of banking.

I went back to Vince's den, and he had to yank off his headset again.

"Ventura. Joyce is from Ventura."

"So?"

"One of my book groups is in Ventura." I explained that Ventura was a small city on the California coast, not far from Santa Barbara where Joyce went to college. I often visited book groups by Skype or Zoom. The Ventura group was one of my favorites and we met a couple of times a year. "It's a small enough place that one of them might know Joyce or her mother."

"There you go. You have something to do. Besides your writing, of course." Vince shot me a meaningful look at the writing comment.

"I'm working on my writing."

"Sure you are." His smile told me I wasn't convincing. He turned off his computer. "I didn't get far on Claudia. I'll keep looking when I get back."

"Where are you going?"

"Dentist. Then the gym."

"What about the cats? They have a vet appointment at one."

"Oh, that's right. I forgot. Sorry about that."

"No problem. It's so much fun forcing them into their carriers and hauling them around."

"I'll make it up to you." His blue eyes danced.

"Like the other night?" The memory of our post-River Edge lovemaking made me smile.

"Who knew a retirement home could lead to such, um, *effects?*"

"Let's move in," I teased as I kissed my husband. "Say hi to the folks at the dentist."

Back at my desk, I dashed off a text to Tonya Rhodes, coordinator of the Ventura book group, asking if she had time to talk.

"Absolutely," she responded less than a minute later. "Call me anytime." I punched her name in my contacts list.

I took Tonya through an account of Randy's murder and his wife's spending time in Ventura during the summer and fall. When I asked her if she knew Joyce, Tonya told me something I hadn't expected to hear:

"I do. She came to our book group a couple of times. You met her in August, at the last Skype session we had with you."

TWENTY-SEVEN

"You're kidding! She was at the book group?"

"She was. You don't remember her?"

"No, I don't. Funny, because I would think she'd have looked familiar when I saw her at the memorial service. But apparently I didn't make an impression on her either, as she gave no indication that she recognized me."

"She was very quiet."

I didn't know how quietness impacted memory, but I let the matter go. "Did you know her pretty well?"

"No. I didn't know her at all till Amy brought her to the group. Joyce was a bit younger than most of us, but she and Amy were in the same high school class. Plus Amy lives next door to where Joyce's mother lived before she passed away. But tell me, Hazel—why are you asking about this?"

"I'm helping Vince with some preliminary research. You know, he writes true crime." In the group, we spent much time talking about our personal lives, especially our spouses.

"Do you think Joyce killed Randy?"

"I have no idea. All I'm doing is getting background information for Vince. He wants to know everything about everyone involved."

"We all know you get involved in investigations. We just never mentioned it, mainly because you haven't."

"Well, I haven't committed to investigating this one. Back to the matter at hand—you said Joyce attended the book group a couple of times? Until she came back to Richmond?"

"No, she left before that. She didn't like the books we were reading."

Was my book one of the ones Joyce found unworthy of her time and attention? Tonya and I observed a *don't ask, don't tell* policy. "What can you tell me about her?"

"Quiet, low key, boring. Sorry to sound unkind, but no one minded when she left. She wasn't unpleasant, but she wasn't pleasant either. But still waters run deep, as they say. According to Amy, Joyce and Mick Jacoby were a hot item at one time. He's kind of a legend in town, one of those classic bad boys, sexy as all get out."

"Quiet, low key, boring teams up with bad boy." I reached for a pen and scrap of paper and jotted down the name Mick Jacoby. Why, I didn't know. He was probably part of Joyce's distant past.

Tonya went on. "Amy told us that the day Joyce's mom died, she, meaning Joyce, first made funeral arrangements, then went out on a date with the undertaker. She returned the next morning—in the same outfit."

"Not very ethical of either of them." I didn't share about finding Joyce in bed with a still-unidentified someone. Apparently Joyce hadn't been a faithful wife.

"No. Luckily the undertaker's uncle owns the funeral business, so he didn't have to worry about losing his job."

"So Joyce stayed out there for a while, cleared out the house, and put it on the market? Is that right?"

"I think it's still on the market."

"Did her mother have money?"

"I don't think so. She lived in kind of a middle class

neighborhood. Maybe even lower class. You know one of those places that was nice at one time?"

"She could have been a miser."

"You're right. I had an aunt who lived in a hovel and she was loaded."

"Did Joyce have any other family?"

"I don't think so." Tonya chuckled. "Why don't you write a mystery, Hazel?"

"As a matter of fact, I'm writing one right now." I didn't go into my hard-luck story about being dropped by my publisher.

"Great! A lot of us in the romance group like mysteries."

When Tonya and I wrapped up our conversation, I sat for a minute, trying to marshal my thoughts. I knew more about Joyce than I did before. But how helpful would the information turn out to be?

My computer clock read twelve-thirty. I went to the utility room and pulled the cat carriers off the storage shelf before searching for the rascals. I was convinced they "knew" the schedule for their annual checkups and made themselves scarce. Once in their carriers and in the car, they expressed their displeasure with inharmonious meowing. Thankfully the trip to the animal hospital was only a mile.

In the examining room, I took pictures of Morris cowering under a bench, hoping we'd forget about him. A suspicious Olive wandered around on a counter, sniffing. I posted the pictures on Instagram and Facebook.

The vet pronounced the scamps sound and healthy. Despite their vowing to hate me forever, Morris and Olive forgot about their torturous experience once they arrived home and were rewarded with treats.

Thinking that the humans in the household needed a treat as well, I scanned my pantry shelves for baking ideas. A can of pumpkin caught my eye. With Thanksgiving coming up, pumpkin seemed perfect. Thanksgiving made me wonder about the current status of Lucy and Dave's relationship. She'd been tight-lipped about it ever since she first told me. Did she regret confiding in me? I wanted to ask how things were, but wasn't sure how to frame the question, and hoped she didn't take my avoiding the subject as a sign of not caring. Vince and I usually spent Thanksgiving with Lucy and her family. Would we this year? Turkey day was ten days away.

I assembled the ingredients for pumpkin bread and slid the loaves in the oven to bake. For the next hour, the aromas of the fragrant bread, redolent of cinnamon and cloves, wafted from the kitchen. I worked on Claudia's assignment, putting together what I hoped was compelling dialogue.

Vince arrived home. "What smells good?"

"Pumpkin bread." I pointed to the loaves cooling on the counter. After reporting the good news about Morris and Olive's glowing health, I recounted my conversation with Tonya.

"So you actually met Joyce before?"

"Yes, on Skype. Incredible, isn't it? I bet any money that Joyce killed Randy. Or she got that hot guy to do it. Do the police know who he is?"

"Not as of this morning."

I turned my attention to the pumpkin bread. "Want some?"

At Vince's enthusiastic "sure," I cut two slices for us.

"Excellent, as always," he said after scarfing down the warm bread. "I'll have more."

I handed him a second helping. "So the spa is the Inn by the Bay?"

"Yes. Oh, I know that look. You want to go there."

"It's a two hour drive at the most. Joyce could easily drive to Richmond, kill her husband, and drive back to the spa."

"What do you think you'll find that the police haven't?"

"People will tell Lucy and me stuff they wouldn't tell the police. And Lucy has a personal connection. Her mother-in-law used to go there all the time before she passed away. In fact she took Lucy with her a couple of times. Thanksgiving's coming up. I'm sure Lucy would want to take them something in Constance's memory."

"Well, if you and Lucy go together—"

"You don't have to keep reminding me to have someone accompany me," I said.

"I'm concerned about you."

"I know, and I appreciate it. But I won't do anything dangerous. I promise."

I sealed my promise with a kiss, a kiss perfumed with pumpkin and spice.

TWENTY-EIGHT

"Interesting that you'd already met Joyce on Skype," Lucy said after I filled her in on my conversation with Tonya Rhodes. "Even if you underwhelmed each other."

"Vince did some research on Claudia. He didn't find anything we didn't already know. No criminal record. She keeps a tight grip on her privacy. Her blog posts yield nothing personal."

"Anything on her husband? Kids?"

"As we know, her husband's a musician, plays the trumpet. According to his website, his current gig is at a club in Virginia Beach. Vince didn't say anything about the kids, but he's still looking. Of course, we know about her daughter and grandson in Short Pump."

"Oh, I checked the cards—no Rons or Robs," Lucy said.

I groaned. "We need answers. Are you up for a trip to Inn by the Bay to check out Joyce's alibi? Maybe dig up some dirt?"

"Sure. When?"

"As soon as we can. I thought you might like to take a gift for the director. I know your mother-in-law went there frequently. Didn't you go with her a few times?"

"Yes, I did. I don't know if the director would remember me, but gifts never hurt. I'll put together a nice basket. Thanksgiving-themed."

"We'll go in on it together. So when can you go?"

Lucy checked her iPhone calendar. "Can't do it till Thursday. My schedule's full the next few days and I can't change anything. Sorry to slow things down."

"That's okay. The police could nail the killer by then. And, like Vince said, I can always work on my writing."

On Tuesday morning, I worked on a plan for Murder on Tour's upcoming year. I read the emails the group's members sent in response to my recent request for suggestions. All agreed with my idea to read mysteries set in European countries from the Communist regime, preferably penned by authors native to the countries. Trudy had been to Hungary and the Czech Republic the year before and had brought home a copy of *Quarantine in the Grand Hotel*, written in the thirties by a Hungarian author. I noted the title she had found on her current tour of Croatia, *The Return of Philip Latinowicz*.

Time for a stab at Facebook as a research tool. I hadn't found the right Joyce Zimmerman on Facebook. But I might be able to unearth Joyce Bennett. If we had mutual friends, they could provide useful information. Lots of Joyce Bennetts, but none struck me as the one I sought.

I tried Mick Jacoby, for no reason other than it was something to do. Knowing where he lived or what he looked like would help. Tonya's "bad boy" description could apply to several of the Mick Jacobys who smiled at me from their profile pictures. I asked myself why I was even interested in the man. Tonya indicated they'd split up —but she didn't know how long ago.

On to Twitter. Joyce didn't tweet under any of her names. But if she wasn't on Facebook, she likely wouldn't be on Twitter. But—

much to my surprise—I found a picture of a Mick Jacoby on Twitter. With Joyce.

Neither of them had a Twitter account. One Dan Ferguson had tweeted this gem four years before. Dan listed Florida as his residence in his profile. The sand, surf, and swimsuits told me the setting was a beach, likely in Florida. Mick and Dan flanked Joyce, each cupping one of her breasts with one hand while holding cans of beer aloft in the other. Charming.

Joyce and Mick stood at about the same height. Joyce's bikini showed lots of skin. Mick sported a white blond buzz cut and hid behind mirrored sunglasses. Tattoos decorated his arms and chest. Dan, inches shorter than his companions, had a dissipated look. That and an over-hanging belly showed a fondness for alcohol.

I replied to the tweet, asking Dan if he knew anything about Joyce and Mick.

So their relationship thrived as recently as four years before—a relatively short time. Did Mick have a role in Randy's death? It didn't hurt to consider everyone.

At one o'clock Vince walked by my den. "Let's have lunch. Grilled cheese sandwiches?"

"And tomato soup?"

"Sure."

"Take a look at this picture." I tabbed back to the Twitter photo of Joyce, Mick, and Dan.

Vince laughed. "Classy threesome."

TWENTY-NINE

Like most authors these days, I often found myself tethered to social media. After lunch, I checked Twitter to see if Dan had replied to my inquiry. He hadn't. I stayed on Twitter for a while, tweeting and retweeting.

Time for a break. I drove to the mall, wanting to see what Richmond Books had in the way of book-related gift items suitable for holiday giveaways to my readers. After roaming around the store for close to an hour and not settling on anything, I spotted a display of felt tote bags and quickly purchased several before changing my mind.

Before leaving the store, I checked my books on the shelves in the Romance section, seeing if any needed my autograph. Randy and Lorraine so distracted me on the day of the book signing that the task had slipped my mind. Several copies needed my flourish. Felicia Brimwell, the store's author coordinator, stood behind the information desk in the center of the store. After handing me a roll of "autographed by" stickers to affix to the front covers of my books, we fell to discussing Randy's murder.

"Do you think Claudia did it? It happened just a few hours after she slugged the guy over there." Felicia waved toward the café. "I did, of course, have to tell the police about that."

"Of course you did," I said. "I sure hope she didn't do it and is only a victim of bad timing."

"Me too. It would be such a loss to the writing community. Although I guess she could still write from prison." Felicia fiddled with a dangling silver earring. "Did you mention a mystery writing class Claudia was teaching?"

"Yes, it started last week." I briefly described the class. "Lorraine Popp is taking it. And Randy was going to."

"So you're going to write mysteries?"

"Yes, I'm thinking of broadening my writing."

"Good. You're such a great writer. I can see you and Claudia signing together. The lines would be out to the parking lot." Felicia held out an arm toward the main entrance.

Before I could get out a "thanks," Felicia said, "Lorraine Popp surprised me. I was a little worried when I first met her. She's sweet, but kind of spacey. But she did great."

"Yes, she did." I didn't add that Lorraine owed her success to Lucy and me. "She's a debut author and on her way to becoming a name to notice. Oh, and I'm so sorry I forgot to post the pictures on Instagram."

Felicia waved a hand. "Now that I think of it, I'm surprised Lorraine wasn't sitting with Claudia and Randy in the café after their signings. She sat by herself at a table right behind them, reading a book."

"Oh?"

"Yes, Claudia—" Felicia stopped to help a customer and I went back to my signing task. When Felicia returned, she said, "Now where were we? Oh, the café. The funny thing is that Claudia had been so keen on including Lorraine in the signing that I thought they were buddies, or that Claudia would be her mentor. Especially since you say Lorraine's taking Claudia's class."

"But they sat at different tables in the café?"

"Yes. Strange. I almost didn't recognize Lorraine, because she was wearing a beret and a denim jacket in the café. She hadn't been when signing."

"Probably Lorraine didn't want to sit with Randy. I don't think she was too hot on him. Neither was I, for that matter."

"Why was that?" Felicia asked.

Was it a good idea to call attention to the altercation I had with Randy at Lorraine's signing table? Had Felicia heard it? If so, she hadn't reported it to the police. Figuring that being open could yield useful information, I said, "Randy ridiculed our writing. He was pretty obnoxious."

When a half dozen customers queued up at the information desk, Felicia tended to them and I finished signing my stack of books. Not expecting to learn much more, I decided to walk through the mall.

Midway through the food court a woman caught my eye. It was easy to see why. She was drop-dead gorgeous with her cascade of black hair and cut glass cheekbones. Her snug-fitting sapphire sweater displayed her assets to advantage. She sipped a drink through a straw and stared into the middle distance.

"Hi, Sherry."

I could describe the expression that crossed Sherry's perfect features as I disturbed her reverie in one word: alarmed. She quickly stood and gathered her purse, drink, and disposable plate that held remnants of a pizza slice. Then she fled.

"Wait, Sherry. You forgot your book." I picked up a Richmond Books bag and waved it at her. But she kept moving, only stopping to toss her plate in the trash.

A heavyset man sitting nearby raised his eyebrows. "I guess she didn't want to talk to you," he said cheerfully.

"Guess not." Sherry took a right turn at the end of the food court. "But she left her book."

"She'll probably be back for it." The man bit into his calzone.

"I'm going to try to catch up with her." I took off, making the same right after the Sunglass Hut that Sherry had.

She hadn't been wearing a coat or jacket, making me think she worked in one of the stores. Mall stores these days catered to the young, so I got some curious looks as, one by one, I visited them. Likely customers and sales associates assumed I was shopping for my child. Or grandchild. At least I didn't have to dodge the hordes of shoppers, mostly teenagers, who populated the place on weekends.

In Macy's, I walked around the perimeter of the store and up and down the aisles, head swiveling, hoping to catch sight of the elusive Sherry. No luck.

After forty-five minutes, I gave up my search and returned to the food court. The calzone-eating man had left. I pulled Sherry's book from the bag I still clutched. *How to Be an Effective Volunteer in Today's World.* Sherry needed a manual for volunteering? I'd done my share of volunteer work and never once consulted a manual. It was something you just *did.* I didn't find a receipt in the bag or between the pages of the book.

Richmond Books was adjacent to the food court. I left Sherry's book with a cheerful young man behind the counter at the front of the store. He wore his shiny brown hair coiled in a man bun. His face wasn't a familiar one, and he didn't recognize me from my many signings at the store, so likely he was a recent employee.

"Oh yes, Sherry bought this a little while ago," he said.

"You know Sherry?" I asked. "I tried to catch up with her but lost her. Does she work in the mall?"

"I think so, she wears a badge. Macy's, Sears, Penney's . . ." He trailed off, shrugging. "I know her from church."

"That's something I need to do, find a church. Do you like yours?"

"I love it! My parents never took me, but my girlfriend talked me into going a few months ago and it's the best thing that ever happened to me."

"You certainly sound happy. What church is it?"

"Grace of God Community Church. It's on Courthouse Road, other side of Hull."

"Is it a friendly church?"

"It's super friendly. Very bible-centered. And lots of people your age, with nursery facilities for your grandkids."

"Good to know." I smiled at the age reference. "I'll check out the church. Grace of God Community Church, right?"

The young man nodded, eyes shining.

"I'm worried about getting Sherry's book back to her. Do you know her last name? Maybe I can find her on social media."

"No, sorry, Ma'am. I haven't known Sherry for long. But she comes in here often, so I wouldn't be too worried about it. If she doesn't pick it up before Sunday, I'll tell her about it at church."

"Sounds good. You may see me there some Sunday. With my grandkids."

"I hope so, Ma'am."

There was that irksome "Ma'am" again. I pictured my alter-ego Marjorie Adams with a passel of grandkids, delighting in the "Ma'am" label.

In the car, I googled Sherry's church, noted the address, and aimed my Honda Insight toward Courthouse Road.

THIRTY

Judging from Google's description and the building's size, Grace of God Community Church was one of those mega churches that televised their Sunday services. Generous amounts of wood and glass created several soaring vaulted roofs. No doubt religious symbolism played a part in the design.

Lucy sang in the choir at her church and I sometimes attended, especially when she gave a solo performance. Her pastor favored intellectual sermons that made me snooze. In fact, one morning after a sleepless night my head fell against the man next to me. He'd smiled indulgently, but his wife bristled.

"Hazel Rose, as I live and breathe!" A woman came around a long curved desk in the church entrance hall and threw her arms around me in a bear hug.

So much for my plans to use my Marjorie Adams alias. Aloud, I said, "Lola Mays? How wonderful to see you. I didn't know you worked here."

"I've only been here a couple of months."

Lola Mays, one of my beta readers and all-round cheerleaders, bore an uncanny resemblance to an aging Betty Boop. The c-shaped curls framing her round face recalled the beloved cartoon character.

The bag of potato chips, package of Oreo cookies, and twenty-ounce beverage container beside Lola's laptop no doubt explained the twenty or so extra pounds padding her frame.

"So what brings you to Grace of God?"

"I met a woman named Sherry who goes here, and she raved about this place." I feigned a senior moment. "I don't remember her last name. An attractive young woman with long dark hair." I touched a point by my hip to measure a length of hair.

"That sounds like Sherry Guanzon."

"That's it!" I exclaimed with triumph. "Sherry Guanzon."

"Let me give you a tour." Lola called a woman who walked behind the desk a moment later, ready to take Lola's place while she played tour guide.

"Impressive," I said several times as she led me through room after room—rooms for Christian education, a gym, fellowship hall with kitchen, and a massive auditorium for worship services.

"Sherry is such a sweet, sweet person," Lola gushed. "So is her mother. And her little boy is simply *adorable*. But something strange happened one Sunday—". Lola looked around. "I don't want Pastor Frank to hear me. He doesn't like it when I gossip." No one seemed to be in the vicinity but Lola took the caution of lowering her voice before going on. "This woman showed up here, screaming at Sherry."

"What was that about?"

"She wanted Sherry to stay away from her husband."

"What did the woman look like?"

"Tallish. Of course, I'm so short everyone is tall to me. Long blond hair. Kind of plain. If she was worried about someone like Sherry, she should glam herself up a bit."

"I guess. What about Sherry's husband? Was he with her?"

"I'm not sure she even has a husband. She attends with her little boy and her mother."

Tour over, I thanked Lola for her time.

"So, Hazel, when will I have another story to read?"

"Do you like mysteries? I'm going to be writing them now."

Lola's big eyes, framed in what had to be false eyelashes, widened. "Nothing gory, I hope."

"Nothing gory." I smiled, adding, "And there will still be plenty of romance."

She handed me a brochure. "I hope to see you here on Sunday. Bring your husband. Bring your family and friends."

"I'll definitely be here on Sunday," I said, meaning it.

"I think Sherry was having an affair with Randy," I said without preamble when I arrived home. "And, when things went awry, she killed him."

"Interesting conclusion." Vince showed no surprise at my pronouncement. "How did you arrive at it?"

When I told him about my strange encounter with Sherry Guanzon and the ensuing search through the mall, he said, "Are you sure it was her?"

"Sure, I'm sure. She looked so alarmed, like I was coming to arrest her. You know, at the signing, I tried to photograph her with Randy, Matt, and Lorraine. Sherry refused to be in the picture."

"So she's camera shy. Lots of people are."

"Someone who looks like Sherry shouldn't be camera shy."

"She might not realize she's beautiful."

"You're right," I allowed. "If she has poor self-esteem, she might think she's unattractive."

"Nothing you've said explains why you think she killed Randy."

"Oh, well, there's more. I went to her church and—"

"What? You went to her *church*?"

"Yes, that's how I learned her last name. Wait'll you hear what I found out." When I finished, I said, "So I'm thinking that Sherry had a thing going with Randy and Joyce went to the church to warn her off him."

"But that's guesswork on your part. Plus it's a scenario that points more to Joyce killing Randy than Sherry killing him."

"Yes, okay, Joyce is still on the suspect list. But why was Sherry so spooked when she saw me?"

"I have no idea."

"Should I tell Fish?"

"Tell him what? There's nothing to tell him."

As I fumed about the lack of information to feed the police, Vince said, "Why did you go to that church on your own? You said you weren't going to do that."

"Sorry, but it was a spur-of-the-moment thing. Besides, what's going to happen to me in a church?"

"Next time, call me. Your spurs of the moment could get you in trouble, especially if Sherry *is* a suspect. I worry about you."

"Next time I will. Promise. I appreciate your caring about me." I blew my husband a kiss. "What do you think about the idea of Sherry being a volunteer—or planning to be one?"

Without waiting for an answer, I said, "I'll email people I know who work in non-profits. Someone might have heard of her. Sarah Rubottom has volunteered for just about every non-profit in Richmond."

"You're going to bother her while she's traveling?"

"She just has to answer a question. It's not like I'm expecting her to do anything."

"You used to do volunteer work. Why did you stop?"

"I don't know. Got busy, I guess." I often chided myself to get back into that world.

"If writing doesn't keep you out of trouble, and obviously it doesn't, volunteer work might do the trick."

"Maybe," I said absently. "George might know Sherry from one of his volunteer gigs. But he's probably busy with his grandsons now."

"Email him."

"No, he tends to be terse in his emails but forthcoming in person. I'll tackle him in the morning."

Vince's thumbs-up gesture signaled approval. "I'll see if I can find anything on Sherry," he said.

"Thanks." How could I get to the bottom of the mystery surrounding Randy Zimmerman's death? The missing puzzle pieces remained missing.

"Oh, I almost forgot—". When I got through the bit about Lorraine sitting behind Randy and Claudia in the Richmond Books café, I added, "So she must have heard some interesting stuff, like what Randy said to get himself slapped."

"But Lorraine didn't report this to the police," Vince said.

"No, she didn't. Hmm. That café can get pretty noisy, so maybe she didn't hear anything. Still, it seems like she would have."

We were fresh out of insights. Sighing, I said, "Well, I have stuff to do on my computer."

Dan Ferguson replied to my earlier tweet about Joyce and Mick: "Sorry. Lost touch with those two. They came through Florida four years ago and I haven't heard from them since."

When I asked where they lived, he immediately replied, "Not sure. Sorry, Babe." He didn't ask why I wanted to know and I didn't enlighten him.

Returning my attention to Sherry, I emailed Sarah Rubottom and a couple of others in the non-profit sector to see if they knew, or knew of, a Sherry Guanzon. I explained the reason for my interest to Sarah, but not to the others.

Sherry might have provided her workplace on social media. But the Sherry Guanzons I found on Facebook, Twitter, and Instagram bore no resemblance to the stunning Sherry I sought.

I sat, waiting for inspiration. It came almost at once. Randy. See if she's Facebook friends with him.

But she wasn't. Unless she was one of those exasperating people who lived life under multiple names. Like Sherry was her middle name, or she was really a Veronica but preferred Sherry. I scanned the photos of Randy's friends but, again, I saw no one who resembled the glamorous Sherry.

Nothing was easy.

THIRTY-ONE

"Lorraine was sitting right behind Randy and Claudia in the Richmond Books café?" Lucy stopped for a light and looked at me. "Why wouldn't she tell the police about it?"

"Beats me. It's not the kind of thing you forget."

We puzzled over Lorraine and Sherry's inexplicable actions as we made our way to the library for our second writing class.

When the light changed, Lucy hit the gas pedal. "I remember Lorraine picking up a jacket and purse when she left the signing table that day. I thought she was leaving the store, but I guess she decided to unwind in the café."

In the library, we walked down to the lower level. A smiling woman stood at the bottom of the steps.

"Evelyn!" We hugged. Turning to Lucy, I said, "This is my cousin, Lucy Hooper. Lucy, this is Evelyn Estes, one of my most loyal readers. And Claudia's as well. She stood in Claudia's long line at Richmond Books last week."

"I just ran into Claudia," Evelyn said. "I saw on Facebook that you're taking her mystery writing class. You're not giving up romances, are you?" From her stricken look, I took it she didn't favor the idea.

I explained my foray into the mystery genre. "I've been thinking about doing this for a while. Don't worry, there'll still be plenty of romance."

"Hmm. I guess that's okay." Evelyn shifted her pile of books from one arm to the other. "Did you know Claudia's one of my neighbors?"

"No, I didn't."

She leaned closer, like she had classified information to share. "No one in the neighborhood has ever seen her husband."

"Well, he's a musician and travels a lot."

"Yes, a *lot*. Write a mystery about it. You could call it *The Case of the Missing Husband*."

"Claudia never says much about him but I had the impression the marriage was a good one," I said, leaving out my own reservations about the relationship.

Evelyn raised her eyebrows and gave us a knowing look.

"Maybe he's been there and you've missed him," Lucy said.

"We have a couple of old biddies on the street. One of them lives next door to Claudia. The kind who sits by the window all day and doesn't miss a thing. Believe me, she'd know if the husband showed up."

"Maybe they split up," I said. "I could have drawn the wrong conclusion about their marriage."

"I see you've met my neighbor."

I spun around. "Claudia!" How much had she heard? I hoped my bright greeting canceled out my no doubt guilty look. "Evelyn and I have known each other for quite a while. She's one of my favorite readers."

"And one of my favorite neighbors. Time for class, ladies." Claudia turned and walked toward the conference room.

Before moving on, Evelyn exhorted me to get another book written, and fast. She and Lucy exchanged "Nice meeting yous."

Once settled in the meeting room, Claudia asked for updates on our works-in-progress. Lorraine lost no time raising her hand.

"Yes, Lorraine."

"I've decided what I want to write about. Hazel helped me find my niche." She shot a smile at me. "Genealogy. Like I told Hazel, I have ancestors who were criminals." She gave brief accounts of the deeds of her ne'er-do-well relatives. Her enthusiasm both surprised and delighted me.

"That's a wonderful idea, Lorraine," Claudia said. "Keep us posted on your progress. How about you, Matt?"

"Um, nothing new."

"I enjoyed your story," Claudia said.

"I did too," Lorraine chimed in. "Especially the period legal details."

"If you want it critiqued, we'll do that at the last class," Claudia said.

Matt didn't say "whatever," but his shrug gave the impression of indifference.

Eileen had reached fifty thousand words on her manuscript. Lucy's schedule hadn't allowed a minute to write, and my scant progress stirred little interest. Likely Lorraine and Eileen saved Claudia from despair over our unproductive class.

Claudia moved on to the subject of dialogue. "Use dialogue to tell your story," she advised. "Let the characters tell your readers what's going on. For example, 'I saw your husband hit on his secretary at the office party' is more interesting than presenting the same information in the narrative voice: 'Jane was disgusted when she saw her friend's husband hitting on his secretary at the office party.' "

"You can also use dialogue to develop your characters." Claudia picked up a Robert B. Parker book from a stack on the table. She did the same with an Elmore Leonard title.

"These two crime authors are renowned masters of dialogue." She passed the books to Matt on her left and continued clicking from slide to slide of her PowerPoint presentation until she declared it time for a break.

"It looks like Lorraine listened to you after all," Lucy said. We were walking around the parking lot during our break.

"It's wonderful to see her so fired up."

"What Evelyn told us was interesting."

"Yes, it was." Lest Claudia suddenly materialize, I lowered my voice. "I wonder if Claudia heard any of our conversation."

"I sure hope not. Not when we were talking about her husband."

I paused, thinking this the perfect segue to a discussion, or even a remark, on the status of Lucy's marriage. Had her personal problems, and not a busy schedule, caused her lack of progress in writing? Eileen's walking up to us put the kibosh on that opportunity.

"How's the investigation going?" She stage whispered.

Lucy and I filled her in on the various findings and doings in a very amateur investigation. When I described my afternoon adventure at the mall playing hide-and-seek with Sherry, followed by the visit to Grace of God Community Church, Eileen said, "I've been to Sherry's church and liked it. But it's too far to go every week."

"Were you there the day a woman screamed at Sherry?"

"No. I missed that one."

"I'm thinking about going on Sunday. Want to join me?"

"Sure," Eileen agreed.

"Not me," Lucy said. "I'm reading at my service."

"I'll pick you up on Sunday at ten," I said to Eileen.

"I have some time now," she said. "Let me know if I can help with the investigation."

"I have an idea," I said. "Settlements. The police have been researching Randy's cases, looking for disgruntled defendants and plaintiffs. But I'm wondering about people who won cases. Or ended up with nice settlements."

"But maybe the settlements weren't nice enough?" Eileen guessed.

"Exactly. See if anything changed—if an unhappy plaintiff died recently, maybe his or her family would focus on Randy."

"I'll get right on it." Eileen sounded like I'd handed her gold. Her eyes danced. "I remember Trudy saying that often Randy's clients didn't want to settle, but Randy would strong-arm them into it. There was a court case and the jury members were commenting a lot to each other, saying the plaintiff didn't appear to be in that much pain. One of the jury members told the judge about the comments."

"Jurors aren't supposed to talk amongst themselves about the cases they're sitting on," Lucy said.

"Doesn't mean they don't," Eileen said.

"So they agreed to settle because they thought the jury was prejudiced?" I asked.

Eileen nodded. "Although there could have been other factors involved."

I took my phone from my purse. "Want to see something sleazy?"

"Sure," Lucy and Eileen chorused.

I accessed my Twitter account and showed them the picture of Mick Jacoby and Dan Ferguson cupping Joyce's breasts.

"Eww, that *is* sleazy," Eileen said.

Lucy agreed. "So that's Mick Jacoby, huh? But do we care about him?"

"I don't know. He's not the same guy from the memorial service. I don't *think*. Anyway, Dan doesn't know where they are. Of course, we know where Joyce is."

"Matt's sure devoted to his phone," Lucy said, glancing at Matt and Lorraine, standing under an overhead light. He talked and scrolled at the same time, a testament to multi-tasking. The three of us laughed as we walked back into the building.

"I wonder if Matt's accusing Lorraine of killing Randy." At Eileen's startled expression, I pulled her aside and filled her in on Matt's behavior from the week before.

Eileen's eyes widened behind her glasses. "Be careful."

As I took my seat in the meeting room, I asked, "Claudia, when's the next Sisters in Crime meeting? I'm sure some of us would like to go."

"January. Check their website or Facebook page."

"Thank you," I said, puzzled by Claudia's snippy tone.

We read our homework assignments aloud. Most of us had no trouble creating dialogue between two strangers at a bus stop, but Lorraine's newfound enthusiasm for writing hadn't yet extended to a conversation on the page. Eileen did so well that I wondered if she chatted at bus stops on a regular basis.

At the end of the class, Claudia approached Lucy and me. "We need to talk. Can we meet at Café Sweetbrew tomorrow?"

"I can. How 'bout you, Lucy?"

"Sure. Eight o'clock."

"Fine." Claudia slung her messenger bag over her shoulder.

"What the hell," Lucy said after Claudia exited the room at a brisk pace. "What's with the snotty attitude?"

"Who knows." I picked up my bag and notebook. "I guess we'll find out tomorrow."

"First Sherry, now Claudia." Lucy grinned. "You're having a time of it with women today."

"You're right. Randy's women."

THIRTY-TWO

Lucy took a different route home: the winding, two-lane River Road, lined with luxury properties overlooking the James River. I once read an article stating that sometimes your brain tells you to do something different, like taking a different route. What did Lucy's brain have in mind when it directed her down River Road?

"I wonder what Lorraine and Claudia were talking about," Lucy said. In the library's parking lot, the two women had lingered by Claudia's SUV.

"Writing's my guess. Probably Lorraine is asking Claudia for advice."

"At least Matt didn't waylay us. I didn't even see his monstrous SUV. Must have hightailed it out of there."

"Lucy, I'm thinking about starting a study group for our class."

"A study group? Like in college?"

"Kind of. Lorraine needs a lot of help with her assignments. Next week we're doing character development. So I thought—"

"Yes, it's fine to help her. But your real motive is finding out what she heard in the café."

"Well, yeah. But if we can help her as well, it's win-win."

"Sure. Set it up." Lucy sounded distracted. "This guy's tailgating me."

I turned. Someone drove perilously close to Lucy's Prius. "It's hard to see anything, especially with that spoiler in the way."

Suddenly, light flooded our car.

"God, now he's on my bumper with his high beams on." Lucy adjusted her rearview mirror to reduce the glare. She let loose a few choice expletives as she honked her horn.

"Why don't you turn into one of these driveways?"

"No." Lucy sounded adamant. "I'm *not* letting him win. We'll turn at the exit for Chippenham, like we would normally."

I understood Lucy's feelings about not wanting to be bullied, but didn't think it a good stance to take on the road, especially at night.

"You're referring to the driver with the masculine pronoun. It could be a woman."

"I'm being generic, Hazel."

"I hope he—or she—doesn't follow us down Chippenham."

Lucy honked a couple more times, but the driver maintained a close distance.

"Can you see what kind of car it is?" Lucy asked.

"No. It's blinding in here."

Finally, the exit for the Chippenham Parkway loomed ahead. As Lucy turned, the offending vehicle roared off, continuing on River Road. I caught sight of a light-colored sedan, but the driver drove too fast for me to get so much as a digit of the license plate.

"Damn. I couldn't see the plate at all. I don't even know if it's from Virginia."

In my driveway, Lucy cut the engine and we sat, laughing ruefully.

"If we were born Southerners, we could joke that it was some rude Northerner," Lucy said.

"But since we're Northerners ourselves, we don't want to do that." Lucy hailed from upstate New York and I grew up in New Jersey.

"At least whoever it was is gone. Probably some jackass in a hurry. Or overburdened with testosterone."

"Do you think this has anything to do with the investigation?" I asked.

"No. He would have done more. In crime fiction, there's often a scene where someone tries to run the detective off the road."

"Do you want me to get Vince? We can follow you home."

"Oh no." Lucy waved a hand. "I'll be fine. We got rid of him. The tailgater, not Vince."

"We're still calling him he."

"Well, you do call a him a he, don't you?"

We laughed. Belly laughs that left us clutching our sides.

"I hope it wasn't Matt," Lucy said, gasping for breath. "He might have another vehicle besides that SUV."

"Call or text me when you get home."

"Will do. See you in the a.m. at Sweetbrew."

"Yeah, bright and early."

<hr>

Vince disagreed with Lucy's notion that someone trying to scare us off the investigation was unlikely. "Don't be too sure it isn't someone who feels threatened. We can't discount the possibility. But it could just be some jerk who thinks he owns the road."

"You're also assuming the driver was male."

"It was *probably* a male," he amended. "I'd sure feel better if you and Lucy stuck to the well-lit, four-lane roads and avoided River Road."

"Oh, we will. Don't worry about that."

"What is it? You look like you're struggling to say something."

"Yeah, I guess I am. I'm wondering if it was Matt Rowan."

"Why him?"

Vince's reaction to learning about the conversation Lucy and I had with Matt in the library parking lot the week before was predictable.

"Why didn't you tell me this before?"

"He backed off. We attributed the incident to his emotional state. Besides, he drives an SUV. At least he did last week. So, unless he has another vehicle, it probably wasn't him."

"If it happens again, call the police."

As promised, Lucy texted me. "Home!"

When Vince asked about the class, I started with Evelyn Estes's revelation about Claudia's husband and moved on to Claudia's puzzling attitude, Lorraine's discovering her "niche," my assigning settlements to Eileen, and Claudia's wanting to meet again at Café Sweetbrew.

"Maybe Claudia will explain herself when you see her in the morning."

"I hope so. Oh, and Eileen and I are going to Sherry's church on Sunday."

"I'm glad you're traveling in pairs."

I told Vince about my idea for the study group. "It was wonderful to see Lorraine so excited about writing. When we left, she and Claudia were in the parking lot, talking about writing."

"How do you know what they were talking about? Did you hear them?"

"Well, um, no. I guess I, well . . . *assumed*. And I don't need to hear the definition of *assume*."

Before getting ready for bed, I emailed Lorraine, Eileen, Lucy, and Matt about the study group. I pretended to brush off the tailgating incident, but it continued to haunt me. I slept little that night.

THIRTY-THREE

"What's keeping Claudia?" Lucy checked the time on her phone. "It's eight ten."

I glanced at my own phone. "She hasn't texted, called, or emailed."

We sat at the same window table at Café Sweetbrew we had the week before. While we waited for Claudia, we munched on bagels and sipped Sweetbrew's daily brew.

"You'll never guess what Vince found out about Sherry." Lucy looked expectant, but didn't hazard a guess. "Her husband's in prison!"

"In prison? What for?"

"Drug trafficking. He's serving a ten-year sentence."

"Interesting."

"Hello, ladies." We looked up to see the smiling face of Matt's wife, Susan. Her liberal application of makeup seemed better suited to more formal business attire than the casual look she presented: jeans, athletic shoes, and a sweatshirt jacket emblazoned with "Alaska." The short, tousled hairstyle with the honey-colored highlights probably required frequent visits to a pricey salon—and I guessed she'd been to one in the three days since the memorial service. I remembered the chin length style with long bangs.

"Hi, Susan," I said. "Join us."

"Thanks. I only have a few minutes, but I'd love to chat." She put her coffee and orange scone on the table and pulled out a chair. "Matt's enjoying the writing class. Although he thought he'd be taking it with his friend." Her mouth twisted.

"It must be so hard for him," Lucy said. "Being lifelong friends and all."

"I'm pretty broken up about it myself," Susan said. "I met Randy a while back when I had breast cancer. He was on the board of the cancer association and I met him at a fundraiser. We struck up a friendship."

"I'm sorry to hear about your cancer," I said.

"It's a thing of the past. I'm cancer free!"

"That's wonderful." I leaned forward. "Tell us how you met Matt."

"Randy introduced us. And Matt introduced him to Joyce. One good turn deserves another." Susan's eyes and mine met. "I can't tell you how shocked I was to see Joyce and that guy together the other day. What was she thinking?"

"Do you know who he is?"

"I haven't a clue. I guess she was so distraught over losing Randy that she turned to someone, anyone, to take away the pain."

Quite a charitable assessment of the situation, I thought. Trying for a nonchalant tone, I asked, "Were you and Matt close with Randy and Joyce as couples?"

"No, not too much."

We waited a beat for Susan to elaborate. Instead, she took a large bite of her scone. To fill the silence, Lucy said, "I'm enjoying Matt's story."

"Yes, Lucy's been raving about it." This was the first I'd heard Lucy mention Matt's literary effort, but a little deception never hurt. "I hope to get to it soon."

Once Susan finished chewing, she smiled. "Thanks for your kind words. I'm so proud of Matt. He says I should write a financial thriller. I was a financial planner before taking early retirement."

Early indeed, I thought. I pegged Susan to be in her late forties.

"You should be taking the writing class with Matt," Lucy said.

"I would, but I'm super busy right now. My dad died recently and I'm his executor."

"I'm sorry about your dad," Lucy said. "And being an executor is quite a responsibility. Do you have a large family?"

"No, just me."

"Claudia, our teacher, should be here any minute. If you're interested in taking a class in the future, she might be starting another one." Then, lest it sounded like Lucy and I were teacher's pets, I added, "Claudia and I are friends and get together often."

"I wonder where she *is,*" Lucy fussed.

"Speak of the devil," I quipped when a ding alerted me to a text. "She can't make it. Something came up," I said as I read. "That Claudia's one busy woman." My overly bright delivery made Lucy give me a what's-up look, but I'd wait till we were alone before sharing Claudia's actual message. I bit into my everything bagel, savoring the tartness of the cream cheese.

"Susan, are you on social media?" Lucy asked.

"Yes, Facebook. I'm not too active, though." Susan sipped her coffee. "Mostly with my high school class. We had a reunion this year and we all connected on Facebook."

"Where did you go to high school?" I asked.

"Near Roanoke." Susan named a city in the shadow of the Blue Ridge Mountains in Southwest Virginia. Changing the subject, she said, "Matt says you're a romance writer transitioning into mysteries. And Lucy, you're going to write something set in the corporate world, is that right?"

I was surprised Matt had shared so much information with his wife. In my experience, men were more general than detailed when reporting on conversations. Or was that sexist? Had Matt confided his suspicions about me to Susan? Her expression didn't let on that he had, but she could be gifted with a poker face.

"Right," I said. After Lucy and I elaborated on our goals for the writing class, Susan mentioned Eileen's clean-living PI. "And he says one of you is using genealogy as a theme."

"Yes, Lorraine."

"That should be fascinating," Susan said. "Researching my family tree's on my bucket list."

Like with Lorraine, I told Susan about the relatives my sister had unearthed. Unlike Lorraine, Susan found my experience of finding family members late in life fascinating.

"You say one of them lives right here in Richmond? You're so lucky. Do you see her? Or him?"

"Him. Yes, I expect to see Brad on Thanksgiving." I slanted a look at Lucy, not sure about Thanksgiving, or her current status with her husband.

"Susan, do you know about our book group?" Lucy asked. Was the change in subject a deliberate ploy to avoid the question of Thanksgiving?

"I don't." Susan finished her scone and wiped her fingers on a napkin. "It sounds interesting," she said with little conviction when we finished describing the Murder on Tour group. "Well, ladies, it's been fun talking with you. I have to go pick up my car in the shop. I was in an accident last week."

"I'm sorry," Lucy said. "Is everything all right?"

"Oh, yes. Just some body damage to the car. I was fine and so was the guy who hit me."

"Do you live nearby?" Lucy asked as we exchanged cards.

"Yes, not far. I walked here." She laughed. "I need the exercise after indulging in that scone."

Susan walked out the door and toward the alley that ran behind the café.

"Why on earth does she plaster on so much makeup? She's

retired. News anchors don't go that overboard, at least not the ones on the shows I've appeared on."

"Beats me." Lucy surveyed her burgundy nails. "Tell me about Claudia's text that you were obviously adlibbing before."

I handed Lucy my phone, and she read the text: "'Meet me at the Best Café at the Museum. Noon sharp.' My, my. Quite magisterial, isn't she?"

"Yes, I don't like this bossiness. She acts like we're her minions. But I do want to find out what's going on with her. Can you go to the museum? You said you had a full schedule. I could get Vince to go with me."

"Claudia might clam up if Vince is there."

"There's Eileen. But the museum should be safe. They have lots of security guards."

"No, I'll go with you. I can take time for lunch. But I'd better get moving now."

We carried our dishes to the bussing station before stepping outside. "How 'bout I text her that we can't meet till one?"

Lucy grinned. "A little passive aggressiveness?"

"Never hurts." I sent off the text.

"It's funny, Claudia was fine until last night, wasn't she?" Lucy asked.

"She was fine on Sunday night. Something happened between then and last night that made her go off on us."

"There's something she doesn't want us to find out," Lucy said. "It could be about her husband. She saw us talking to Evelyn Estes and may have guessed that Evelyn gossiped about the missing husband."

"And we don't know what Claudia heard before we saw her." I scrolled through my emails. "I have some answers about Sherry. But no one has heard of her. Sarah said she emailed VAFRE and will let me know if anyone there has." VAFRE was the acronym for Virginia Association of Fund Raising Executives. Since fundraising execs worked for non-profits, and non-profits relied on volunteers, VAFRE was a potential source of information.

"Maybe Sherry was only starting to be a volunteer," Lucy said. "Or she bought the book for a gift."

"I wonder if there's any significance to her husband being in prison."

My phone dinged. "Claudia says one is fine. Says 'Don't be late.'"

Lucy bristled. "She better get off her high horse."

"She'd better damn well show up. We have better things to do than run around for meetings with her. And my story isn't going to write itself."

"Did you know Matt was married before and has two adult children?" That was more or less my husband's greeting when I arrived home.

"No. But I know little about him other than he's surgically attached to his phone."

"Besides his undergraduate and law degrees from the U of R, there isn't much about him. He's been at Hannan and Hannan his entire career."

"Like I said before, his behavior toward Lucy and me was probably driven by emotion."

"People commit crimes in the heat of emotion. Don't let down your guard around him. I may have to start driving you to your class. Speaking of driving, Matt has a 2015 Ford Explorer. His wife has a 2016 Toyota Avalon that's in the shop for repairs after an accident."

"Yes, Lucy and I chatted with his wife this morning." I ran down that conversation, plus the one via text with the dictatorial Claudia. "So I'm guessing Matt isn't our tailgater. But I'm not clearing him yet."

During my daily walk, I came upon George Monahan and Opa the dog. Perfect timing.

After greeting man and dog, I described my interactions with Sherry, both at the mystery signing and at the food court. "Do you know her? I thought you might have run across her while volunteering."

"No, I don't know her." George's blue eyes twinkled at my description of Sherry. "And it sounds like I would remember her."

"I'm concerned about her book."

"Why be concerned? She can either retrieve it or buy another. You tried."

"Yes, I tried. But somehow I don't think my efforts were enough."

George knit his brow. "Sounds to me like you're investigating Randy's murder."

We arrived at our respective driveways. Olive walked up and rolled over on the ground. For some reason, Olive and Opa tended to ignore each other. As I rubbed the cat's tummy, I said, "No, George, I'm like Olive. Curious."

"You know what they say: 'curiosity killed the cat.'"

"They also say 'satisfaction brought it back.'"

THIRTY-FOUR

The Virginia Museum of Fine Arts, dubbed "The Museum" by the locals, was arguably one of the finest art museums in the country. I'd spent many a delightful and inspiring afternoon touring the collections and exhibits.

But as I drove down Grove Avenue to the museum, my mind was not on the Impressionists or Faberge eggs—it was on the annoying and mystifying Claudia. What prompted her to summon Lucy and me in such an imperious fashion? Could we expect her to give us a clue, a confession—*something*?

Lucy followed me into the parking lot and we walked along one of the ramps leading to the museum's entrance. The expected security guard stood just inside the building, giving me a feeling of comfort. Lucy and I headed for the membership desk and turned right for the Best Café.

"So where is she?" Lucy asked when we didn't find Claudia in the café. "She demands our presence, then leaves us cooling our heels." We went back out to the concourse.

"Here she is." I pointed to the woman walking toward us, a long black sweater over jeans with knife-edged creases. Pressed jeans? I hadn't seen them in eons.

"You're fired!" Claudia announced as she neared us.

I looked at Claudia, then at Lucy. "Excuse me?"

"You didn't tell me about your discussion with Randy at Richmond Books." She glared at me, face flushed. "Your *true* discussion."

"We talked about writing and about your upcoming class. How we were all looking forward to it. That was our 'true' discussion." I made quote marks with my fingers, a gesture I found annoying.

"Then you lied by omission."

Too bad I lacked a politician's gift for dodging challenging situations. "Ask Matt. He was there."

"How do I know he didn't kill Randy?"

"At this point we don't know who killed him."

"Randy put down your writing. He laughed at you. At Lorraine as well."

"Yes, he did."

"That means both you and Lorraine had motives to kill him. And here I go, asking you to investigate. Why, you could be planning to kill me, too."

"Claudia, I'm under no obligation to tell you anything. You're not the police."

Lucy piped up. "What were you and Lorraine talking about last night in the parking lot?"

"She cornered me by my car. Tried to blackmail me."

"Blackmail?" I laughed. "Lorraine? Why?"

"Said she has information I wouldn't want made public. She probably killed Randy for dissing her work but she wants it to look like I killed him."

"What information does she have?"

"I don't know. I didn't want to encourage her by asking."

Lucy gave Claudia a level look. "Did she actually blackmail you? Name a figure?"

Faltering, Claudia said, "Um . . . well, not *exactly*."

"Claudia, what's this all about?" Lucy asked. "What has happened? Everything was fine until last night, and then—."

"How did you find out about our conversation with Randy?" I interrupted.

"Someone told me. Someone who was standing in my line."

"Evelyn Estes?"

"I'm not at liberty to say." Claudia sniffed. "I bet you killed Randy. Or Lorraine did."

"Claudia." Lucy kept her voice low, but the steel in it was clear. "You can't hurl wild accusations like that."

"Lucy's right," I said. "You can't go around accusing people of murder. You have nothing to base it on."

"I trusted you," she shrieked. "Both of you."

We were attracting attention. A couple of teenaged girls with multi-colored hair broke into gales of laughter. "I trusted you. Both of you," they parodied Claudia's dramatic delivery before disappearing into the café.

"Claudia, we have to go someplace quieter or else tone down this conversation," I said.

Ignoring my advice, she stood rooted to the spot and repeated her earlier declaration. "You're fired!"

"Fine. We're fired. Have a nice day."

Lucy and I walked quickly to the exit, feeling many sets of eyes tracking us. I had planned to grab some lunch in the café, but getting as far away from Claudia as possible made the lunch idea unappealing.

"What's her *problem*?" Lucy cried once we stepped outside. "Has she gone off the deep end? And what's with the 'You're fired' bit? Is she channeling Donald Trump?"

Lucy referred to the catchphrase made famous by real estate tycoon Donald Trump on *The Apprentice*, a reality television show he'd hosted until his stint in the Oval Office.

"As if she could fire us," I said. "She's not paying us and we never even agreed to investigate. My guess is there's something she doesn't want us to find out."

"Is it whatever Lorraine's allegedly blackmailing her about?"

"Good question. I'm going to give Lorraine a call." I took out my phone and located her in my contacts.

When prompted to leave a voice mail, I said, "Lorraine, it's Hazel. Lucy and I just saw Claudia, and she's upset about something. We saw you talking with her last night and wondered if you knew anything. Call me when you get a chance." I left my number and pressed the end button.

"I bet this has to do with the conversation Claudia and Randy had in the café that day," I said. "If Claudia smacked him, there must have been some fiery words exchanged. Lorraine probably got an earful."

"Well, if she has blackmail in mind, you don't think she's going to tell you about it, do you?"

"No. And if she's into extortion, that explains why she didn't tell the police she was even in the café."

"It's still hard to imagine Lorraine blackmailing," Lucy said.

We looked at each other and laughed at the absurdities we were facing at every turn. "My guess is that it was Evelyn Estes who told Claudia about my conversation with Randy," I said. "She was in Claudia's line at Richmond Books."

"So were scores of people."

"Yes, but Evelyn was there last night in the library. That doesn't prove it was her, but it's pretty likely."

Lucy took a moment to answer her phone. From what I could surmise of the conversation, one of her employees needed advice about handling a difficult temp. Part of the secret of Lucy's business success was her skill in dealing with challenging people. She dispensed the advice and calmed down the employee.

"Lucy," I said once she finished playing mom. "Are temps the same as contractors?"

"Yes, sort of. But most contractors are placed in high-paying jobs. Not like the ones I fill."

"Might someone refer to a temp job as a contracting job?"

"Sure. It sounds classier. For the reasons I stated. Why do you ask?"

"Lorraine said she contracted with the state before they hired her as a regular employee. But she's worked other places. At the memorial service Rhea mentioned a temp Randy had yelled at and fired. I think I told you about that. Maybe not. This was a while back, maybe before you took over the account. In fact, it might have been *why* you landed the account, because Randy was so unhappy with the temps other agencies sent."

"And you think this temp that Randy yelled at and fired was Lorraine? Out of all the temps out there?"

"It's a long shot. But long shots are all we have going for us right now. Remember the story Lorraine told me about a woman at the post office who complained about Randy, the boss from hell?"

"Yes."

"I kind of felt like she was making it up. Or that she was talking about herself, substituting this fictitious woman."

"A variation on the 'asking for a friend' gambit."

"Exactly. Especially when Rhea didn't recognize the description of the woman that I gave her. Anyway, I thought you might take some pictures of Lorraine to Randy's office and show them to Rhea. There are the ones I took at Richmond Books and there's her author picture."

"Ok, I'll do it. Send me the pictures from the store."

"I'll do it now." I found the photos and texted them to Lucy. A couple of emails caught my eye. "I've heard from everyone but Matt about our study group. We'll meet at The Beanery on Friday at seven. Matt's free to join us."

At Lucy's "Okay with me" I sent the email.

Lucy checked the time on her phone. "If we're going to the spa tomorrow, I have to get going. I have a ton of work at the office. I'll pick you up at ten. Okay with you?"

"Okay with me. While I'm here, I need to renew my membership."

"You're going back in there and risk another confrontation?"

"I won't let her intimidate me."

"Good for you."

"One more thing, Lucy. George says he doesn't know Sherry. And I'm sure he would remember her if he ever met her. Any man would."

We fell silent, mulling over the situation. I took a deep breath. "Did you really read Matt's story?"

Lucy snickered. "No, I fibbed. Then hoped Susan wouldn't ask a question that revealed my lie."

"We should read it. It might help somehow. I'll tell you one thing, I've had it up to here with being accused of killing Randy."

"I know. We have to find out who did."

"It doesn't feel like we're going anywhere."

"The class should be especially interesting now," Lucy said. "I'm surprised Claudia didn't expel us."

"I don't know if she could. At any rate, I wouldn't miss a minute of it."

THIRTY-FIVE

The run-in with Claudia fueled my writing and I produced ten pages in two hours. As I backed up my work, Lucy called.

"I just got off the phone with Rhea. I emailed her the photos of Lorraine. Rhea is *sure* Lorraine was the same temp Randy screamed at and fired."

"She's absolutely sure?"

"Absolutely sure. Said Lorraine's hair was reddish back then, but it's definitely her."

"So that means she knew who Randy was that day at Richmond Books," I said.

"Looks like it. But you said he didn't recognize her either."

"No. Or else, like her, he pretended not to. I'm sure his not remembering her, coupled with his ridiculing her book, might have set Lorraine off."

"The question is how much did it set her off?"

"Exactly. I don't want it to be Lorraine. I like her."

"Me too. We don't like Joyce."

I laughed. "Yeah, let it be her. Of course, I'm not too crazy about Claudia at the moment. Still . . ."

"Your obligation."

"Right."

"By the way," Lucy said, "I know you'll ask if I told Fish what I learned about Lorraine today. I did."

"I wonder how she'll explain herself."

"Did she return your call about Claudia?" Lucy asked.

"Yes, she did. Said she and Claudia talked about writing and only writing. I thought she might unintentionally reveal something useful, but she didn't."

"Do you suppose Claudia's husband killed Randy?"

I groaned. "Let's not add another suspect to the mix."

"Did you see Claudia when you went back in the museum?"

"No. She was probably in the café, fuming. By the way, there're some interesting exhibits coming up. I'll email you the details." I paused for a nanosecond before saying, "On to Sherry—you know, Matt might know how to get in touch with her. Although I'm pretty sure Randy introduced them that day at Richmond Books, so maybe not. Still, he might be worth a try."

"Are you sure you want to talk to him?"

"I know I don't want to talk to him. But if he can move things along, I'll grit my teeth and do it. I'll call him in the morning before we leave for Inn By the Bay."

"See you then."

THIRTY-SIX

Thursday dawned with a downpour, but by eight o'clock the sun broke through the clouds. I stood at my kitchen window, absent-mindedly eating yogurt with blueberries as I gazed at the watercolor the rain had created with autumn's palette and soggy leaves.

Upstairs, I dug Matt's business card out of my purse and dialed his cell number. I didn't know if I should call during a business day, but figured he could call me back if I was impacting his billable hours.

"How's the investigation going?" he asked.

"I don't know, Matt. You could ask the detective in charge." I didn't use Fish's name as it would suggest a familiarity I didn't want to admit. "Did you get my email about having a study group for the writing class?"

"Yeah, I got it. I had enough of study groups in law school."

"Well, if you change your mind, we're meeting at The Beanery tomorrow night at seven."

"Okay."

"Matt, I'm hoping you can help me. I need to get hold of Sherry."

"Sherry?"

"Yes, Randy's friend. That attractive young woman he introduced to us at Richmond Books."

"Gotcha."

"I had the funniest experience the other day. I saw Sherry in the food court at the mall. She looked alarmed to see me and ran off."

"No kidding? Strange. But why do you need to get hold of her?"

"She left a book from Richmond Books on the table. I took it and tried to track her down, but couldn't. I want to make sure she gets it. And I'm curious why she seemed so afraid of me. She was so friendly that day at the store."

"I don't know. Unless . . ." Matt sounded like he was carefully choosing his words. "I hate to think it—"

"You mean she could've killed Randy?" I finished his sentence. Now Matt could entertain thoughts of Sherry as a suspect.

"I can't think of any other reason for her to act like that."

"But what would be her motive? Weren't she and Randy great friends?"

"I don't know. I've never met her before or heard Randy mention her. Possibly she's a client, or former client."

"If so, she was a grateful one, judging by the charming banter she and Randy shared."

"Did you leave her book at the store?" Matt asked, ignoring my comment.

"Um, yes. Yes, I did."

"She probably went back there and got it. Else she could buy a new one."

"Yes, you're right. I'm not that worried about the book. But it's disconcerting to have someone be afraid of me."

The Sherry discussion was running out of steam, so I moved on. "How's Susan doing? Lucy and I had a nice chat with her yesterday."

"Yes, she mentioned that."

"Did you two often get together with Randy and Joyce?" I had posed this question to Susan and wanted to see how Matt would respond.

"Now and then. Susan wasn't crazy about Randy. They were great friends for a while. They met when Susan was undergoing treatment for her breast cancer and Randy served on the board of a cancer non-profit."

"So what happened to their friendship?"

"Not sure. Eventually Susan was declared cancer-free. Joyce and I worked near each other downtown and kind of hung out during lunch. I'm not sure of the sequence of events, but I introduced Randy to Joyce, and Randy introduced me to Susan.

"I think Randy and Joyce regretted their marriage. Don't know that for a fact. Just an idea. I think he always had a thing for Susan. Again, don't know that for a fact. So for the four of us to get together was kind of uncomfortable."

"Why did Randy and Joyce stay married?"

"Money, I would guess."

"Did they have a pre-nup?"

"I'm not sure. Randy mentioned getting one drawn up, but I don't know if they did."

I'd tried for a nonchalant tone with these questions. Switching to a bold approach, I asked, "Do you think Joyce killed Randy?"

"Joyce? No way." Matt's voice rose. "That's nuts, Hazel. Joyce wouldn't kill anyone."

But I would. Interesting how Matt felt so sure Joyce wouldn't kill anyone, while he felt comfortable suggesting I was a cold-blooded killer.

Matt continued. "I guess since Joyce is the spouse the police are watching her closely. But there are thousands, millions maybe, of folks in the world who don't kill because they're in unhappy marriages."

I considered his heated words. "But you know something, Matt? Some do."

"You're right. Some do."

My conversation with Matt took longer than expected, so I had to dash to get ready for the trip to Inn by the Bay. I heard Vince on the phone, but beyond a couple of loud laughs, I only caught a word here and there. Likely Dennis was on the other side of the conversation with a report on Lorraine and her response when questioned about knowing Randy while pretending she didn't.

Thirty minutes later, Vince and I met in the kitchen. He was off to speak to a criminal justice class at J. Sargeant Reynolds, dubbed J. Sarge, a local community college.

"Who were you talking to?" I asked.

"Dennis. According to Lorraine, she worked at Randy's firm for a week and only dealt with office staff. Some guy did fire her, but she didn't remember him as Randy."

"Sounds specious to me." I poured coffee into two travel mugs.

"The part about being there for a week is true. They checked it out."

"But how do you forget the person who fired you? And, from what Rhea told me at the memorial service, it was a pretty humiliating firing."

"Well, we can't answer that one yet," Vince said.

When I spotted Lucy's silver Prius through one of the side windows that flanked the front door, I gathered my purse and travel mugs. "Lucy's here. Gotta go."

"Be careful," Vince said as we kissed.

"I'm always careful."

Not always.

THIRTY-SEVEN

A cellophane-wrapped basket, adorned with a gold bow, took up most of the back seat of Lucy's car.

"Gorgeous basket. The director at the spa will be thrilled." I set the mugs in Lucy's beverage holders. "I brought you coffee."

Giant cotton puffs dotted a blue sky. We said little while Lucy negotiated a route requiring exits and lane changes that were easy to miss. Once settled on the interstate, I updated her on Lorraine's visit to the police.

Lucy's response to Lorraine's not remembering that Randy fired her mirrored my own: "What a bunch of BS." After a beat, she asked, "Did you talk to Matt?"

"Oh, yeah. I forgot about him. Let's see . . ."

"Interesting about Randy, Joyce, Matt, and Susan with their couples dynamics," Lucy said when I ran down the conversation. "An expanded version of what Susan told us yesterday at Sweetbrew."

"Yes, I couldn't help but wonder—"

"If the couples' rearrangement was okay with everyone?" Lucy completed my thought.

"Exactly. Perhaps Susan envisioned living her cancer-free life happily ever after with Randy. And when Matt introduced Randy to Joyce, was he matchmaking? Or had he been surprised when the two of them got married?"

In West Point, the town's paper mill loomed across the Pamunkey River. No matter how many times I passed this gangly industrial complex, the view of plumes of smoke spewing from cylindrical stacks vaguely frightened me. I hoped the exterior hid a wonderful and welcoming workplace.

We arrived at Inn by the Bay. Lucy had made an appointment with the director, Vanessa Laurie, who met us in the lobby. Vanessa appeared to be in her mid-fifties. Her luxurious head of auburn hair brushed the shoulders of an expensive-looking hot pink active suit. Multi-colored athletic shoes that also appeared pricey completed her vibrant outfit. As the Inn's clientele was well-to-do, Vanessa likely wanted to project an upscale image.

"It's wonderful to see you again, Lucy. And you must be Hazel. I'm one of your fans." We shook hands.

"Happy Thanksgiving!" Lucy presented the basket. From what I could see through the orange cellophane, the basket contained a bottle of wine, a can of plum pudding, a package of gourmet stuffing, a coffee table book on Thanksgiving traditions, and other items too small to identify.

Vanessa beamed. "How lovely! Let's go back to my office." We followed her down a hall lit by sconces with etched translucent shades. In Vanessa's office, she placed the basket on a credenza behind her desk. Prints of Chesapeake Bay scenes hung on the pine-paneled walls.

"What can I get you?" Vanessa asked as we settled into visitor chairs. "I have some lovely herbal tea."

"Herbal tea sounds good," I said. Vanessa dropped tea bags into ceramic mugs and added hot water from a dispenser. She invited us to help ourselves to an assortment of condiments set out on a small table. We bypassed the sweeteners and wrapped the tea bag strings around spoons to squeeze out the liquid. The inn's logo emblazoned the mugs.

Vanessa sat at her desk and got right to the point. "I understand you're here about one of our guests, Joyce Zimmerman."

"Yes," Lucy said. "I'm sure you know about the murder of her husband, Randy Zimmerman?"

"Yes. Such a tragedy. We all felt so bad for her."

"We do too. She's a dear friend. And you know how the police focus on the spouse. Bad enough to lose your husband, but to be a suspect . . ." Lucy trailed off, perhaps for dramatic effect.

"I know, I know," Vanessa murmured.

Lucy went on. "We're trying to help her out. And help you out as well. I'm sure you don't want anyone to think you had a killer as a guest."

"Heavens, no!" Vanessa crossed her heart with a ring-laden hand, nails covered with hot pink polish. "But the police have been here and questioned several of us. Discreetly, of course. And we vouched for Joyce. She was here the whole weekend. We showed a movie on Saturday night after dinner and I know she was here for that."

"You saw her?" I spoke for the first time since we'd sat down.

"I did."

"By the way, this is excellent tea," I said. "What kind is it?"

"It's a custom blend made especially for us. We sell it here. I'm happy to give you some on your way out."

"Thanks. Back to Joyce, did she have any particular friends here? Someone she talked to?"

Vanessa thought. "Joyce was quiet, kept herself to herself. But I did see her talking to this one woman. Although I'm sure the police interviewed her."

"Yes," Lucy said. "But she might not have told them something minor, something personal."

"Tell you what I'll do. I'll email this woman and ask her if she'll talk to you. How's that? In fact I'll do it right now."

"Great," I said.

"Let me just look up her record." A few clicks and taps later, Vanessa proclaimed, "Sent!"

"Did Joyce speak to her attendants?" I asked.

"It's doubtful. They told the police she didn't do more than say hello, goodbye, and thank you. And I believe them. Your friend was laconic, to say the least."

We spent a few minutes talking about Lucy's late mother-in-law.

"She was such a dear woman, one of our most loyal guests," Vanessa gushed. "We all miss her." She glanced at her laptop. "Ah, here's your response."

When Vanessa read the response and shook her head, I knew that potential source of information was a non-starter. "She says she told the police everything she knew, and she isn't talking to anyone else. I'm sorry."

"And she was the only one Joyce talked to?"

"She's the only one I recall. Oh! Why didn't I think of this before? I don't know if this will help, but after the movie, I walked through the community room and heard a spirited discussion about pre-nups."

"Pre-nups?" That got my attention. "Was Joyce involved in that?"

"She was. I may have taken this out of context, but it sounded like someone's sister was getting married and her fiancé wanted her to sign a pre-nup. Joyce said, 'Try to talk your sister out of it. If she ever gets divorced, she could do badly.' She was quite intense about it, which is why I noticed."

In the lobby, Vanessa gave us a supply of the herbal tea that boasted a blend of relaxing and energizing herbs. Did that mean we'd be suspended between the two states? Vanessa also gifted us with vouchers for comp weekends for two. I wondered if Dave would benefit from that treat. I wondered about Dave, period. Lucy's errant husband was fast becoming the proverbial elephant in the room.

Lucy and I embraced Vanessa and we started to leave the spa. But Vanessa wanted a status report on my writing.

"Well, I love mysteries as well as romances," she said when I told her my plans. "The one you wrote about the women cruising through the Greek Islands prompted the cruise my husband and I made last fall through the same islands. It was a *wonderful* experience. I hope you don't mind my saying this, Hazel, but I didn't like your latest romance as much as the others you've written." She leaned closer and stage whispered, "Kind of formulaic."

"I don't mind you saying that at all. It's one of the reasons I'm switching to mysteries."

THIRTY-EIGHT

"The pre-nup idea is intriguing," Lucy said. "It sure gives Joyce a powerful motive. She could have hired someone to do the deed."

We were sitting in a dark booth in a dark corner of a restaurant in West Point. The lunch rush over, we shared the place with an elderly couple. As we read the menu, we reviewed our visit to Inn by the Bay.

"It strikes me as being a crime of passion, not something pre-meditated." I closed the menu and placed it on the scratched linoleum table top. "And Vince said there's no record of a pre-nup. Nothing in the house or in Randy's office. No safe. And they haven't turned up a safe deposit box. Joyce claims she knows nothing about it."

"Joyce could have found it and destroyed it."

I groaned. "I wish we could eliminate possibilities, but we're adding to them."

"It looks like Joyce was at the spa when Randy was killed. So who else—" Lucy paused when our server appeared. Our orders placed,

Lucy picked up where she'd stopped, not missing a beat. "Who else could have done it?"

"There's Matt."

"Yes, there's Matt. We shouldn't rule him out because he and Randy were friends."

"That what Vince says. We don't know how things were between them. And Matt has no alibi to speak of. He spent the evening at home, with Susan."

The server delivered our salads, and we set to spearing lettuce and chopped vegetables.

Lucy said, "There are a bunch of murky sorts, like lawyers, defendants in lawsuits, and maybe plaintiffs in lawsuits who didn't like what Randy did for them."

"And me, based on his needling me at Richmond Books."

Lucy waved at the air. "But we know you didn't do it. As for Lorraine, we don't know her as well."

"I can't see Lorraine doing it. I know we can't dismiss her. Still." I chomped on a pepperoncini pepper and winced at the heat. "Don't forget Sherry."

"Yes, Sherry. But why would she kill Randy?"

"I have no idea. Why would she avoid me?"

"Um . . . she thinks you killed Randy?"

"Why would she think that?"

"Did she hear your conversation at Richmond Books?"

"I don't know. I wasn't even aware of her until Randy tried to imitate Frankie Valli. Poorly, I might say." I described Randy's rendition of "Sherry," a sixties-era song made famous by the Four Seasons. "She came up from behind me, so I don't know if she'd been standing there or just walking by. Even so, Randy and I were hardly coming to blows."

Our review of suspects going nowhere, we discussed non-murder matters such as the book group, writing, and Lucy's business, avoiding talk of Dave or Thanksgiving.

As Lucy drove out of the parking lot, I said, "If Joyce hired someone, wouldn't the hit man—or woman—use a gun? Professionals use guns, with silencers."

"Have you ever heard of a hit woman?"

"There was a TV movie called *Hit Lady*, back in the seventies. Yvette Mimieux, remember her?" I described the plot. "The character had another job, she was only a hit woman on the side, and—"

"What, it's more acceptable that she only moonlighted and didn't kill full time?"

"No. I'm just telling you the story. Anyway, she's hired to kill this guy, a union leader. But she doesn't want to do it."

"Gets an attack of morals?"

"I guess. Can you see Joyce, Claudia, Lorraine, or Sherry supplementing their incomes by taking gigs as hit women?"

Lucy laughed. "But it's like we said before—they would have used guns. No one would pay someone to hurl a brass statue at a targeted victim."

We digressed into a conversation about popular stars of the sixties and seventies who'd faded into oblivion. One by one I researched them on my phone. That diversion occupied us until we reached Richmond.

I checked my email. "Speaking of Sherry, here's something from Sarah. 'No one at VAFRE knows Sherry. She could do private volunteering, like tutoring.' At any rate, it looks like that line of inquiry has dried up."

"Don't worry, we'll get something else."

"Lucy, can we go by Randy's house?"

"Why?"

"I want to see if anything's going on."

"We may run into Joyce. Or Ruby."

"I know, but I still want to see if anything's going on. Let's chance them seeing us. What can they do?"

"Is that Joyce?" Lucy asked as we approached the house and saw a tall woman with long blond hair standing on the lawn, leaning on a rake.

"It sure is. And she doesn't look happy."

Joyce was talking to a man of about her same height, wearing a red plaid shirt. The set of Joyce's jaw and her pursed lips suggested the conversation wasn't a friendly one. The man leaned in close, making her step back.

"That shirt!" I shrieked. "Lucy, that's the guy Joyce was screwing at the memorial service. He's wearing the same shirt." I ducked down in my seat. "Don't let them see us."

"She's so focused on the man I doubt she'd notice a lion walking by." Lucy grabbed my arm. "Look at that guy in the bushes."

I raised my head enough to see where Lucy pointed. A young man crouched behind a tall boxwood at the corner of Ruby's house, next door to Joyce's. He held up a phone, no doubt recording the altercation. The bush likely hid him from Joyce's view, but I guessed that gaps in the foliage allowed him to see well enough.

"I wonder if he's Ruby's son," I said. "Was he the one with her at Sweetbrew that day she confronted Claudia?"

"Could be."

"Let's go around the block again."

"I hope no one calls the police, reporting a lurking car."

"Just one more time."

Cars lined either side of the narrow street, making it a tight squeeze for two cars going in opposite directions. We circled the block and once again approached Joyce's house. The plaid-shirted man was nowhere in sight, leaving Joyce to her leaf gathering. From the jerky swipes with her rake and set to her jaw I took it her anger from the encounter lingered. I turned my head so she wouldn't see me.

"I don't see the guy who was hiding in the bushes," Lucy said.

"What happened to the plaid-shirt guy?" I turned this way and that as Lucy cruised along the street.

"You mean the one walking right in front of us?"

"He's sure taking his time," I said. The man lit a cigarette and took several deep drags before taking it from his mouth, holding it between thumb and index finger. He glanced at Lucy's license plate and his mouth formed a mischievous smile.

"You better not try anything, Buddy," Lucy muttered.

"If this was one of my romances, I'd have him trying something. He's such a classic bad boy with that rumpled hair, two day growth, scars—"

The man finally moved out of our way and opened the door of a beat-up silver sedan.

I ran out of Lucy's car, slamming the door.

THIRTY-NINE

"Hey, was that you who followed us the other night?" I asked as I approached the man.

He crossed his heart with the hand holding his cigarette. "Me?"

"Yes, you. On River Road. You were tailgating us with your brights on." I glanced at his license plate, committing it to memory, and praying for my memory to hold until I returned to Lucy's car and could write it down. I didn't feel brave enough to take a picture with my phone. "It was you all right. Same license plate."

I was bluffing, but he didn't know that. And if he was the tailgater, he wouldn't challenge me on the plate, effectively admitting to the deed.

"Wasn't me, darlin'. But I'd follow you anywhere." He winked as he gave me the once over. "Hey, haven't we met before?"

Close up, the scar I'd noticed at the memorial service looked fresh. I hadn't seen the two that crisscrossed his forehead. Fight? Scuffle with an animal?

"Got it! The other day at Randy's memorial service. You kinda got lost on the way to the little girls' room and barged in on a big moment." He hooked a thumb at Lucy, who stayed in the car, watching us. She had lowered her window enough to hear our conversation. "I can handle two of you. I love cougars."

Ignoring him, I turned and saw Joyce still raking. "Lucy, can you park the car? We need to talk to Joyce."

"Oh, so you're friends of the widow lady. Hey, I've done it with three women before. More the merrier." He hooted.

I moved to the sidewalk on the other side of the street and quickly texted the license number to myself. Lucy drove to the end of the block and parked. The man, still laughing, got in his car and maneuvered it out of the tight space. It didn't faze him when he hit the vehicles in front of and behind him before peeling off.

A middle-aged man who had been raking leaves ran to the sidewalk and yelled at the driver, now turning the corner. "That was my car you banged into, you moron." He added some colorful adjectives and nouns that network TV would have bleeped.

"I have his license number if you want it," I called across the street.

The man assessed the damage to his bumper. Waving a hand, he said, "Nah, he didn't do enough to worry about. But that's the second time in a week he's backed into me."

"Oh?" I walked over to the man so I didn't have to shout. "He's a regular visitor?"

"Yeah, lately anyway." A gleam appeared in his eye as he added, "Ever since Randy Zimmerman got himself killed. I guess the grieving widow needs some comforting. If you know what I mean."

I did know what he meant and, from what I'd witnessed at the memorial service, I didn't doubt it was true. "Really?" I prompted, hoping to learn more.

"The wife took a casserole over to the grieving widow." The man hooked his thumb in the direction of his house, where I pictured "the wife" laboring over a hot stove, producing casseroles. "Bitch slammed the door in her face."

The man segued into a tirade about leaf blowers. Lucy

approached, fire in her eyes. I said goodbye to the man, and Lucy and I walked toward Joyce's house.

"I'm absolutely furious with you," Lucy said, keeping her voice low. "Why would you accuse that man of following us?"

"I know, I know, it was a dumb thing to do. But I'm sure it was him. Did you see the way he looked at your plate and leered at us?"

"Yeah, but he could just be some jerk who thinks he's God's gift to women."

"He is kind of hot. And he seems to like older women. Perfect character for a story."

"So now you're going to put yourself in harm's way to get a good story?"

"Lucy, let's talk about this later. Joyce might go back inside and refuse to open the door to us."

"Hi, Joyce," I called from the sidewalk. Lucy echoed my cheerful greeting.

"What do you want *now*?" The unsmiling woman held the rake before her, whether as protection or weapon I wasn't sure. Although it was one of those flimsy rakes that could only do minimal damage. Preferring to avoid even minimal damage, I stayed on the sidewalk and prayed that Lucy did the same.

"We wanted to be sure everything was, well, okay." My voice faltered under her withering stare.

"Everything's okay." Joyce continued her leaf gathering. As bandages circled the base of both of her thumbs, she'd been raking long enough to develop blisters.

"Let us know if we can help you in any way," I said.

She shot us a baleful look, but said nothing.

"Get off Joyce's property." Ruby Landis charged out of her house and up to us. "The police are on their way."

"We're not on her property. This is a city sidewalk." Lucy didn't raise her voice but the don't-mess-with-us tone was unmistakable.

"You've caused this poor woman enough trouble. Please leave. See, I said *please*."

Joyce threw the rake on the ground and went in her house without a backward glance. Dismissed, we trekked back to Lucy's car. "How rude," Lucy said. "Whatever she's going through doesn't excuse such boorish behavior."

"Agreed. She and Ruby could use a good etiquette manual."

"Do you think Ruby called the police?"

"Probably not. But in case she did, let's beat it out of here. I don't need another run-in with them, especially at the same location as before."

"No police yet," Lucy said as we buckled our seat belts. "Should we go to Sweetbrew?"

"Sure, why not? At this point we're putting the owner's kids through college."

When we approached the corner to turn onto Westover Hills Boulevard, a police car passed us.

FORTY

Café Sweetbrew's supply of pastries had dwindled down to plain bagels and black and white cookies. Neither appealed to me. I only spotted two other customers, unusual in a place often abuzz with coffee enthusiasts.

"I betcha anything that guy's the one who followed us the other night," I said once Lucy and I settled at "our" table by the window.

"So you said. And by the way, I'm still furious with you. Confronting someone like that, accusing. If he was the one following us, we could be in danger. I sure hope he was only in a hurry and didn't mean to threaten us."

"I understand, Lucy. But I had to get a look at his license plate and I could hardly do that without saying *something*."

Lucy sighed. "I hope you don't do anything like that by yourself. And don't tell Vince. Especially after your recent solo adventures."

"No problem. I won't." I sipped my decaf latte.

Lucy's voice softened. "We don't want anything to happen to you, Hazel."

"I appreciate that, Lucy. Really, I do. And I give you my word— no more incidents like that."

It occurred to me that I was breaking promises with little thought. At least twice I'd promised Vince I wouldn't investigate on my own, only to do so. I vowed to do better at honoring my promises.

"But apparently Joyce and lover boy have been having an affair for a while—at least since Randy was killed," I said after running down my conversation with the neighbor.

"Show me that picture again. The one of Mick Jacoby, Joyce, and Dan Ferguson."

When I pulled up the Twitter photo Lucy used her fingers to enlarge the image. "I thought he might be the same guy we saw today. But I can't see it."

"No, the guy in the picture doesn't have scars, but I think they're pretty recent. And the hair is totally different. The mirrored glasses throw things off, too."

Lucy studied the picture. "Nice body. I guess Joyce likes those classic bad boys."

"Yeah, Randy may have been a bad boy, but in a different way."

"But back to classic bad boy's license plate—what was that all about? You said you couldn't see the license plate on the car the other night."

"No, I couldn't. I was bluffing. But I wanted to get his plate number. He may have been the one tailgating us."

"Why do you think that?"

"For one thing, did you see the way he smiled when he saw the *Lucywho* on your plate? And another thing, he was driving a silver sedan. Light-colored."

"So do thousands and thousands of people."

"Wait, there's more. Seeing him with Joyce today made me wonder if the two plotted to kill Randy. Could be that he did the dirty work while Joyce was getting pampered at Inn by the Bay."

"Ah, that's where the possible pre-nup comes in."

"You got it. The only way Joyce could get out of the marriage with Randy's money was for him to die. And he didn't appear to be ill or in danger of dying anytime soon on his own, so Joyce and her lover helped things along. Those two could have been planning to kill Randy for a long time."

"It's a great idea as ideas go. All you need is proof. And lots of it."

"We'll find proof. Lots of it."

"Such an easy task." Lucy rolled her eyes.

"Now, how about that guy in the bushes? I'd love to get hold of his video. I'll see if he posted it on Facebook. I need his name." I busied myself on Facebook. "Ruby Landis has a friend, Adam Landis. He looks pretty young. What do you think?" I passed my phone to Lucy.

"Yeah, he could be the guy in the bushes. In fact, he's the guy Ruby was with last week. They sat right over there." She pointed to a table on the other side of the café. "He hasn't posted anything since July. But then kids don't use Facebook much anymore, especially if their parents are on it."

"So where would he post a video? YouTube?"

"Yes, YouTube." Lucy handed me my phone. I brought up the video-sharing website.

"Bingo! Here it is. Posted less than an hour ago."

I started the video. After two seconds, I shut it off. "It's too quiet in here. We should watch this in the car."

We drained our drinks, returned our mugs to the counter, and rushed outside.

Once in the car, Lucy started the engine. "I don't want to watch it here. We're too close to Joyce's neighborhood."

"Let's go to my house. Vince can see it as well."

We huddled around Vince's laptop while he pulled up the video.

"What are you doing here?" Joyce shielded herself with the rake.

"I want my money, honey." The man drew close to Joyce. *"How 'bout inviting me inside—hmm?"*

"Your money?" Joyce gave a half laugh. *"I'm not giving you any money, so don't start hounding me."*

"Randy's gone now. You said it was worth fifty grand to get him out of the way."

"I never said that! Mick Jacoby, are you saying that you killed my husband?"

"So he *is* Mick Jacoby!"

A couple of "shhs!" and hand flaps cut off my jubilant proclamation.

"Well, I have it on record that you did *say that."* Mick Jacoby smirked. *"I have other things on record as well."*

"Get out!" Joyce shrieked as she raised the rake.

Mick wrested the rake from her and threw it to the side.

"You better get me my fifty grand." He included a few four-letter words of a sexist nature.

"I don't have fifty grand and even if I did, I wouldn't give it to you."

"Next time I come over you'd better have it." He added one more expletive for good measure.

The next few seconds showed Mick Jacoby walking away with a swagger. Joyce picked up the rake and shot daggers at him, but she didn't appear to be shaken. I'd have been a wreck after an altercation like that.

The video stopped at a point that must have been a matter of seconds before we'd cruised down the street a second time, catching Joyce furiously raking and Mick Jacoby walking in front of Lucy's car, blocking our way.

"He sure looks different from that Twitter picture," I said.

Vince picked up his phone and dialed. "I have to tell Fish about this." Ordinarily Vince would have told me to call Fish. But this video had enough gravitas to warrant the big guns—a retired detective. I gave Vince Mick's license plate number to pass along.

Vince spent several minutes talking to Fish, whom he called Tom. Then the three of us analyzed the unpleasant encounter between Joyce and Mick.

"What's this about money?" I asked. "Did she say she'd pay fifty grand to have Randy killed?"

Lucy stretched out her legs and crossed her ankles. "She said she never said that."

"But did she? He hinted that he had recorded her saying that she would."

"And recordings of other things as well."

Vince spoke up. "He didn't answer her question about killing Randy."

"That's right," I said. "He didn't."

"So how long do we have to wait to hear something?" Lucy asked.

"It could take a while," Vince said. "Fish will bring them both in for questioning, but he has to find them first. I say let's eat."

"Let's go out," I said. "Want to join us, Lucy?"

"Sure."

Would she say something about Dave, such as "Let's ask Dave to meet us there" or "I'll call Dave and tell him I'll be home later?"

What she did say was "Dave's working late." Her flat delivery discouraged questions.

Vince went to the front door. "Let me get the mail before we go." A few minutes later, he returned with an armful of envelopes and catalogs. He dumped the load on the kitchen table and sorted it into three piles: his, mine, and recycling.

I undid the flap on a business-sized envelope and pulled out the enclosed sheet of paper. The message, composed of letters cut out from newspapers and magazines, read: "Mind your own business or you'll be next."

"Oh my God." I read the message to Vince and Lucy.

"Drop it on the table," Vince said, his voice gruff. "Envelope, too. You've got your prints all over them." After reading the brief threat, he used his keys to turn the envelope over. "No return address."

"The zip code is 23229, in the West End," I said. "But that doesn't mean anything. It's easy enough to travel over there."

"This envelope was written on a typewriter."

"Looks like it," Lucy said. "But you can use courier font on a computer."

"The 's' is raised." Vince's finger hovered over the "s" in "Rose." "Let's go down to headquarters and give this to Fish. First, I'll put it in a ziplock bag."

"Maybe we can eat downtown. Lucy heard about a new Italian place. Is it open for dinner, Lucy?"

"Yes, let's try it."

We didn't get to talk to Fish because he was questioning someone: Mick and Joyce, perhaps? Detective Garcia took the bag containing the envelope and sheet of paper.

"Any prints?" Her question came out like a bark.

"Mine, and you have them on file," I said.

We left without running into Mick, Joyce, or anyone else we knew.

Once seated in the restaurant, we lost no time in speculating about the letter sender.

"A letter with pasted-on letters is way too creepy," Lucy said.

"I wouldn't be surprised if Mick sent it. It's just the sort of sleazy thing he would do."

That netted me the inevitable "You need proof."

I huffed my annoyance at the proof reminder. "Well, it must be the same person who killed Randy." Not a brilliant deduction, but the only one I had at the moment.

Lucy and I feigned interest in Vince's talk to the criminal justice class at J. Sarge. Feigned because we wanted to talk about *our* day. We did just that over lasagna and Greek style spaghetti. I started with the visit to Inn by the Bay and ended with our mini visit with Joyce, editing out the confrontation with Mick.

"Where do you think a pre-nup could be?" I asked.

"Would Randy's lawyer have copies?" Lucy asked.

"Probably not," Vince said. "But who is the lawyer? That's a job for Fish."

I sighed. "There are too many loose ends. How on earth does it all fit together?"

"The questions never stop, do they?" Vince smiled. "That's what an investigation is all about."

At eight o'clock, Vince learned from Dennis that Fish and Detective Garcia were questioning Joyce and Mick. I went to bed at ten and started Claudia's *Virginia Menace*. It was as good as her previous Astrid Gordon adventures, but it couldn't take my mind off what was happening at Richmond Police Headquarters. After reading the same paragraph three times, I put the book aside. At eleven, I heard Vince's phone ringing downstairs. Dennis, I hoped. I petted Olive as I waited for Vince to come upstairs. Ten minutes later, he appeared, sat on the bed, and told me the Joyce-Mick story.

"Joyce said she and Mick had an on-again, off-again relationship for many years. Recently it was on-again. She told him she was unhappy with Randy, but couldn't divorce him because of the pre-nup which she deeply regretted signing. When Mick asked how much she'd pay someone to kill Randy, she thought he was kidding. She said, 'Oh, fifty thousand.'"

"Post-coital banter, I suppose. But Mick took it to heart. It's hard to imagine Joyce being fun and light-hearted. But back to the pre-nup —hadn't Joyce told the police she didn't know about a pre-nup?"

"Yes. Now she says Fish only asked her where a pre-nup *was*, not specifically if she'd signed one."

"Oh, wow!" I laughed. "That sounds like something a lawyer would say. I wonder if she learned that kind of dodging trick from Randy."

Vince continued. "As for Mick, the police found him living with his aunt over in the East End. In fact, his car is registered to her. He has a record a mile long—assault, property damage, drug possession, drunk driving, you name it, most of it in California—but he has an alibi for the night of Randy's murder. He was in the hospital after getting into a fight at the Moonshine Inn."

"The Moonshine Inn?" I rolled my eyes. "Not surprising. He looks like a good candidate for that place." Vince and I had gone under cover to the infamous bar when investigating the murder of a family member.

"He had to get stitches in his forehead and the side of his face. He was admitted at five forty-five in the afternoon and they kept him there till eleven."

"That explains his facial scars." I leaned back against the pillow and tried to collect my thoughts. "What about this recording he claims he has of Joyce saying she'd pay someone fifty grand to kill her husband?"

"There's no recording. He claims he was just messing with her. According to Fish and Garcia the guy's a dumbass and wouldn't think to record anything until it was too late."

"And he probably didn't predict that anyone would record his little altercation with Joyce today." I pushed my tousled hair out of my eyes. "So were Joyce and Mick released?"

"Yes. Despite the video, Fish doesn't have proof of any wrongdoing. Joyce didn't press harassment charges, but she did get a restraining order against Mick."

"What if he violates the order? He's hardly a law-abiding citizen. Dumb or not, he could still be dangerous."

"Unfortunately, it's a wait-and-see situation." Vince stood, said "See you in a few minutes," and left to turn off lights and indulge the cats with a bedtime snack.

Despite the late hour, Lucy wanted timely updates.

"Joyce might never be free of Mick," Lucy said once I ran down Vince's summary of the couple's evening at police headquarters.

"Assuming she even wants to be."

"Any news on the threatening letter?" she asked.

"*Nada.*"

"Whoever sent it obviously doesn't want you investigating. Maybe we need to stop."

"Lucy! It's not like you to be a quitter."

"I know, I don't want to quit. On the other hand, I value my life. And yours. We could pretend we've stopped investigating."

"We've been pretending all along that we haven't even started investigating."

"True."

"I wish we could discover something that would move us further along."

We didn't know it then, but we were making progress. A funny, and inescapable, thing about progress: it often required wading through quicksand.

FORTY-ONE

"They didn't get any prints off that paper with the threatening message. Only yours. The envelope had other prints, but probably from the post office folks."

"The sender was smarter about prints than the receiver," I said. "But I won't be intimidated by someone childish enough to cut out letters and paste them on paper."

"Better intimidated than dead," Vince rejoined.

"I feel like a character in a mystery with those cutout letters. I guess whatever they do on the page comes from real life."

On Friday morning, we sat in the kitchen, the remains of our breakfast littering the table. My mind focused on one track: who sent the threatening letter I'd received the day before?

Vince said, "You may be getting too close and someone feels threatened enough to threaten you."

We lapsed into silence as we sipped our coffee. My eyes swept over our outdated kitchen with its Formica countertops and harvest gold appliances. *House Hunters*, who viewed granite countertops and stainless steel appliances hallmarks of an acceptable kitchen, would take one look at our place and run screaming. As for our bathrooms—enough said.

"Well, I'm going to devote today to writing." I put my mug in the sink. "Remember that we're going to The Beanery tonight for our study group."

"I remember."

I spent several hours working on my story, breaking for a quick lunch. Olive and Morris periodically walked on my keyboard. Despite their distracting ways, I counted them as my muses. They helped me come up with names for my fictional couple: Zack and Zoey Hunter. Hunter seemed appropriate not only for Olive, a huntress extraordinaire, but for sleuths looking for a killer.

A sinus headache sent Eileen home from work early. When she texted regrets about missing the study group, Lucy, Lorraine, and I replied with variations of "Hope you feel better."

As I tore Romaine lettuce into bite-sized pieces for salad, Vince heated our leftovers from the previous night's Italian restaurant.

"You know, we don't have a plan for the meeting tonight."

"What's the topic for your next class?" Vince asked.

"Character development. I guess we could create character descriptions with backstories." I shredded a carrot and tossed it in the salad. "The tricky part will be broaching the subject of Lorraine's previous acquaintance with Randy, and why she denied it. But we'll figure out a way."

After eating and cleaning up, I gathered my purse, laptop, and a book about creating believable characters. Vince saw me off with a kiss and the inevitable "Be careful. Lorraine could be a suspect."

We had little to worry about on that score—but we didn't know that yet.

FORTY-TWO

When Lorraine didn't show at The Beanery, Lucy and I alternated between annoyance and concern.

"I bet she forgot about meeting us," Lucy said. "Not a surprise, really. We know she's kind of an airhead."

"What a week—first Claudia stands us up, and now Lorraine. And this meeting was for her benefit. Of course, she didn't know that."

Lucy snickered. "It was more for our benefit. I just hope she's okay."

"Yeah, me too. Let's go over to her place and make sure." We bussed our dishes that had contained lattes and a brownie that we split. "I'm sick of lattes," I grumbled.

I parked in front of Lorraine's building and called her. "Still not answering. I didn't bother leaving a voicemail. I've left three in the past thirty minutes. Maybe she didn't charge her phone."

"Does she have a landline?" Lucy asked. "Even if she does, I don't have that number."

"Neither do I. Let's go and see if she's there." A frisson of something I couldn't identify fluttered through me. Was it fear?

Halfway up the walkway, I tripped on a crack in the concrete. Only balance skills I didn't know I had saved me from falling flat on my face. Lorraine's building amenities didn't include security, so we had no trouble gaining entrance through the outside door. We walked past a row of mailboxes and a set of stairs leading to an upper level. At the end of a dimly-lit hall, we stopped at the door to Lorraine's apartment.

I pounded on the door and waited. When Lorraine didn't appear, I pressed the buzzer. Still no answer. When Lucy tried calling, we heard the phone ringing inside.

The door that led to the rear parking lot opened to admit a tall woman with a full, rounded figure, who looked to be in her seventies. She hefted two recyclable bags of groceries. Dark green leek leaves poked out of one.

"Looking for Lorraine?" she asked.

"Yes, we're part of her writing group. She was supposed to meet us at The Beanery at six-thirty." I checked my phone. "It's seven twenty now."

"She was here a while ago and I just parked next to her, so she must be nearby. Maybe she's taking a shower."

That possibility switched my concern back to annoyance. Was she so dirty that she had to keep us waiting?

"I have a key," the woman said. "But let's give her a few more minutes. I'll just put these groceries away." She opened the door across from Lorraine's and disappeared inside.

At seven-thirty, I pressed Lorraine's buzzer for several seconds. "This is ridiculous," I said when my efforts continued to fail. "Either she forgot, or . . ." I couldn't finish my speculation. Lucy knocked on the neighbor's door.

The woman introduced herself as Vivian Rawlins, unlocked Lorraine's door, and opened it a few inches. "Lorraine," she called.

Silence. Such silence.

Cautiously, Vivian stepped into the living room, Lucy and I close behind.

An odor redolent of fish and a cruciferous vegetable assailed our nostrils. A desk faced the door. A swing-arm lamp illuminated the workspace that included a laptop, printer, cell phone, and stacks of paper.

Lorraine had paired a turquoise conversational grouping—sofa, loveseat, and chair—with gold shag carpeting, reminiscent of the seventies. Lamps with low-wattage bulbs topped the end tables that flanked the sofa. Copies of *Writer's Digest* fanned across the top of a rickety-looking coffee table.

"Lorraine," Vivian called again. "It's Vivian. Are you here? Is everything okay?" She walked down a short hallway leading to the single bedroom.

I peeked behind the desk and gasped. "Oh, no."

Lorraine lay flat on her back with a long dark scarf pulled tightly around her neck. I couldn't make out her facial features in the dim light—not that I wanted to.

Vivian rushed back into the living room and pushed me aside. She knelt by Lorraine and felt her pulse. "She's gone. Call 9-1-1." She waved her arm at me.

"Are you sure?"

"Yes, I was an EMT. Call 9-1-1."

Lucy called the emergency service. Her voice trembled, but she managed to convey the necessary information. Vivian supplied the address.

"I need to get out of here." My voice sounded raspy to my ears.

I ran down the hall, Lucy at my heels. Outside, I gagged and took several deep breaths of the cool evening air. It took a few minutes, but the waves of nausea subsided.

"You okay?" Lucy asked.

"I guess. You?"

"Yeah. A bit shaky, but I've got a strong stomach."

We looked at each other, stricken by this second death in the space of two weeks. Our teeth chattered. It was cool, but it was shock that made us tremble so, not temperature.

"Let's go wait by the car." I lowered my voice as we walked. "I don't know what happened to Vivian, but I don't want to hang around here, with a killer possibly lurking. Too many bushes and trees. Just like at Randy's."

We leaned against my car, waiting for the crime scene troops to arrive.

"Yeah, it's a replay of finding Randy's body," I said, adding, "Nighttime version."

———

The rest of the evening passed in a blur. The usual cadre of crime scene players arrived and assumed their assigned roles. Fish and Garcia showed up and questioned Lucy and me. We didn't see Vivian Rawlins again, but presumably they questioned her as well.

A boisterous crowd gathered behind the crime scene tape. There was much hectoring of a small man with rimless glasses and a receding hairline—the landlord, judging from the comments being hurled at him.

"You don't give a *damn* how safe your tenants are," one woman shrieked. A portly man wearing a baseball cap and shaking his fist in the air suggested anatomically challenging actions the landlord could try.

I told Fish everything I could think of about Lorraine, including her newfound enthusiasm for writing and genealogy. I told him about observing her talking to Matt and Claudia. Still shielding Claudia, I left out her claim that Lorraine had tried to blackmail her and hoped that omission didn't trip me up later. An image of Fish charging me with obstructing an investigation danced before my eyes. Would handcuffs be involved?

"Tell me more about Lorraine's interest in genealogy," he said.

"I don't know much to tell. She said she and her mother had researched their own family tree and that she planned to incorporate it into her writing."

Fish fell silent and regarded me with one of his goofy grins. I didn't add anything to my account about Lorraine. I had nothing to add, anyway.

"So, Ms. Rose, why am I finding you at these crime scenes? First Mr. Zimmerman's, now Ms. Popp's?"

What did he expect me to say? That hunting for dead bodies was my new hobby? I settled for an elaborate, European style shrug.

<hr>

When Lucy and I were finally let go, Vince came to pick us up. Most of the onlookers had drifted away.

"Your car should be safe here overnight," he said.

"No, I don't want to leave it here. I need to take Lucy home. Why don't you follow us?"

"Sure you'll be okay?"

"I'm sure. Let's go, Lucy."

Once on the road, Lucy and I gave in to our exhaustion, limiting our conversation to "I can't believe it!" and "Her poor mother."

Vince waited on the street when I pulled into Lucy's driveway. She and I agreed to go to police headquarters together the next day to sign our statements.

"I'll pick you up," Lucy said. "Oh, and the book group—we need to let them know."

"We'll set up a Zoom call. I have a signing in the afternoon at Book Nook."

"Are you up for that?"

"I will be. It'll take my mind off all this."

At home, Vince and I hugged for a long time. When we broke apart, he said, "I'll fix you some tea. Go downstairs and relax."

"If only."

I settled in my recliner and Morris curled in my lap. A few minutes later, Vince handed me a steaming mug. "Chamomile. I added a little honey."

"Does Lorraine's mother know?"

"Yes, she does."

"I can't take this in. Why kill Lorraine?"

When Vince didn't offer an explanation, I said, "All right, I can think of a few whys. Claudia, for one: if Lorraine was truly blackmailing her, she put herself in harm's way, for sure." I wrapped my hands around the mug, soothed by its warmth. "I sure hope that's not the answer."

"I'll call Dennis in the morning for an update," Vince said. "Maybe one of the neighbors saw or heard something. They're still interviewing them. All I know at this point is that the medical examiner estimates the time of death as between six and seven."

Vince continued. "I investigated a murder there back in the early nineties. Another strangling, this time a man strangled his wife. The place was on the shabby side, but still genteel, as they say."

"Still is. More shabby than genteel."

"Back then, the security was pretty non-existent. I don't know if they've improved it since then."

"They haven't," I said. "You can walk right in the front entrance and to the doors of the apartments. And there are lots of bushes and trees outside. Another similarity to Randy's place—lots of places to hide."

Morris purred as I stroked his back. My tense muscles slowly relaxed. "Do you think this is connected with Randy?"

"Maybe, maybe not. Their connection wasn't strong. But it is suggestive."

"Suggestive is right."

I sipped my tea as we talked. When I finished, I announced, "I'm going to bed."

Eileen called, interrupting my nightly ablutions. "Are you and Lucy okay? I just saw the news."

"We're okay, but we're exhausted. Still in shock." After offering the sketchiest of details, I assured Eileen that we'd fill her in the next day. Amazingly, I remembered to ask her how she was feeling.

"Still under the weather. I just took more Tylenol."

The impact of the evening's events hadn't set in. Still, to my surprise I fell asleep in seconds and slept for eight hours without waking.

FORTY-THREE

Bright sun streamed through the bedroom window on Saturday morning, making me feel cheerful. Then I remembered the night before. As if it sensed my mood, the sun drifted behind a cloud and the room darkened.

Vince sat in the kitchen, local paper in hand. I poured coffee and brought my mug to the table.

"Let me guess the headline: 'Hazel Rose, local romance writer, found *another* dead body last night.' "

Vince's smile was rueful. "That's pretty much what it says."

"Maybe we'll have a good turnout at the signing today. Bloodthirsty types will want to check me out."

"I just got off the phone with Dennis, and—".

I leaned forward, not wanting to miss a syllable. "Do tell."

"Someone saw a woman with long blond hair go into Lorraine's building about six-thirty. The witness lived in the complex and was coming home from a run."

"Did this witness give more of a description? I'm thinking that could be Joyce."

Vince ran a hand through his hair. "No, he wasn't sure what she was wearing. Or if it was even a woman. At the time, he wasn't paying much attention."

"Will Joyce be questioned?"

"I would think so. Your writing class as well."

"I wonder if Claudia will still have the writing class on Tuesday."

Vince shrugged his answer to my rhetorical question. Glancing at the calendar on the refrigerator, he asked, "You said you have a signing today at the Book Nook?"

"Yes. Two o'clock."

"That should take your mind off things. I'll go with you and hang out in that café across the street."

My phone dinged. "A text from Lucy. She wants to set up a Zoom call at noon with the book group. She says we can do it in the car after we sign our statements."

"Okay," I texted to Lucy. "Pick me up at ten forty."

Grace Street in Downtown Richmond was eerily quiet, with little vehicle or pedestrian traffic. Inside headquarters, Fish and Garcia greeted Lucy and me—he with his usual effusiveness and she in a more brusque manner—and escorted us to their respective desks for the signing ceremony.

Out on the street again, we had time before our Zoom call, so we walked several blocks to the Virginia State Capitol. We spoke little as we roamed the grounds surrounding the imposing white building that rose atop Shockoe Hill, overlooking downtown skyscrapers and the James River.

We returned to Lucy's car and she launched the Zoom meeting on her iPhone. Once Trudy, Sarah, and Eileen joined us, I shared the news about Lorraine.

After the expected expressions of shock, disbelief, and distress, Sarah said, "I need to call her mother at River Edge." As I'd expected, Sarah took the news of Lorraine's death the hardest.

Lorraine and her mother had lived in Sarah's neighborhood for several years.

"Fish called me this morning to question me about Lorraine," Eileen said. "I didn't have much to tell him. I'm sure he'll check out my alibi. Thankfully, I borrowed some Tylenol from my neighbor and we chatted for a bit."

By turns, Lucy and I brought the group up to speed on recent happenings: Claudia's "firing" us, the threatening letter, the Joyce and Mick incident, Joyce and Randy's possible pre-nup, Claudia's notion that Lorraine tried to blackmail her, Eileen's looking at Randy's settlements.

"Much as I hate to say it, we have to consider Claudia as a suspect," Lucy said. "If Lorraine was in fact blackmailing her. Blackmail's a pretty good motive for wanting to get someone out of the way."

Sarah raised her voice in protest. "It's ridiculous to even think of Lorraine blackmailing someone."

Sarah wanted to shield Lorraine from a suspicion of blackmail, even if the woman was dead. And my need to protect Claudia from a murder charge made me a less than objective party.

"We need to step up our efforts to find this killer," I said. "Come up with proof of, well, *something*."

"I'm still looking at those settlements," Eileen said. "I haven't figured anything out yet but I'll tackle them again this afternoon. There are tons of them. Randy was one busy attorney."

"Did you ever find out anything about Sherry Guanzon," Trudy asked.

"No, but I found out where she goes to church. Eileen and I are going there tomorrow. Maybe we can get something out of her." I checked the time on my phone. "I have to get going in a few minutes. Let's hear about Trudy and Sarah's trip."

Eileen said, "Sarah, I love your new do." Sarah's short bob was a departure from the long braid she usually wound around her head, coronet style.

"Thanks. I had it done the other day in Florence."

By turns, Trudy and Sarah shared the highlights of their European jaunt. "We're in Venice now and about to go out exploring," Sarah said.

Much as I loved my adopted city of Richmond, Italy—or anywhere without a murder to solve—sounded infinitely better.

A steady stream of fans approached the table I shared with three romance authors at the Book Nook, a converted Cape Cod house squeezed between towering office buildings in Richmond's West End. I sold out of the store's copies of not only my eight successful novels, but my latest so-called "flop." Several customers commented on my finding not just one, but *two* dead bodies, but business was brisk enough to keep the curious from lingering at my table and pumping me for inside information. People gathered in groups and cast furtive glances my way. I caught them a couple of times, but tried to ignore them.

But spending an afternoon with my "tribe" of authors and readers lifted my flagging spirits and restored my energy. My face ached from smiling.

At four-thirty I left the store and walked across the street to the café where Vince had holed up with his laptop, indulging in coffee drinks and pastries. Deciding to boycott lattes, I ordered a strawberry smoothie and joined Vince at a table in a far corner.

"As I predicted this morning, my notoriety resulted in a good turnout," I said when Vince asked how the signing went. After describing the event, I asked, "Any news?"

"They checked alibis. Matt spent last evening at home with his wife. Joyce's alibi is also a weak one—she was with her next-door neighbor, the infamous Ruby Landis, who backs up Joyce's claim that they spent the evening together from six o'clock on. They ate pizza and watched a movie. As for Claudia, she was home alone all evening."

"Oh, dear. Can anyone vouch for her?"

"Maybe a neighbor will."

"What about Sherry?"

"I didn't hear about her. Despite your suspicions, there's no reason to question her."

"The woman's sure an enigma. Maybe Eileen and I will get a break tomorrow at Grace of God and learn something useful." I sipped my smoothie as I considered our prospects. "We just might crack this case wide open."

FORTY-FOUR

Grace of God Community Church's parking lot was full. I found a space in the overflow lot and nosed into it.

"Let's hurry," I said. "There's a better chance of catching Sherry by surprise and getting her to talk before the service than after."

According to Eileen, the church observed a come-as-you-are dress code. Not wanting to take that policy literally, I wore a cotton blouse with a blazer and black jeans. Eileen chose blue jeans and a long, multi-colored sweater. Judging by the bustling crowd in the lobby, we were overdressed. One young man wore what could only be pajamas.

Congregants balanced Styrofoam cups and plates loaded with cookies and Cheetos. Lola Mays presided over a table holding a pot of chrysanthemums, a guest registry, a basket of programs, a roll of name tags, and marking pens in assorted colors.

When Lola saw me, her face lit up with joy. "Hazel, I'm so happy you joined us." Once released from her enthusiastic hug, I turned to Eileen.

"Eileen, this is Lola Mays. She's the church receptionist and one of my beta readers."

"Haven't you been here before?" Lola asked Eileen.

"Yes, but not in a while. We're here today because Sherry Guanzon—"

"Oh yes, it was Sherry who told you about our wonderful church. She's inside with her son and her mother. Such lovely people! The service will begin in a few minutes. Please fill out a name tag and sign our guest register." She waved a hand at the table.

After completing our name tags with a red marker, we signed the register and grabbed programs from the basket. We sat in the back of the immense auditorium and scanned the crowd for Sherry. Eileen had never seen her so it was up to me to pick her out. But the size of the crowd made the task impossible. According to statistics, church attendance in the country was low—but not at this church. I people-watched as more congregants poured in, taking in the diversity of races and cultures. Still no Sherry.

The service started with the choir, accompanied by a contemporary band, singing a rousing rendition of a hymn. The singers stood on a three-tiered platform and I picked out the Richmond Books clerk with his man bun on the top tier. Lyrics projected on a pull-down screen took the place of hymnals.

At one point the clergy gathered on the stage. Eventually all but one remained. As he approached the podium to give the sermon, I checked the program for his name. Pastor Frank, he who frowned on his employees gossiping.

To Pastor Frank's credit, I never once nodded off during his contemporary message focused on relationships, with all the conflicts, challenges, and positive aspects. He even made me forget about Sherry—temporarily. As soon as he recited the prayer that concluded his sermon, I again scanned the gathered members. No Sherry.

When the service ended and everyone spilled out into the hall, I saw Lola and made my way over to her, Eileen following close behind.

"Well, how did you ladies like our service?" Lola asked.

"It was very uplifting, inspirational," I said. "But we didn't see Sherry in there."

"Sherry had a family emergency and had to leave early." Lola looked regretful.

"Oh, I hope everything's all right," I said, feigning concern.

"Oh, so do I. They're such wonderful people."

"What a waste of time and gas," I fumed as we walked to the car. "I'm sure Sherry was not eager to see me and the family emergency was an avoidance tactic. I guess she saw us when we arrived and ducked out."

Eileen agreed. "She's looking mighty suspicious. Oh, well. I liked the sermon."

"I did too. It made this excursion worthwhile."

We stopped at River City Diner for brunch. Over silver dollar pancakes, scrambled eggs, and turkey sausage, we brainstormed ideas about the suspects.

It was a short storm.

***

Several months before, I'd submitted a short story to an anthology, *Tales of Love and Mystery*. The theme was romance in mysteries. Foreshadowing of my genre transition, perhaps?

Per the submission requirements, I agreed to read and rate three stories. Roseanne Dempsey, the anthology editor, had attached the stories in an email. Needing a diversion from the faltering investigation, I printed them out, settled in my recliner, and started reading.

One tale about mistaken identity was so enjoyable that it ended too soon and I yearned for more from the author. The second submission was dreadful. Couples join a swingers meetup and get more than sex—namely murder. The third story was so-so, set in an amusement park where the Tunnel of Love becomes an unamusing Tunnel of Murder.

The stories were blind submissions, with the author names removed in the information section of Word. I rated all three, giving the highest marks to the first one, trying for kindness and honesty for the second, and suggesting a rewrite for the third.

That project had distracted me for a while, but as short stories were, well, *short*, they didn't distract for long. I spent an hour on my romance writing workshop, updating the PowerPoint presentation with the new resources I'd acquired since my last workshop.

In my dreams that night, Randy and Lorraine's killer taunted me with the demented laughter heard in horror films.

FORTY-FIVE

The snail-like pace of the investigation was getting to me. That thought greeted me the second I woke up on Monday morning, making me vow to do whatever it took to get this investigation, now a double one, on a track leading somewhere.

But what could I do that the police couldn't? I thought I could get people to talk and reveal stuff they'd never even whisper to the police. But, so far, such revelations hadn't happened. Joyce wouldn't communicate with me, and neither would Claudia or Sherry. Lorraine hadn't offered much to help things along. Nor had Matt.

Clearing Claudia of suspicion in order to pay back a family debt had motivated me to play amateur detective. I also needed to clear myself of suspicion, although I seemed to be at the bottom of Fish's suspect list.

The ego deflation I'd suffered after being dropped by my publisher no doubt made me want to prove myself in a big way. Plus, crime-solving could enhance my first attempt at writing a mystery. Quite a mix of reasons drove me along this path.

And there was my deep-rooted desire to seek justice. I hadn't known Randy, not even met him until the day of his death. My brief acquaintance with him was not a warm one. But he was a human being and his killer needed to be caught and punished.

Years before, when I decided to investigate Carlene Arness's death, Lucy had reminded me how I'd had a strong sense of justice even as a child. She'd said something along the lines of: "I remember visiting you when we were kids and you'd be livid about something you read in the paper, a crime, or someone getting a bad deal." I smiled at the memory.

Lorraine's murder pushed the stakes higher. It also made things more personal for me. Lorraine, by turns charming but exasperating in her cluelessness about her writing life, had brought out my maternal side. A challenging woman in life became even more challenging in death.

No doubt about it—the two murders were related.

Yeah, yeah, that's all well and good. But what are you going to do?

My inner critic. I knew she'd show up eventually. "Good question," I said.

"What's a good question?" Vince put a mug of coffee on my nightstand and kissed me.

I plumped the pillows behind me and sat up before reaching for my coffee. "I'm going to Zelda's," I announced.

"Why there?" Vince got under the covers next to me. Morris and Olive leaped on the bed. Olive nestled against my foot and commenced a grooming session. Morris joined her.

"I don't know. Inspiration, I guess. That Bernie—Joyce's boss from Kellogg Publishing—she saw Joyce with some guy at Zelda's."

"The guy from Randy's memorial service?"

"Yes. I'm thinking, hoping, that something will come to me if I go there. Plus, it's a neat place and I haven't been in a while. I might use it in a scene for my story."

"Your story's set in Costa Rica," Vince reminded me.

"Oh, right. Well, next story."

Vince put his arm around me and pulled me close. The cats,

finished with their ablutions, each took a lap. We all stayed like that for a while, saying nothing.

Church Hill was a historic district of Richmond, home of St. John's Episcopal Church where Patrick Henry gave his famous "Give me liberty or give me death" speech.

Unlike in downtown Richmond, a couple of miles to the west, parking was plentiful in Church Hill—and free. Zelda's Cafe greeted me with the heavenly aroma of freshly roasted coffee beans, an aroma that made me reconsider my latte boycott.

I chose a cheese and pepper quiche to accompany the coffee drink. Banners from Virginia colleges—Virginia Commonwealth University, University of Richmond, University of Virginia, College of William and Mary, and Virginia Tech, to name a few—covered the walls, along with relics of the past, like a framed ad for vanilla milk shakes at ten cents. Zelda's produced their brew in a large roaster that I guessed was already an antique in my grandmother's day. The vintage item presided by the front window.

I sat at a scarred wooden table next to two men who said grace together before tucking into their sandwiches. The server delivered my quiche, garnished with an assortment of fruit, and an oversized cup of foam-topped latte. I took my time eating, savoring the delicious combination of egg, cheese, roasted peppers, and onions. Other customers arrived, some staying while others left carrying lunches in paper bags, holding coffee containers aloft.

I pictured Joyce, maybe at the table for two in the corner, deep in conversation with . . . who? Would she show up today with her mysterious companion? Somehow I hadn't considered that possibility. If she arrived to find me, sipping a latte, invading her space, I didn't expect a cordial greeting.

As I swallowed my last bite, I toyed with the idea of splurging on one of Zelda's homemade pastries. A call from Lucy put that idea on hold.

Not wanting to disturb the other customers—the two men next to me now took turns reciting passages from their bibles—I stepped outside on the sidewalk. "Hi, Lucy. What's up?"

"Bernie called. Guess who it was with Joyce at Zelda's. You'll never guess."

"Tell me."

"Matt."

"Matt? Matt Rowan?"

"The very one. Bernie got her lunch from one of the food trucks today." Food trucks lined up on the streets of downtown Richmond each day for lunch hour.

Lucy continued. "She saw the guy she'd recognized from Zelda's and from the memorial service. She introduced herself, they talked and exchanged cards. Sure enough, it was Matt Rowan. When Bernie mentioned meeting him a while back at Zelda's, he said he and Joyce met occasionally to review a manuscript that Joyce was editing for him."

"You won't believe this, but I'm at Zelda's right now."

"Why? Expecting the two of them to show up?"

"I guess. I thought I might find out something. And I have, thanks to you."

"So you think Joyce and Matt kept up their relationship?"

"Who knows what they kept up or if they even had a relationship beyond meeting at food trucks."

Lucy laughed. "Joyce sounds like a busy woman, juggling a husband along with Mick Jacoby and Matt."

"Well, Zelda's is a good place for a clandestine meeting. And I think Joyce and Matt's meetings were clandestine. I bet they met here often, and not just for editing purposes. Remember those guys at the memorial service who said Matt wanted to divorce Susan?"

"Yes, but then her father dying and leaving her money put the kibosh on that idea."

"Maybe Matt decided Joyce was more important than money. Plus, with Randy dead, Joyce would have his money. So Matt could be the killer. Of Randy, anyway."

"Didn't Matt have an alibi?"

"Yes, but it was an iffy one—he and Susan spent the night at home." A young man with rumpled hair and a two-day growth on his face went into Zelda's. "I'll show some pictures to the person working at the counter. Maybe she'll have some tidbits to share about Joyce and Matt. What, I can't imagine. But you never know."

I went back in the coffee house and waited until the disheveled young man collected his coffee. When I found the photo of Randy and Joyce on his Facebook page, I enlarged it and handed my phone to the young woman behind the counter. "Do you recognize the woman in the picture?"

After a moment, she said, "I'm not sure."

I pulled up Matt's Facebook profile. "How about him?"

"He looks kinda like my Uncle Jim."

Striking out. I ordered an oatmeal raisin cookie, paid for it, and took it back to the table.

The two men sat with closed bibles. It was a long shot, but I asked, "Do you two come here often?" I smiled at the sound of a clichéd pickup line from the singles scene.

"We're here every day," one of them said. He was thin with a neatly trimmed white mustache. "We live around the corner."

When I showed them the photos of Joyce and Matt, they both nodded with no hesitation.

"Yes, they've been here before," the second man said in a deep voice. In contrast to his fit-looking friend, his belly overflowed. His hair would benefit from a shampooing.

"Often?"

The first man made a waffling motion with his hand. "From time to time. Last week, I think."

"Did they seem like lovers?"

"Could be. They often seem to be comforting each other. They always sit over there." He pointed to the exact spot I'd imagined them being. "Last time we saw them, she was crying and his hand covered hers."

Number Two man spoke. "Sometimes they have what looks like a manuscript. A notebook filled with white paper." That corroborated what Bernie had said about Joyce editing Matt's manuscript.

"Are they friends of yours?" Number One man asked.

"Acquaintances. The woman's husband was murdered recently. Randy Zimmerman."

"Ah, yes."

"So maybe that's why the man was here, comforting the woman," Number Two man said.

"Yes," I said. "That's my guess. The man, Matt, was a lifelong friend of Randy's. You said he and the woman were here last week?"

"Last week, maybe two weeks. Hard to keep track of time. What do you think, Harold?"

"I think it was last week," Harold said.

"And Lorraine Popp was murdered the other night," I said.

"Yes, I heard that on the news," Number One man said. "Any connection between them?"

"They knew each other."

"Why are you interested in them?" Harold asked.

"I'm a writer. Always on the lookout for the human interest angle."

FORTY-SIX

The Chimborazo Medical Museum presided over Richmond National Battlefield Park, site of Chimborazo Hospital, the largest Civil War medical facility. The museum housed exhibits on medical equipment and hospital life from the time of the Confederacy.

Needing to burn the calories I'd consumed at Zelda's, I walked up and down the brick-paved sidewalks of Church Hill, fading autumn leaves fluttering around me. When Broad Street came to an abrupt end, I reversed course. Cutting over to Grace Street, I found Richmond Hill, a community center offering daily prayers for Richmond and the surrounding metropolitan area. They also provided a number of personal retreats for a modest fee. A retreat sounded appealing to my beleaguered brain and spirit. I added "spiritual retreat" to my mental to do list.

On the south side of the James River, I drove through the Forest Hill Historic District and detoured off the main street to Lorraine's apartment building. The structure, one I'd never seen in daytime, bore the look of an office building with its ubiquitous red brick and white trim. No historic merit. Crime scene tape still stretched across the area in front of Lorraine's unit, but I saw no signs of forensic activity. Or any activity. The bustle and chaos of Friday evening might have happened in a dream. Too bad that wasn't the case.

Thinking that Fish could pop up like a jack in the box, I stayed in the car. I'd rather he didn't catch me in snooping mode.

When the rousing notes of *Steppin' Out* heralded a call, I pulled my car to the curb and stopped the engine.

"Hi, Eileen."

"I found a case that might help us. Back in 2006, a truck rammed into Randy's client's car. In late 2007 they settled the case for ten million dollars. The plaintiff, John Evangelista, died recently. Surviving was his daughter, one Sharon Guanzon."

"Bingo! Good job, Eileen. Now we have to track her down and make her talk." I sounded like a gangster.

"What day of the week did you see Sherry?"

I thought. "Tuesday, around two o'clock."

"It's likely she has a regular schedule and takes the same lunch hour and eats in the food court. We have nothing to lose by hanging out there."

"Nothing but time."

"Tomorrow's Tuesday, and I'm off, so I can go. Although I *should* work on my class assignment—"

"Oh, the class assignment!" I exclaimed. "I forgot all about that."

"And your romance writing class."

"I don't have anything to do on that. I've taught it before, so I just need to update it a bit."

"We'll work the assignment in somehow. I'll go to the mall with you and see if we can spot her."

"It would be a big help if we knew where she works. I didn't find her on social media."

"I'll see if I can find her." After a minute, Eileen said, "There's a Sherry Guanzon on Instagram—at least she matches the description you gave me—but her account is private so I can't see her postings."

"Nothing's easy. Eileen, I'm by Lorraine's apartment building now—"

"Be careful, you don't want that Fish guy to catch you snooping around."

"I haven't seen him. Or anyone. And I'm staying in my car. You know something? There's a huge similarity between Lorraine and Randy's properties. Lots of bushes and trees. If we were criminals, these would be great places to be one."

That evening Claudia called.

"Hazel," she cried. "I'm sorry I was so rude to you and Lucy last week."

"It's okay, Claudia." It wasn't, but I needed all the information sources I could get. "You were upset."

"Still am. I had to go and talk to Fish again. I'm so sick of him. I always enjoyed chatting with him for my research, but . . ." Claudia trailed off and took a deep breath. "Anyway, it's a whole other thing being treated like a suspect. He had heard about Lorraine and me talking after class last week and I'm *pretty* sure it was you and/or Lucy who clued him in on that tidbit." Claudia's voice rose in pitch with each syllable.

I knew from Vince that Claudia had talked to Fish earlier in the day. She was right about my statement prompting him to question her. Did the stress of multiple questionings explain her increasing agitation?

"Claudia, you started this conversation with an apology. Now it sounds like you're getting worked up all over again. What's going on?"

Claudia heaved a deep sigh. "I can't take another session with Fish. It was bad enough to be a suspect in Randy's murder, but now there's *Lorraine*. At least my neighbor can verify my alibi. She saw me taking out my garbage around seven-thirty."

Claudia couldn't have so much garbage that it took her more than a few minutes to take care of the task. Still plenty of time to dash over to Westover Hills and back. But I was supposed to be rooting for her, so I kept quiet on that point.

"I have to get out from behind the eight ball, that's all there is to it," Claudia said, the distress of multiple questionings clear from her tone.

"Yes, well, I'm kind of behind the eight ball myself, at least in Randy's murder." When was the last time I'd heard the eight ball expression? Most people say they're at a disadvantage. Not as colorful, but more straightforward. But we writers liked to jazz up the language when we could.

"So I'm sure you and Lucy haven't stopped investigating?" I caught a coy note in Claudia's voice.

"We never started." I mimicked the coyness.

"Start now. I'm willing to pay you for your services."

"Thank you, Claudia, but save your money for the pros. See you in class tomorrow night."

But Claudia wasn't ready to end our conversation.

"Um, Hazel . . . I never told you the whole story."

"Oh?" I waited for Claudia to share her "whole story."

FORTY-SEVEN

"Lorraine didn't actually try to blackmail me—but I thought she *might*."

"So what did she say that made you think she *might* have had blackmail in mind?" I asked.

"Remember my telling you about that day at Richmond Books? In the café, after the signing?"

"I do."

"Do you remember what I said?"

"Let's see. You and Randy used to meet to critique his work. Then he stopped meeting you and wouldn't answer your emails. You didn't hear from him until he registered for your class and wanted you to read his completed manuscript. So you confronted him in the café, he laughed at you, and you slapped him."

"Nothing wrong with your memory." Claudia gave a half laugh. "Okay, there's more to the story. First, I had no idea Lorraine was there. She said she was sitting right behind me. She hinted that she recorded our conversation."

"When did she do this hinting?"

"Last week after class."

"Are you sure she recorded you?" I thought of Mick Jacoby's faux recording. And Vince never mentioned the police finding such a recording on Lorraine's phone, or on a separate recorder. Maybe, like Mick, Lorraine flung empty threats about.

"Well, no."

"This doesn't sound like Lorraine at all."

"I know. She seemed so sweet and ditzy. Well, she wasn't, I can tell you that right now."

"Claudia, there's something I don't get. Even if Lorraine recorded your conversation, it doesn't sound like you and Randy said anything worthy of blackmail. What else have you left out?"

Claudia took a deep breath and began. "Randy and I met several times over the summer. I kind of fell for him. One day, we had lunch at the Omni, downtown." She paused before going on. "I could feel the chemistry between us. At one point, his hand covered mine and my whole body tingled."

I held the phone away and coughed to cover up my laugh. The body tingling bit was too much—hopefully Claudia didn't take up romance writing.

She continued. "When I suggested that we book a room, his eyes lit up. 'I'll take care of the bill and you get us a room.' So I went ahead and got the room. Then I waited. And waited. And waited some more. The jackass stood me up. After I shelled out nearly two hundred dollars!"

"Did you ask him why?"

"Not then. I was furious. I didn't call, text, or email. I stayed for two hours before leaving the hotel. I didn't hear from him until two weeks before the class, when he registered. He had the audacity, the unmitigated *gall*, to ask me to read his finished story—like the whole thing never happened."

"Do you think he was called away that day, like for an emergency?" My attempt to excuse Randy's behavior sounded lame to my ears. Claudia's snort confirmed my feeling.

"Are you for real? If he had an emergency, couldn't he have told me that? We had phones."

"What happened next?"

"That brings us to that day at Richmond Books. He's going around singing my praises. Then he shows up in my line with that woman with the boobs."

"Her name is Sherry," I said, not liking to identify people by their body parts.

"Whatever. I told him I wanted to talk to him when I finished signing. We met in the café. It took me a while to confront him because he started out with this long, convoluted story idea." Claudia described the idea, the same one Randy had shared at Lorraine's signing table perhaps an hour before telling it to Claudia. I recognized the premise: rich guy dies and leaves his fortune to his only son. Lo and behold, another son turns up, creating a moral dilemma for son number one.

I held back a sigh, hoping Claudia would move on to the confrontation scene. Instead, she segued into Randy's pressing her to ghostwrite his legal thriller. I listened, trying to practice patience and, finally, she came to the "big scene."

"When I asked him why he stood me up that day, he said, 'What day?' He looked amused. When I said 'At the Omni,' he laughed. He *laughed*. 'Sorry, Claudia. You're a brilliant writer, but I like my women younger. No offense.' "

"Oh, God," I said.

"Oh, there's more. He goes, 'I was thinking a roll in the hay might be nice, what the hell, but I just couldn't do it.' He sounded like I was repulsive." Claudia's voice caught. "So I got up, slapped him hard, and left. I never even noticed Lorraine behind us.

"The whole thing was so humiliating. I had liked Randy, really, really liked him. That day at the Omni I thought we were ready to take things further. He'd been so nice and charming until then."

"I'm so sorry that happened. But I have to ask about your husband: where's he in all of this?"

Claudia's tone turned rueful. "I love my husband, but he's away all the time. I've had lots of affairs, none of them serious."

"So Lorraine may or may not have had a recording. But you said she didn't try to blackmail you?"

"No. I got in my car and left before she had the chance. She laughed at me as well. What if she had sent that recording, assuming it existed, to my husband or kids? And these days you have to worry about stuff showing up on the Internet. Still, she didn't actually blackmail me and, well, with her being dead and all, I don't want to besmirch her memory."

"Claudia, have you told all this to the police?"

"No. Well, some of it. Not all. But I didn't kill either one of them. I know I have motives, but I also have alibis."

Not very good ones.

Claudia fell silent for a moment before announcing, "I'm going to go to Fish and tell him *everything*."

Vince was on a conference call, so Lucy got the scoop on Claudia first.

"She has motives up the wazoo for Randy's killing," Lucy said. "I'm not sure why she would kill Lorraine if Lorraine didn't blackmail her."

"You know, if this was a book, neither Joyce nor Claudia killed either one of them. It would be someone who isn't even on our radar."

"I take it we're back in Claudia's good graces," Lucy said. "Well, it'll make being in the writing class easier."

We talked about Eileen's and my planned surveillance at the mall. Lucy cautioned us to watch out for our safety. "You don't know this woman or who her friends are. And how are you going to get her to talk to you? She obviously wants to give you a wide berth."

"We'll have to find a way to narrow the berth."

"Did you tell her you've carried on without her blessing?" Vince asked when I summarized my conversation with Claudia.

"No. I'm not telling her anything unless it's necessary. She's strictly on a need-to-know basis."

Vince shook his head. "Claudia's made a lot of bad decisions, except for one—telling all to Fish. I hope she follows through on that."

As it turned out, she did.

FORTY-EIGHT

The next day Eileen and I arrived at the mall, hoping Sherry would show up. We chose a table in the food court that afforded a good vantage point for checking the passing parade of mall customers and employees.

"I'll get us some lunch," Eileen said. "What do you want?"

"A slice of pizza and some water. No ice. Let me give you some money."

Eileen waved a hand. "No, I'll get it."

"Let's be on the lookout for a babe in a tight sweater." I opened a copy of the *Richmond Times-Dispatch* and held the paper up to hide my face during our surveillance. Better to spot Sherry before she spotted us and bolted.

A steady stream of customers passed through the food court, some stopping at the various vendors, some bound for other parts of the mall. Eileen returned with a tray of pizza, salad, and bottles of water. I arranged the paper so I could still hide behind it while munching my pizza. I absorbed little of the news.

When I shared Claudia's stunning admissions with Eileen, she said, "Whew! The woman's quite a drama queen. And she has a heap of motives."

"Yeah. Weak alibis, too. I sure hope this case breaks soon and Claudia is off the hook. It's tough trying to clear a suspect who may be guilty."

Changing the subject, I asked, "Did you get the email I sent to the book group about Lorraine's funeral?"

"Yes, next Monday at eleven at her church. That Presbyterian one near where she lived. Seems like a long time to wait. Was it because they wouldn't release her body?"

"No, they would have had it this Friday, but with Thanksgiving being this week, they had to wait till Monday."

We fell to discussing our holiday plans. Passersby might have thought Eileen was conversing with a newspaper. She and her mother planned to visit relatives in Charlottesville for the holiday meal. "And I guess you're spending the day with Lucy and her family?"

"Oh, yes. Looking forward to seeing everyone again." Was Thanksgiving at Lucy's going to happen? I didn't want to share my cousin's troubles. Eileen was a friend but not a confidant. Besides, it was Lucy's story to tell, or not. I felt a prick of annoyance that she'd left me hanging about the plans.

"This is exciting!" Eileen exclaimed. "My first stakeout."

I found it rather boring, but didn't want to dampen Eileen's enthusiasm, so I merely smiled and nodded.

It took thirty minutes of lowering the paper and raising it again before I announced, "There she is. At the pizza place."

This time Sherry wore a canary yellow sweater paired with a short black skirt and tights. She made her purchases and carried her tray to a nearby table. Was the slice of pizza and soda on the tray her daily lunch fare? Not a nutritious choice. Granted, pizza crusts littered my plate, but I didn't indulge on a regular basis.

Sherry sat with her back to us so Eileen and I had no trouble taking seats at her table before she saw us. She gulped and started to get up.

I held out my hand. "Please, Sherry. Stay. We just want some information." I introduced Eileen.

The muscles in Sherry's face tightened. "What information? I don't know anything."

Strange claim to make, I thought. She wore a Macy's employee badge with her name stamped on it. Aloud I said, "We need to find out what you know about Randy Zimmerman. And how you knew him."

Cringing, she started, "I knew him—"

"Is everything okay here, Sherry?"

A security guard loomed over our table. I marveled at his quick transition of expressions: menacing for Eileen and me, adoring for Sherry.

"Everything's fine, Ralph." Sherry's pearly teeth sparkled. "Thanks so much for checking."

"Just want to keep you girls safe." Ralph shot a parting warning glance at me before swaggering off to find other women needing a proverbial knight in shining armor, modern-day version.

"You were telling us how you knew Randy," I prompted when Sherry gave me a blank look.

"Oh, yes, the Infinity Center. My mother goes there, and so does his aunt. He used to bring her in the morning. Now his sister does."

"Why so afraid of me?"

"George Monahan told me about you. How you're a detective. *Unlicensed* one, but that you've been successful. George warned me because I've said so many bad things about Randy to so many people, and that if you found out, I'd be a suspect in his murder. He also said your husband was a retired homicide detective."

Hmm. George. He denied knowing Sherry. I needed to have a chat with him.

"But you and Randy were so friendly that day in Richmond Books." I pointed toward the store to my right.

"Yes, well." Sherry's hair shimmered as she flung it over her shoulder. Taking a deep breath, she told us pretty much the story we thought she would, about how Randy had pressured her father into accepting a settlement.

"It wasn't fair! It *just* wasn't fair! He could have held out for so much more. And then my daddy died." Tears filled her eyes and ran down her face. She took a tissue that Eileen handed her, mopped her face, and blew her nose.

"Did your father die from complications from the accident?" Eileen asked.

"No, not really." Sherry's voice went flat. "He had cancer."

We murmured "So sorry" and for a moment none of us spoke.

"And you showed up at my church!" Sherry broke the silence.

"We wanted to talk to you," I said.

After a pause, Eileen said, "Tell us how you and Randy became friends."

"He started bringing his aunt to the Infinity Center about six months ago. He went to my daddy's funeral and apologized to my mother and me for the pain he caused us. We forgave him. He said he was on the board of a cancer non-profit. I feel that I should volunteer after my experience with my father. So that's what I plan to do, at the non-profit Randy mentioned."

"Is that why you had that book on volunteering?" When Sherry nodded, I asked, "Did you find the book? I left it in the store."

"I did."

"Where were you the night Randy was killed?" Eileen asked.

"Where I am every night. At home with my kid and my mom."

"So they can vouch for you?" Eileen persisted.

From Sherry's expression of alarm I knew we needed to back off. She'd started to relax and Eileen got her all riled again. I tried for a light tone. "I'm sure your mom and your kid would back you up."

"So I am a suspect," she cried. My tone wasn't light enough.

"You're not a suspect in our eyes." I hoped Eileen wouldn't add anything to refute my words. "But if you know anything, anything at all, that would help the police find who killed Randy and who killed Lorraine—"

"Lorraine?"

"Yes, Lorraine. She signed a book for you that day at Richmond Books."

"Oh, yes, Lorraine! She was killed?"

"Yes, the other night, in her apartment. Strangled."

Sherry's hand, fingers tipped with bitten nails, flew to her mouth. "Oh, my God!"

"Sherry, if you have any information, it's your duty as a citizen to tell the police."

Sherry said nothing. It occurred to me that her husband's incarceration could make her wary of the police.

"You can call Crime Stoppers and be anonymous," I said. "Do you know anyone who could have killed Randy?"

"Probably lots of people. I don't know if he made amends to everyone he pissed off. I'm sure if you reviewed his cases, you'd find plenty of possibilities."

Thankfully, Eileen didn't share that she'd done that very thing.

"I heard through the grapevine that a woman came to your church and screamed at you. Wanted you to stay away from her husband."

Sherry's eyes fluttered heavenward. "Yes. Joyce."

"Did you know it was Joyce at the time?" Eileen asked.

"I did. I met her once at the Infinity Center."

We spent a few minutes talking about Randy and Lorraine, then shifted to more mundane topics: Sherry's job, her son, her mother, her church. Nothing about her imprisoned husband and I hesitated to broach that subject.

"So are you coming back to the church?" Sherry asked. Something in her tone hinted that she wanted the answer to be "No."

Eileen and I said as one voice, "It's kind of far."

Back in Eileen's car, I said, "I don't think Sherry killed Randy."

"I don't, either."

"But if you're harboring ill will toward someone, you need to be discreet. I hope she's learned that lesson."

Halfway home, Eileen had to brake suddenly when a teenager, backpack strapped across his back, loped across the road in front of us. Eileen yelled a few expletives out the window before driving on.

"I need to talk to George," I said. "I'm pretty pissed that he claimed he didn't know Sherry."

"Probably protecting her. Like she said."

"I guess."

FORTY-NINE

The mere idea of being a damsel in distress didn't sit well with me. But, as Vince said when he insisted on accompanying Lucy, Eileen, and me to the library, "There've been two murders in your small class and we're no closer to knowing who's responsible. I don't want anything to happen to the rest of you."

"I know, I don't either. It's hard to be brave once the sun goes down."

Lucy and Eileen also loathed being damsels in distress, but agreed when I texted them about Vince playing bodyguard. Eileen usually preferred driving on her own, as she visited her mother at assisted living between work and class. "I hate that we need protection," she wrote, "But it doesn't hurt to have the law by our side."

Lucy echoed Eileen's sentiments. "The whole thing is getting more and more like *And Then There Were None*. We don't want to reenact an Agatha Christie plot." Lucy referred to Agatha Christie's famous story about ten people getting invited to an island only to be killed, one by one.

En route to the library, Eileen and I replayed our earlier

encounter with Sherry for Lucy's benefit. I'd already caught Vince up on the Sherry aspect.

"What about George?" Eileen asked. "Did you ask him why he pretended he didn't know Sherry?"

"Not yet," I said. "I'll deal with him in the morning."

Vince told us about his day spent at the Library of Virginia, researching for his current project.

"Is it about that couple who kidnapped a man and his mistress and locked them in their basement for a month?"

At Vince's "yes" Eileen said, "I grew up in Richmond and remember when that happened. I was pretty young, but my parents talked about it a lot. They knew someone connected with the mistress."

In the library, the four of us trooped down to the lower level. "I'll be using one of these computers." Vince gestured toward a bank of computers that would let him keep an eye on us through the glass wall of the conference room. "Looks like Claudia's having a pow wow with someone in there. Is that Matt?"

Claudia and Matt sat at the table. Matt monitored his phone activity while they talked. "That's Matt," Lucy said.

"We'll come get you when we go on break," I said to Vince.

To no one's surprise, the conversation in class centered on Lorraine.

"Does anyone know when her funeral is?" Claudia asked.

"Monday at eleven at Southside Presbyterian Church," I said.

"It's so unbelievable!" Claudia cried. She pressed her lips together like she was trying to hold back tears.

"Matt," I said. "Weren't you and Lorraine talking last week during break?"

"Yes. She was all excited about her genealogy ideas and said she might try solving Randy's murder by looking up all our family trees. I warned her against that, said it could be dangerous." He shot me a meaningful look before adding, "She might have been kidding, though."

"How about you, Claudia? Hazel and I saw you and Lorraine talking by your car last week. Did she say anything about doing her own investigating?" Lucy sounded offhand, but I knew better.

"No."

That was a pretty quick no, Claudia.

"We talked about writing, writing in general. She didn't tell me anything like she told Matt." Claudia's eyes met mine for a split second.

Matt piped up. "Hazel, last week Lorraine said you gave her the genealogy idea. Did she say anything to *you* that could be helpful?"

"No. In fact when I mentioned genealogy she didn't even seem interested. Apparently she thought it over and decided that it appealed to her."

Both Matt and Claudia gave me long looks like they suspected I was lying. I held my ground and didn't add—or subtract—anything from my brief account.

"Let's talk about character." Claudia's relief at being back in teacher mode was palpable. She fired up her PowerPoint presentation and gave us pointers on creating great characters. She covered the sleuth, secondary characters, victim, killer, and suspects.

"Create characters readers will care about and will root for. Characters are often more important than the plot," Claudia said. "Readers love characters and if you have a series, they'll be looking for their favorites with each book."

"That may be the case for contemporary mysteries," Eileen said. "But when I read the works of, say, Ross Macdonald, he hardly describes his detective at all."

"Good point," Claudia said. "Yes, story took precedence over character with writers of previous eras. Today's readers want a good story, but they'll remember the characters long after forgetting the plot."

Claudia clicked through her slides, elaborating on her bulleted points. "Give each suspect a secret that makes him or her look suspicious. The secret doesn't have to relate to the murder. Perhaps the suspect committed a white collar crime, like embezzling. Or is having an affair and doesn't want it known."

I mentally reviewed the roster of suspects in Randy's and Lorraine's murders. Which of them harbored a secret?

At the break, Lucy, Eileen, and I collected Vince. He logged off his computer and accompanied us up the stairs and outside. Matt was nowhere in sight.

"Vince," I said, lowering my voice, "According to Matt, Lorraine told him she was all excited about her genealogy ideas and that she might try solving Randy's murder by looking up the family trees of everyone in the class."

"She hadn't done any genealogy research. Not recently."

"She hadn't?" Lucy said. "How do you know that?"

"I talked to Dennis a few minutes ago. Fish was quite interested in what you had to say about Lorraine's interest in genealogy. But she hadn't been on any of the usual databases in several months. She's registered on several genealogical sites."

"But there are other places for research," Eileen said. "Google, for one."

"She hadn't been doing anything on her home or work computers. Maybe at the library, but Fish and Garcia couldn't access her online activity there."

"They can't?" Lucy asked. "Why not?"

Eileen the librarian fielded that question. "When we turn off the public computers, everything gets wiped, including browsing history and saved documents."

"What about security cameras?" I asked.

"We do have them, but I doubt they can capture a computer screen. And for the most part, they're pointed toward the stacks, not the computers."

Claudia approached us, interrupting our conversation. When she saw Vince, she gushed, "Oh, Vince, we'd love to have you join the class and give us writing tips on police matters."

"Oh, I wouldn't want to interrupt your lesson plan."

"It's not a problem," Claudia assured him with a dismissive wave. "We'll forego the writing prompts." She winked at us and added, "I'm sure these ladies wouldn't mind."

"I don't mind." I was always happy to forego writing prompts. When Vince joined us in the conference room, he introduced himself to Matt. If my reports about Matt had swayed Vince's opinion of the man, he hid his feelings as the two exchanged cordial handshakes.

We enjoyed a spirited discussion with Vince as he shared his expertise on police procedure. Matt especially opened up, asking a number of questions. Vince knew quite a bit about historical police procedure as well.

Claudia asked Vince if he knew how the murder investigations were proceeding. His mild yet firm "The investigation is ongoing" response stopped further questioning.

We dropped off Eileen before continuing on to Lucy's home in the Stratford Hills section of Richmond. When we pulled into her driveway, she asked, "Are you bringing your sweet potato casserole on Thursday?"

"Um . . . sure."

"Dinner's at four. Come on over any time before that." She opened the door, then hesitated. "As for Dave and me, things are still hanging in the balance. I'm not sure what to do, but I'm hoping that the children and grandchildren, you two, and your cousin Brad, will diffuse the situation."

"Let us know what we can do to help," Vince said. I seconded his offer.

We waited for Lucy to unlock her front door and disappear inside.

"She sounded like she assumed I knew the dinner was still happening," I said as Vince backed out of the driveway. "This should be a Thanksgiving to remember."

On Wednesday morning, I found George Monahan walking down the street, Opa in tow.

We went through our standard morning greetings before I said, "I talked with Sherry yesterday."

"Sherry?"

"Yes, Sherry Guanzon. She told me about your warning her to stay away from me."

George didn't miss a beat. "I wanted to protect her from harm."

"You might have obstructed a police investigation."

"You're not the police."

I laughed. "No, I'm not."

"Like I said, I was trying to help the young woman. I felt sure she didn't kill this Randy, but knew she could look suspicious after airing her anger toward him in such an indiscreet fashion. Besides, she and Randy became friends."

Laboring the point was futile, so I said, "Well, that's it, I guess."

"No hard feelings?"

"No hard feelings." I smiled. "Your heart was in the right place."

FIFTY

While my sweet potato casserole with marshmallows baked, Vince and I watched the Macy's Thanksgiving Parade. As the balloons, floats, and marching bands passed, my mind dwelled on aspects of the investigation, especially Claudia's recent account of her missed opportunity with Randy at the Omni.

Later, we drove beside the James River on our way to Lucy and Dave's home in Stratford Hills. The nearly bare trees allowed an unobstructed view of the river with its scattered rock formations.

My cousin and her husband, wreathed with smiles, greeted us profusely when we arrived at their house, casserole in hand. The two were always friendly and welcoming, but they were overdoing it. Would I have noticed if I didn't know of the conflict between them?

Lucy took the casserole and Dave carried our coats to the hall closet. He looked handsome as ever with his ready smile and warm brown eyes, dark hair sprinkled with gray.

What do you say to a man who's married to your favorite cousin and sexting with a much younger woman?

"Something sure smells good." What I came up with may have

sounded inane but I spoke the truth—fragrant Thanksgiving aromas of turkey and stuffing wafted from the kitchen.

A small army of relatives descended on us, enveloping us in hugs. My cousin Brad Jones introduced us to his current woman friend, Peggy. Her last name didn't stick. And, of course, we had to greet the resident felines, Daisy and Shammy. The more sociable Daisy mingled with the guests. Daisy, a tiny domestic short hair, white with charcoal spots, was gifted with beautiful dark-lined green eyes.

We went upstairs to visit the shy Shammy, taking refuge in a bedroom. Shammy was a long-haired calico, also with beautiful peepers. She had accompanied me on the plane when I moved to Richmond from Los Angeles in 2000. The plan was for the two of us to camp out with Lucy until we got settled. I didn't leave until Vince and I married, over five years later. Talk about overstaying my welcome!

During the time I'd lived with Lucy, the two cats became pals. Much as it tore me up to leave Shammy when Vince and I married, I didn't want to break up the pair. But I visited my old friend often. She was quite healthy at close to twenty, so maybe she had a few more good years. She let us give her a tummy rub, then curled up and went back to sleep.

Downstairs, Lucy shooed everyone out of the kitchen and we sat in the living room, munching on olives, mixed nuts, shrimp, crackers, and a choice of spreads. Too much food, but it didn't stop me from spearing a shrimp or two with a toothpick.

The big topics were Randy's and Lorraine's murders. Lucy's children lived in Northern Virginia and knew little about our local drama. Vince and I brought them up to speed.

"Did Randy and Joyce have a pre-nup?" Peggy asked. She sported a sleek cap of highlighted hair. Cloisonné turkeys dangled from her ears.

"No one can find a record of one," I said.

"Well, I read lots of mysteries and they say it's usually the spouse.

They also say to follow the money. Sounds to me like Joyce had a powerful money motive."

Really, do you think the police haven't thought along those lines? Aloud, I said, "That's what we, I mean the police, are doing—following the money." I reached for another shrimp.

Brad gave me a knowing look, but didn't ask if I was investigating. "Don't they also say, *Cherchez la femme?*"

Brad's French was about as good as mine, which wasn't saying much. But I recognized the phrase—Rhea had used it at Randy's memorial service.

Lucy appeared. "Dave, will you carve the turkey?"

"Sure, hon." Dave grabbed an olive as he unfolded himself from the sofa and followed his wife to the kitchen.

"What does that mean?" Kevin, Lucy's son, tried to say *cherchez la femme* but settled for "What Brad just said."

"Look for the woman," I translated.

"That's sexist," Lucy's daughter Jessica piped up. "Why doesn't anyone ever say *Cherchez l'homme?*" She pronounced it like "lum." "Look for the man," she explained when she saw our blank looks.

"A *homme* could lead to a *femme*," Peggy said. "Or vice versa."

"Dinner is served," Lucy announced.

We gathered in the dining room, oohing and aahing over the food and table decorations. A white ceramic turkey served as a centerpiece, surrounded by a riotous assortment of mini pumpkins, gourds, pine cones, and votive candles. The placemats were oversized maple leaves in oranges, golds and reds. The décor, along with the platter of carved turkey and bowls of stuffing, mashed potatoes, my sweet potato casserole, green beans, broccoli casserole, biscuits, and homemade cranberry relish, were worthy of a magazine spread. My cousin didn't bother with gourmet touches for her Thanksgiving feasts, but the food was always delicious.

"Sit wherever you like," Lucy invited with a sweep of her hand. "And no murder talk at the table." She and Dave took the traditional positions at either end of the table and the rest of us found chairs based on left-handedness or right. Lucy's young grandchildren clamored for the drumsticks.

During the scrumptious dinner, the gathering did a good job of diffusing the tension between Lucy and Dave. Did they know they were diffusing? Were they even aware of problems between their hosts? I wondered.

"Where are the cats?" Jessica asked. "I would think they'd be begging for turkey."

"On the porch," Lucy said. "They'll get their treats later."

Lucy invited us to rest between dinner and dessert, which we could enjoy in the living room. I took advantage of the break by visiting the downstairs half bath. Finding it occupied, I headed upstairs. When I stepped out of the bathroom, Jessica was standing there. My cousin, first cousin once removed, to be precise. "Hazel, tell me . . ." She stage whispered, an unnecessary caution as loud voices and guffaws carried upstairs. "Is there something going on between Mom and Dave? They're being so, I don't know . . . fake?"

"Uh . . . I don't know."

"Come on, Hazel, you're a terrible actress. Please, tell me what's going on."

"Jessica," I said, trying to be as gentle as possible. "I think they're going through a rough patch, but you should ask your mom about it."

Jessica nodded and said, "I'm worried about them. They were so happy together. And now . . ."

"I'm sure they'll work out whatever troubles them." I hoped my prediction would come true.

We hugged and went back downstairs.

Pumpkin or apple pie? I compromised and picked a sliver of both. While I savored the sweet fruit and flaky crust, I chatted with Peggy about our book group, urging her to come to one of our meetings.

"We're on hiatus, but will start up again after the first of the year." I gave her my card.

Lucy sent Vince and me home with plenty of turkey for Morris and Olive. She and Dave maintained their unsettling merry host demeanors.

"There must be a reason I keep hearing that phrase *Cherchez la femme*," I said to Vince on the way home. "Am I getting a message from the universe?"

"Hmm" was Vince's only comment.

"We *have* been looking at women. There's Joyce. Before we had Lorraine and Sherry, but we've eliminated them." I winced at my word choice, considering Lorraine's fate. With reluctance, I added Claudia to the mix. "But Matt's a *homme*. What do you think about Jessica's idea that a *homme* could lead us to a *femme*?"

"Hmm."

FIFTY-ONE

Take a break from real life murder and focus on your fictional one. My inner critic, this time with a helpful suggestion.

I stayed home on Black Friday, avoiding malls and other shopping arenas. This act of resistance enabled my sleuths, Zack and Zoey Hunter, to stumble over the body of the victim. Literally. They were touring a church in Costa Rica's Central Valley, taking selfies, when Zoey fell backwards over the body of one Francisco Ferrari, a tourist from Argentina.

While I had the red metal church in Grecia in mind for the murder, I fictionalized not only the Costa Rican city, but the church as well. Writers were advised not to stage murders in real places. Not good PR for the real places.

Feeling bound by civic duty to frequent the mom and pop establishments, I ventured out on Small Business Saturday and purchased a stack of books for those on my holiday list.

On Saturday night, I sat down with Matt's manuscript. His story of marriage, adultery, and murder was compelling. Not being knowledgeable of nineteenth-century legal practices, I couldn't attest to the accuracy of the period details and had to give Matt the benefit of the doubt.

As for clues about the recent murders, nothing jumped out. When I talked to Lucy, she had finished the story and, like me, hadn't noticed anything significant.

"Those windows are incredible!"

The stained glass windows, twelve in all, that lined the brick walls of the massive Southside Presbyterian Church depicted scenes from Jesus's life and death.

"They had a tour of these windows last spring," Lucy said. "It was really fascinating."

I admired the windows one last time. Lucy and I were at Lorraine's funeral service for detecting purposes, not for admiring church art. Was Randy and Lorraine's killer sitting amongst us? Who could it be?

Not the two women who flanked a petite older woman in the front pew. One of them must be Lorraine's mother, Greta Popp. A group of about six people huddled together in one pew while another cluster took seats across the aisle. One group likely represented Lorraine's workplace. People sat here and there throughout the nave. Eileen couldn't get time off from work to attend.

"There's Susan Rowan. And is that Kat Berenger?" Lucy pointed to two women sliding into a pew across the aisle.

"It is," I said after studying the woman for a moment. "With very interesting hair."

Lucy and I had known Kat Berenger for many years. She was Carlene Arness's step-sister, and she'd been at the Murder on Tour book group the night Carlene died after drinking tea with a hefty dose of cyanide. After that night, Kat never returned to the group. I used to see her at the gym where she worked as a personal trainer.

But since my membership lapsed, our meetings were few and far between.

Kat was famous for a mass of blond curls crowning her head and cascading down her back. But now she sported a chin length do with one of those startling half and half dye jobs. From forehead to crown was white, while the back of her head was jet black. Kind of like the black and white cookies at Café Sweetbrew.

"I didn't know either of them knew Lorraine," I said.

"Where's Claudia?" Lucy asked after looking around and not spotting her.

Vince slipped into the pew beside me. His dark blue suit deepened the blue of his eyes. Lucy wore her usual impeccable business attire, a charcoal gabardine suit. My blazer, short black skirt, and suede boots struck a more casual note.

The service began with an organ prelude. Lorraine's casket, covered with a blanket of flowers, presided at the end of the center aisle. Several bouquets and wreaths perched on pedestals or hung from easels.

The pastor spoke with fondness of Lorraine, a longtime member of his flock. He had managed to close his jacket over his jutting belly, but I feared a button would pop at any moment.

Three people from the church gave eulogies, and a woman with a shock of white hair and black-framed glasses represented the contingent from the workplace.

No one spoke of Lorraine as a writer. So when the pastor asked if anyone else wished to speak, I stepped forward. My writing career had accustomed me to public speaking, but I usually had the chance to prepare myself. I kept my words brief, painting a picture of Lorraine as a talented writer with unquenchable curiosity. I overdid it on the unquenchable curiosity bit, but figured that hyperbole at a funeral was acceptable. Given my brief acquaintance with Lorraine, I didn't have much material.

The service ended, to reconvene at a local cemetery. Kat rushed over to our pew and hugged Lucy, Vince, and me in turn. We all exchanged versions of "It's so *wonderful* to see you again."

"Ladies, if you'll excuse me," Vince said as he moved away from us. "There's someone I need to talk to."

Seeing Fish standing in the back row of pews, I pegged him as the someone. I turned to Kat and said, "Your hair . . ."

She laughed. "You don't know what to say, I can tell."

"It's sure different. How long have you had it this way?"

"A couple of months. I'm still getting used to it."

"But the leopard touches haven't changed," Lucy said. Kat favored a leopard motif and included it with each wardrobe change. Today her knee high stiletto-heeled boots and oversized satchel bag bore the big cat's rosettes.

"Never," Kat said with a laugh. "We need to catch up. Are you coming back here for the lunch?"

"Yes. We'll chat then."

Susan joined us. "I didn't know you all knew each other," she said.

"Oh, yes," Lucy said. "We go back a long way. And how do you and Kat know each other?"

"The gym. She's my personal trainer."

"You're doing a good job, Kat," I said. "Susan's quite toned."

Both women beamed at my praise. And did Susan actually flex her muscles or did I imagine that?

I looked from one woman to the other and asked, "How did you know Lorraine?"

"From the gym," they answered in unison.

At the graveside service, Lucy, Vince, and I offered our condolences to Mrs. Popp, who turned out to be the petite woman in the front pew of the church. Greta Popp, gifted with an abundance of silver curls, was close to eighty if not beyond. Tears hadn't smudged her makeup—but some people grieved in private.

"Hello, Mrs. Popp. I'm Hazel Rose, I knew Lorr—"

"Oh, yes, Hazel Rose! Lorraine always spoke so highly of you."

Mrs. Popp gripped my hand with surprising strength and leaned forward. "We need to talk."

"Yes, Mrs. Popp. We'll talk at the lunch."

"Call me Greta." She released my hand. I held it at my side and flexed my fingers to get the blood flowing again.

"Mrs. Popp wants to talk," I said to Lucy and Vince on the way back to the church. "I want to talk to Kat and Susan as well. Since they both knew Lorraine, they might know something. But I'll talk to Mrs. Popp first."

"I'll talk to Kat and Susan," Lucy said. "And those folks from Lorraine's job. I know a couple of them."

"Be careful," Vince cautioned.

"We will," I assured my husband. "I'm sure you and Fish will keep an eye on us and everyone else."

A long table in the church fellowship hall groaned with the usual fare found at funerals: cold cuts, various salads, breads, deviled eggs, an assortment of pastries, and that Southern staple—ham biscuits. An adjacent table held an urn of coffee, pitchers of water and iced tea, and a selection of condiments.

Before I could grab a plate, Greta Popp approached and placed a hand on my arm. Burgundy polish covered her well-shaped nails.

"Hazel, I think the sanctuary would be a good place to talk."

"I think you're right." I turned to Lucy and said, "Catch you later."

Vince and Fish sat at one of the round tables set up for the occasion. They were probably surveying the crowd, but skilled at giving the impression they were not. When the pastor walked by, his jacket was open and, as I'd feared, a thread dangled where a button had been. Too bad I couldn't predict other events with such accuracy.

Greta and I took seats in the front pew of the now-empty sanctuary. For a moment neither of us spoke. Greta's closed eyes suggested that she prayed.

When at last she broke the silence, she said, "I can't imagine who would hurt my girl like that."

"Had she mentioned someone—someone who made her, um, uncomfortable?" Not wanting to sound at ease talking about potential murder suspects, I acted tentative.

Greta thought for a moment before shaking her curls. "No."

"Any boyfriends, exes?"

"No." Greta opened her purse and took out a tissue. "If there were, she didn't tell me about them. I'm afraid my girl was an old maid." Did people still use that term for a never-married woman? Apparently Greta Popp did.

We fell silent again. I sensed that Greta wanted to tell me something but struggled with words.

At last she spoke. "Lorraine told me something that had me a little concerned."

"What was that?" I made my voice gentle.

"It was the last time I saw her, that Saturday morning. She had already told me she was using a genealogy theme for her next book. I thought it was a good idea, I never thought much of that quilting theme, she didn't know anything about that. But she and I had done quite a bit of research into our family tree. Write what you know, that's what they say, right?"

When I nodded, she went on. "That day, that Saturday, she told me she had started researching the students in the writing class, looking into their family trees, and had already found some interesting information. I cautioned her about sharing the information with anyone."

"Did she tell you what the information was?"

"Something about a husband in prison. She said she needed to verify it. I don't know if she ever did."

Husband in prison? Sherry? But Sherry wasn't in the class. Besides, Vince said the police couldn't find any evidence that Lorraine had started researching anyone. But, according to Eileen, if she'd researched at the library, they couldn't follow that trail.

A possible way of checking Lorraine's online activity occurred to me. "Greta, did Lorraine use your computer for her genealogical research?"

"No, I don't have a computer. When Lorraine and I lived together, I used hers."

So much for that idea.

Greta's eyes filled with tears and spilled down her face. She blotted her face with her tissue. So much for her perfect makeup. I chided myself for my flippant thought. I put my arm around her and drew her close.

She said, *sotto voce,* "Lorraine said you were a detective. Find out who killed her."

Before I could utter a word in response, she announced, "I'm ready to go home now."

"Do you need a ride?"

"No, my friends will take me."

We returned to the fellowship hall. I pressed my card into Greta's hand. "Call me anytime." I stayed with her until she collected her friends, the two women who'd sat with her during the service.

Kat emerged from the ladies room, nearly colliding with me.

"I wish we could talk, but I have a new client starting this afternoon. We need to get together. Lucy and I had a long talk, mostly about Randy Zimmerman. She gave me all the gory details." Kat waved at the table where they'd been sitting. "First Randy, then Lorraine. I hope their murders aren't part of a trend. So I take it you and Lucy are trying to hunt down the killer, or killers?"

"Well . . . yeah." No use being coy with Kat. She'd been part of my two previous investigations.

"How's Trudy taking it?"

"She's shaken." I explained about Trudy and Sarah traveling. "I had no idea Susan and Lorraine even knew each other. Or that you knew them."

"Lorraine joined the gym a couple of months ago and Susan's been a member forever. They struck up a friendship, sometimes going out for lunch or coffee. A couple of times I heard them talking about genealogy. Susan was devastated about Lorraine's murder. Anyway, gotta go. Let me know if I can help." We hugged. "When are you coming back to the gym? I'll get you a deal."

Hadn't I recently envisioned fighting off would-be adversaries with flabby arms? "I'll think about it."

But would I?

FIFTY-TWO

Susan was nowhere in sight. I piled my plate and took it to a nearby table. For the next hour I talked with various people, including church members and Lorraine's co-workers. To my dismay, Lorraine had told one and all she was hot on the heels of Randy Zimmerman's killer.

Lucy, Vince, and I lingered in the parking lot.

"A husband in prison?" Lucy mused when I shared my conversation with Greta Popp. "Sherry has a husband in prison. But why would Lorraine be researching her? She's not in our class. What about Claudia and her mysterious husband?"

"I researched them," Vince said. "No prison record."

"I don't think Eileen has a husband in prison," Lucy said. "She never even married."

"I'm thinking that someone knew Lorraine was researching and didn't want her to find out about an imprisoned relative," I said. "Or didn't want her sharing the information."

"Or resorting to blackmail," Vince said.

"Vince, will you use your research skills to find out something about the people in our class?"

"Sure. I'll see what I can find out."

"Yesterday I saw George's grandsons cutting through the neighbor's yard. I don't know why I didn't think of this before, but now it occurs to me that if Randy and Matt were neighbors, then they used to cut through each other's yards."

"Like you tried to do that day." Vince scowled at the memory.

"I was trying to check out the surroundings, not cut through. Besides, that crime scene tape was everywhere. So was Ruby." I held up a hand. "The point is, Matt must know Randy's property well, knows all those trees and bushes."

"That may be, but we can't place Matt there during the timeframe of Randy's murder," Vince said.

"I'll scour Facebook again," I said. "It's amazing the stuff you can find out about people on social media."

"It's scary," Lucy commented.

Vince checked his watch. "We should be going."

"But we haven't heard about Lucy's conversation with Kat and Susan."

"I have to get going too, so I'll make this fast," Lucy said. "Let's see . . . I didn't get much from Susan, because she didn't stay long. Kat and I talked about Randy. According to Kat, Susan mentioned him quite often."

"What did she say?"

"She didn't like him. Thought he was obnoxious." Lucy shifted from one foot to the other in her suede stilettos. "I need to get out of these heels. Too high for someone my age."

"Maybe he disappointed her when he didn't move their friendship to a higher level once she was cancer-free," I said. "Pure speculation, I know."

"Susan didn't like Joyce, either, but felt sorry for her, the way Randy poked fun at her."

Vince snickered. "Not a surprise."

"What about genealogy?" I asked. "Kat heard Lorraine and Susan talking about it."

"Lorraine told Susan she was interested in the subject, but didn't say anything specific." Lucy took her keys from her purse. "Gotta go. Let me know what I can do."

"*Cherchez la femme*," I said to Vince as he opened my door. "That phrase keeps playing in my head. Or, as Jessica said at the Thanksgiving dinner, 'Why not *Cherchez l'homme?*' "

FIFTY-THREE

Nothing incriminating about Matt had popped up since my first survey of his social media presence. I scrolled through his Facebook friends list and clicked on Susan's profile picture. Her political leanings conflicted with her husband's, making her household a divided one. In one picture, the photogenic Susan posed in a low-cut black dress with a pink shawl draped over her shoulders. In another, she sported a black leather jacket and matching slacks.

One photo, posted six months before, stopped me short with a feeling of déjà vu. I understood why when I enlarged the photo of Susan and a handsome man who wasn't Matt. According to her comment, the man was one Robert Crain, who she dubbed the "love of her life." I recognized him as the man Susan had been chatting with at Randy's memorial service. What stood out most about the pair were their toothy smiles, the blindingly white teeth. Susan gazed at the man with a glow. She was clearly smitten. I couldn't tell how he felt about her. He enjoyed her adoration, but did he reciprocate?

Penfield High School's thirtieth reunion marked the occasion for this photo opp. It took ten seconds to learn that Penfield High was in

Salem, Virginia, near Roanoke. I remembered Susan saying she went to high school in that part of the state and that the class had a recent reunion.

Over the next hour I researched Susan and Robert. Both received law degrees from the University of Richmond Law School. Apparently the law didn't suit Susan, as she became a Certified Financial Planner and followed that career until she retired.

But the law did suit Robert Crain. After graduation, he joined Trunker and Wells, a Richmond litigation firm, where he stayed.

Susan and Robert graduated from high school and law school together. Were they ever a couple? Did it matter?

"Interesting," Vince said when I ran down my latest findings. "But inconclusive."

We sat at Vince's computer, the Facebook picture of Susan and Robert Crain on the screen in front of us. "There's something about the way she's looking at this guy, like she wants to devour him. It's the same way she looked at him at Randy's memorial service."

When Vince smiled, I held up a hand. "Don't say it—interesting, but inconclusive."

"I was going to say that I wonder how Matt feels about her claiming this Robert as the love of her life."

"Yes, there's that. Some folks sure lead complicated lives. Can you research Susan? I've done about all I could do on the usual sites, like LinkedIn, Facebook, and Google."

"Sure."

I stood and kissed my husband on top of his head.

"Let's go out for dinner," I said.

We indulged in burgers and fries at Walter's, a favorite neighborhood dive. I vowed to walk an extra mile—or two—the next day.

"Tell me what you think about this scenario," I said. "Matt and Joyce wanted to marry. Randy was Joyce's mistake and perhaps Susan was Matt's. But Joyce and Randy have a pre-nup and Joyce will miss out on a boatload of money if she divorces him. So Matt kills Randy—or Joyce does—or they both do. Then after a 'respectable' period of time, Matt figures he'll divorce Susan and marry Joyce. Or— he plans to kill Susan and marry Joyce."

"Awfully convoluted," Vince said.

"Susan could end up as dead as Randy and Lorraine."

Vince gave me a measured look. "Dead is dead."

"Yes, dead is dead." I dragged a sweet potato fry through a puddle of ketchup. "How does Mick Jacoby fit into this? Does Matt know about him?"

"Likely Susan told him about the scene at the memorial service," Vince said. "What about the inheritance Susan is getting from her father?"

"Yes, the guys at the memorial service implied that it was a sizable one—sizable enough to make Matt rethink divorcing Susan."

Vince nodded. "That may alter your scenario."

"So—if Matt doesn't want to divorce her, he might kill her. Sheesh. We'd better catch this killer, or killers, before more people die. But why would any of these people kill poor Lorraine?"

"She was getting too close for comfort, hinting that she planned to poke into family trees and all. Someone might have been nervous about what she'd find out—and what she'd do with the information."

"Like blackmail?"

"Right. Maybe Lorraine didn't try to blackmail Claudia, but she could have blackmailed Matt or Joyce."

We fell silent and concentrated on our food. I didn't know if it was the fat, carbs, or a combination of the two, but I had a sudden insight.

"The short stories! The stories I read and rated for that upcoming anthology—that was where I read something that was similar to my scenario. Let's go, I need to read that story again."

Back at the house, I raced to my computer and zeroed in on the second story, the one I'd thought dreadful. It was about couples who join a swingers meetup. Swingers? Were swinging and couple swapping one and the same activity, one I associated with disenchanted, bored suburban couples? The couples in this story expected to spice up their marriages with casual sex, but a dead body put a damper on their fun.

One of the men, Peter, bullied his wife and another couple into swinging. Devona, the woman not married to Peter, seized the opportunity to kill him while they coupled, making it appear like a heart attack. It wasn't clear how she pulled off the deception and that was one reason for my thumbs down review.

But what interested me this time around was Devona's motive for killing Peter: she wanted her own husband and Peter's wife to be free to marry each other. In turn, Devona could proceed with plans to marry the love of her life. Everyone would live happily ever after. Except for Peter the bully.

The story deviated from my scenario of Matt divorcing—or killing—Susan in order to marry Joyce. Devona, the fictional killer, wants to marry the love of her life.

The love of her life.

Who was a real-life counterpart to Devona? I could only come up with one: Susan.

I sent the story to Vince and to Lucy. Vince agreed that my conclusion about Susan had merit, but added his usual "you need proof" reminder.

"The 'love of her life' expression makes me think of Susan and Robert Crain. The way she looked at him at the memorial service. The picture of the two at their reunion. And she called him the love of her life."

"But these are anonymous submissions, right?" he asked as he checked the information section of Word for the author name, finding it blank.

"I'll try to sweet talk the editor into giving me the author's name."

I emailed the editor, Roseanne Dempsey, asking for the names of the authors I had rated. I only needed the name of the one who wrote the wife-swapping tale, but, in case Roseanne questioned my intentions, I asked for all three names.

"I'm planning a panel for a library program," I wrote. "I know we're not supposed to have the names, but I'd love to have these three on the panel."

Lucy called. "That story was incredibly awful. I wonder who wrote it. Not Claudia, that's for sure."

"No. Joyce, perhaps?"

"If so, hopefully she edits other people's work better than her own. I kept thinking of *The Ice Storm*. Did you ever see that movie? Or read the book?"

"I saw it, but never read the book. Kind of depressing."

The Ice Storm was a disturbing film about dysfunctional upper-class families escaping unsatisfactory lives through sexual experimentation, including couple swapping.

"Let me tell you my current idea for a motive."

When I finished, Lucy said nothing for a moment. "Yes, Susan's emerging as a possibility. But, like Vince always says, we need proof. But how will finding the person who wrote this crap solve the case?"

"At this point we have to consider all possibilities, no matter how remote."

"Sounds desperate to me."

"Yeah, yeah, yeah. I know."

"Okay. Let me know what that woman—Roseanne, is it?—tells you."

"I might have to offer her a spot on the panel as well."

"I haven't heard you talk about a panel."

"No, you haven't. I just came up with the idea."

After my usual morning walk on Tuesday I settled down to write. I made progress and even lost track of time. At noon, Vince appeared in my den, holding a sheaf of papers.

"I may have found your prison connection."

FIFTY-FOUR

"Susan Rowan comes from a wealthy Roanoke family." Vince read from the printout he held. "Her father, Hugh Godsey, made his fortune in real estate."

"So, presumably she *is* coming into money."

"Yes. So might Deborah Godsey Travis, Hugh's daughter from a previous marriage."

"Interesting, especially since Susan told Lucy and me she was an only child."

"She *was* an only child of the second marriage."

We sat in the family room, Morris and Olive each taking a lap. "So who was in prison?"

"I was just getting to that," Vince said. "Susan's first husband was Russell Blaine, who's serving time for armed robbery and assault."

"Really? Tell me more. When did she marry Russell?"

"Married in 2005, divorced in 2007."

"Hmmph."

Was the prison connection with Susan meaningful? Did Russell Blaine have anything to do with Randy and Lorraine—or did it amount to nothing more than a red herring? Was I straying from the matter at hand? Was scope creep finding its way into this investigation? That term took me back to my days as a systems analyst. "Scope creep" happened when a project was not properly defined or controlled.

"And now, Robert Crain." Vince summarized his professional credentials, adding, "He's a widower. His wife died of a heart attack two years ago."

"Ah. So that makes him a catch for Susan. But how can we tie all this together?" Before Vince could weigh in, another connection came to me. "Remember me telling you about Christina Bigelow, the librarian from the Chesterfield County Library? Lucy talked to her at Randy's memorial service. Christina said he was doing research for his next book—a book about a wealthy man."

"I'm guessing you think Hugh Godsey is the wealthy man. There are lots of wealthy men around."

"Christina signed up for my romance writing class."

"So you'll see her tomorrow."

"I can't wait that long to talk to her. Where's my phone?" I nudged Olive off my lap and sprinted up the steps to my den.

After emailing Christina, I tried to resume the morning's productive streak, to no avail. Too many real-life characters clamored for my attention and I compulsively checked my email for responses from Christina and from Roseanne Dempsey.

If I was lucky, Roseanne wouldn't stand on principle and refuse to divulge the names of the short story submitters. Principled people could be such a trial, especially during an investigation.

***

Later, I tried to keep my mind on the writing class, but kept sneaking looks at email on my muted phone. Roseanne Dempsey and Christina Bigelow remained cyberspace no-shows. The next day's romance writing class also vied for my attention.

"Hazel, how do you come up with your writing ideas?" Claudia asked.

"You know, that's one of the most common questions I get from readers," I said.

That statement was true, and it gave me the seconds I needed to tune into the present moment. According to Claudia's syllabus, the scheduled topic was plotting, but it sounded like the conversation had turned to ideas and how writers came up with them.

"Advice columns are great for ideas," I said. "The letters are all about conflict: conflict with spouses, friends, neighbors, in-laws . . ." I named a few more idea generators, prompting Lucy, Matt, and Eileen to chime in with their favorites: travel, newspaper articles, headlines, overheard conversations—good old-fashioned eavesdropping—past experiences, and hobbies to name a few.

What about Randy's idea, the one he'd shared at Richmond Books, first with Lorraine and me, later with Claudia in the café? How did it go? It took a minute to recollect, but I came up with the following: some rich guy dies and leaves everything to his only child, a son. But, lo and behold, another son turns up. Does the first son share the wealth with the second son? Or does he kill him?

Not an original idea, but still . . . where did Randy get it? And was Hugh Godsey the inspiration for the rich guy?

Vince had insisted on once again playing bodyguard, and no one objected. During the break, the entire class traipsed upstairs to the lobby.

Claudia walked up and pulled me aside. "How was Lorraine's funeral? I couldn't make it." She didn't supply a reason.

Matt passed behind Claudia and went outside. Wanting to catch him and ask about Randy's idea, I summarized the service for Claudia, skimping on the details.

"So how's the investigation going?" she asked.

"It's slow."

I grabbed Vince's hand and pulled him off the bench he shared with Lucy and Eileen. "I need to talk to Matt," I said, *sotto voce.*

We found Matt in the parking lot, standing with hands in pockets, no phone in sight. "Hi Matt, how are you doing?" My voice sounded overly bright to my ears.

"Um, okay I guess."

"You've met Vince, haven't you?" I barely gave him time to nod before rushing on. "When we talked about ideas back there, I wondered about that one Randy had about a rich guy who dies and it turns out he has a secret family. You remember that day at Richmond Books when he talked about it?"

"Yeah, I remember."

"Do you know how he got the idea?"

Matt screwed up his face in thought. After a moment, he said, "It could have been a conversation he had with a woman at Hugh Godsey's funeral. Hugh was Susan's dad. According to Randy, the woman said she was from Northern Virginia. Hugh was from there, and he and this woman went to high school together, dated for a while. She said he was the love of her life, even though they both wound up marrying other people."

That "love of her life" expression was popping up on a regular basis.

Matt continued. "Anyway, after this woman's husband died, she got in touch with Hugh. He responded when she contacted him, but he wasn't interested in getting together. Still, she made the trek to Roanoke for his funeral. Now here's the strange part: she asked Susan about a Deborah, Hugh's other daughter. She wondered where she was, why she wasn't at her father's funeral. She said Susan at first didn't seem to know who the woman was talking about. Then she caught herself and said, 'Oh, yes, Deborah's ill and couldn't make it.' But the woman was sure Susan didn't know about Deborah."

"So Deborah is Hugh's daughter from a previous marriage or relationship?"

"Well, no. He didn't have any other children. Only Susan."

"Yes, I remember Susan saying she was an only child." At Matt's questioning look, I said, "Lucy and I talked with Susan one day at Café Sweetbrew."

"Oh, that's right. Anyway, Randy said this woman was kind of—I don't know, dithery. Not quite all there."

"Could be a misunderstanding," I said.

Matt kicked a stone, sending it skittering three feet. "At any rate, no long lost daughter has come forth."

"So maybe Randy took that conversation and created a what-if scenario for a story." Matt and Vince both nodded. I tried to smile, but probably only managed a grimace. Despite my words, I doubted the misunderstanding conclusion and felt a frisson of fear for Deborah Godsey Travis.

By the time the class ended, the only thing I retained was the writing advice: "During the sleuth's confrontation with the killer, convey emotional reactions like panic and fear."

My two previous confrontations with killers had given me firsthand knowledge of panic and fear. I didn't relish a third round.

FIFTY-FIVE

"Ms. Rose, how much, um, *sex* do I need to have in my romance? Do I need any?"

I regarded this woman who was uncomfortable even uttering the word *sex*. An attractive woman in her forties, a mouth pursed in disapproval marred her good looks.

Choosing my words with care, I said, "That's up to you. Remember, physical attraction and desire are important parts of your characters' love journey, and your readers want to experience them. Even if your characters never do more than kiss."

Hearing that she didn't *have* to have a sex scene mollified the woman. Since my fictional baby boomers reveled in sex, I wasn't the best person to coach her, but, with the class's help, we spent a few minutes discussing how she could craft a sex-free story that would appeal to modern day romance readers. I suggested a few authors she could contact for advice.

"Why are you even writing a romance?" one woman asked. "Write one of those cozy mysteries, they never have sex."

A woman who was ninety if she was a day had no problem with the sex aspect—she was working on an even racier version of *50*

Shades of Grey. She and a young woman with pink hair trailing down her back asked questions about talking during sex scenes—should the characters talk? What should they say? How much profanity was acceptable?

Twelve students had made the trek to downtown Richmond for my class at the Richmond Public Library. They gave me their undivided attention, undistracted by texts or Facebook feeds. No sign of Christina Bigelow.

The last minute registration of a student who had burst in as the members were finishing up their introductions surprised me.

Smiling, I said, "Please welcome Susan Rowan."

Susan apologized for her tardiness and kept her introduction brief. Over the next two hours, she took furious notes, but didn't say another word.

Several students surrounded me after class. I fielded questions on showing passion in dialogue and how to create a romantic mood. After talking to the library director about a follow-up program, I gathered my laptop, PowerPoint handouts, and other class materials and started to leave the meeting room.

A slender woman with a mop of dark hair rushed into the room, stopping my exit. Christina Bigelow.

"Hazel, I'm so sorry I missed your class."

"No problem. I have a handout for you."

"Great." Christina took the handout I pulled from my messenger bag. "Sorry I didn't email you back. I've been swamped. You wanted to know about Randy and his research."

"Yes, you mentioned it to Lucy at the memorial service, but she didn't remember who he was researching."

"Hugh Godsey, a self-made multi-millionaire from Roanoke. Randy talked about what an interesting person he was. And that he had some family skeletons."

"Did he elaborate on the skeletons?"

"Just said the guy had an illustrious past." Christina pushed her hair out of her eyes. "Randy thought he only had one child and was surprised to learn that there were two. I guess that could qualify as a skeleton."

"When was he doing this research?"

"I saw him on two different Saturdays. The last time was on the morning of the day he was killed. He was so excited. Said something like 'Wait'll my buddy hears about this.' "

We chatted for a few more minutes before Christina left. I sat on one of the meeting room chairs, reflecting on what I'd learned from our conversation.

Her disclosures paralleled the story idea Randy had pitched at Richmond Books, first with Lorraine and me, later with Claudia in the café. They also supported Matt's account of the woman who showed up at Hugh Godsey's funeral asking about the deceased's daughter.

According to Christina, Randy expressed excitement about his research on Hugh Godsey on the same day he was murdered—the same day he had shared his story idea at Richmond Books.

Coincidence? I thought not.

I stood, picked up my belongings, and walked up the steps to the library's lobby, where Susan sat on a bench, perusing the handout I'd distributed to the class.

"Hi, Hazel." She smiled. "Wonderful class. I learned so much. Luckily I saw your tweet and was able to get in at the last minute." Susan stood and adjusted a burgundy scarf draped around her neck over a black blazer.

As we walked outside, Susan continued to lavish praise, detailing all she'd learned. "I didn't realize you should never start a story with weather. Wouldn't you know it, I did, so I guess I'll have to change it."

"I didn't say never. These are only guidelines—"

"Do you have time for coffee? My treat. I want to pick your brain."

I cringed at the phrase and the literal image it formed in my mind. I preferred "toss ideas around" or even "brainstorm."

"Sure," I said aloud. "Sweetbrew is on the way home."

"Great. See you there." We went to our respective cars.

In the car, I sent a text to Vince: *Can you come to Sweetbrew? I'm meeting Susan there in a few minutes.*

I started driving.

FIFTY-SIX

In a replay of the week before, I drove through the Forest Hill Historic District. This time I did not detour and cruise by Lorraine's apartment. Truth be told, I didn't even think of Lorraine. My mind focused on my conversation with Christina, tying it in with recent conversations and tidbits of information.

At the memorial service, a group of Randy's friends had speculated on Matt and Susan's marriage. One thought Matt had wanted to divorce his wife, but her expected inheritance made him rethink that idea.

Matt thought Susan didn't know about her father's other daughter. Or so he said. Was Matt the buddy Randy mentioned to Christina? *Wait'll my buddy hears about this.* More to the point, would Matt now be less interested in staying married to Susan if she had to split her inheritance with her half-sister? Likely she'd still be loaded. How much money did Matt need? How much did he love Joyce?

As for Susan, did she want to stay with her husband or be free to marry Robert Crain? If the former was the case, she wouldn't want Randy telling Matt about Deborah Godsey Travis—assuming Randy had learned about her. That gave Susan a motive to kill Randy. But if divorcing Matt meant she could take up with Robert, why would she care if Matt knew about the daughter?

And Matt wouldn't be eager to divorce the soon-to-be-wealthy Susan. That meant his life could be in jeopardy—from his wife.

Vince hadn't responded to my text, and he'd be furious if I met with a suspect on my own. Should I keep driving past Café Sweetbrew? I could tell Susan that something came up—I'd suddenly remembered a doctor's appointment. If she really wanted to pick my brain, we could Skype.

But Sweetbrew, a place usually buzzing with activity, should be safe. Although only two other customers were in the place that day Lucy and I went there to view the video of Joyce and Mick Jacoby. A drive-by of the parking lot would tell me how busy the place was.

If Susan wasn't a murderer, she might give me insight on Joyce and Randy. Maybe even Matt. Maybe even herself.

The big question: Had Randy's research into Hugh Godsey's life been his undoing?

Sweetbrew's parking lot was full, indicating lots of customers in the café. I arrived in time to see Susan locking her car, a Toyota the color of the standard house mouse, with her key fob. She'd taken the last spot, so I had to drive around back and wedge my car into a space of questionable legality.

I checked my phone. Still nothing from Vince.

Inside the café, Susan asked, "What can I get you?"

"Oh, I think I'll have some of that tea, you know the cinnamon orange blend."

"Take anything in it?"

"Nothing. And keep the bag in. I like to let it steep."

"Anything to eat?"

"No, thanks."

While Susan tended to the refreshments, I plopped down on a sofa in front of a large window, took my phone from my purse, and accessed my email. I disentangled my hair from the philodendron that trailed from the window ledge and over my shoulder.

Roseanne Dempsey, the anthology editor, had come through with the names I'd requested for the three authors. Two of the names were not familiar to me, but one was:

Susan Rowan.

Not a surprise. I mentally reviewed Susan's story about swinging couples. Devona killing Peter the bully so her own husband and Peter's wife would be free to marry. Devona could then marry the man she coveted. Win-win.

Had Susan taken the write-what-you-know advice literally and fictionalized a murder she'd committed? Or had she written the story first and played it out for real? As the submission deadline for the stories was mid-October, weeks before Randy's murder, the latter must be the case.

And I couldn't forget Matt's revelations about Susan's father and his unacknowledged daughter, a daughter who apparently existed: Deborah Godsey Travis. Yes, Susan now had a prime spot on the suspect list.

And here I was, alone with her. Okay, not alone: groups of men huddled together, finding much to guffaw about. A middle-aged woman dropped a headset, phone, and laptop on a nearby table. A bush-like pony tail of dark hair threaded with white poked from the cutout in back of her baseball cap. Two men discussed their upcoming nuptials with a woman I guessed was a wedding planner.

Could this all be a coincidence and Susan had nothing to do with Randy's murder? Considering my present circumstances, I prayed she was innocent.

I needed time to think. I needed Vince and Lucy. But I had neither thinking time nor the comfort of my loved ones.

Cherchez la femme. Look for the woman.

I had found the woman.

FIFTY-SEVEN

At the counter, Susan passed money to the barista before taking our mugs to the condiment counter against the far wall. She shook something into the mug on her left and swirled the contents, probably with a spoon or stirrer. Guesswork on my part, as my angle didn't allow an unobstructed view of what she was doing. Something white, the size and shape of a sugar packet, fluttered to the floor. Susan bent to pick it up and dropped it in the waste receptacle by the counter.

What was that?

Keeping one eye on Susan, I turned on my recorder app and slipped my phone in my jacket pocket. I was better with phone technology than I used to be. Once I texted a help message to the wrong person. All turned out well, and I lived to tell the story. And improve my phone skills.

Susan didn't touch the mug by her right hand. I kept my focus on both mugs as she picked them up and carried them to where I waited.

Get up and leave.

My guardian angel's warning was clear, not one of her usual

gentle, whispery messages. But I didn't move. I continued to watch Susan, hoping my growing doubts about her were the product of my overactive imagination.

Susan placed the mug in her left hand on the coffee table in front of me. The dangling tea bag made it even more apparent that she intended the brew for me. The aroma from her own beverage was clearly coffee.

"Oh, let me get you a spoon for your tea bag." Susan dashed over to the counter. I contemplated the mug in front of me.

What did she put in my tea?

Could she have simply been dunking the bag? Had she forgotten I'd said "no" when she asked if I took anything in my tea? Best not to assume that possibility. My health and well-being—hell, my life—could be at stake. I pulled the phone from my pocket and sent a text to Lucy. A nanosecond later, I remembered that Lucy went to Northern Virginia for her granddaughter's ballet recital.

I hoped my guardian angel stuck to me like glue.

"Is anything wrong, Hazel?" Susan handed me the spoon before sinking into the sofa. "You look like you've seen a ghost."

"Oh, it's this email from an old friend in California. Someone we knew from work died. Massive heart attack." Unfortunately, I'd heard similar news so often that my fabrication sounded believable.

"I'm so sorry." Susan touched my arm. Her French manicure looked no more than a few hours old. The diamond on her left hand sparkled.

A notification I barely heard over the music and noise alerted me to a text. Should I check it? I felt hard pressed to talk, listen, scheme, and check text messages at the same time. Too much multi-tasking.

"Is that your phone? Don't you need to check it?" Susan asked.

I pulled out the phone, making sure Susan couldn't see any signs of recording.

Are you all right? Vince wrote. *I'm just leaving John Tyler and I'll be there as soon as I can. Let Billy know if you need any help.*

Dang! Vince was giving a guest lecture today at John Tyler Community College and it had slipped my mind. It would take him at least thirty minutes, if not more, to get here.

I'm ok, I'm talking to Susan, I texted back. *Who's Billy?* I returned the phone to my pocket and cautioned myself to turn my attention to Susan. Good manners could extend my life.

"Sorry about that. My husband. Wants me to pick up milk on the way home." *Good, I inserted Vince into the conversation.* I wrapped my tea bag around the spoon before picking up the mug and inhaling the scent of cinnamon, orange, and other spices. If Susan had doctored the brew with a poisonous substance, the aromatic blend masked it. "So, Susan—do you think you'll write a romance?"

"Yes, romantic suspense. Gothic style. Damsel in distress, modern-day version."

That's me right now, I thought ruefully. *Damsel in distress. Maybe.* I pretended to sip my tea, adding a swallow for effect. Was this method acting? I needed to get rid of some of this tea.

"I read a couple of your romances, Hazel. They're so good. Stick with them."

My cue! I needed to talk about something emotional. Noticing that Susan held her mug in her left hand, I came up with a plan that could work—if my luck stayed with me. For good measure, I prayed to the acting gods.

I heaved a mighty sigh. "Susan, did I tell you about my publisher dropping me?"

"No! You're kidding! What happened?"

I shared my sorry tale, embellishing it a bit. Too bad I wasn't a good enough actor to produce tears. When I ended with "I'm so distressed, I just can't tell you," I pressed on Susan's arm to illustrate the extent of said distress.

As I'd hoped, most of her coffee ended up in her lap.

"Oh, Susan." I put my mug on the table. "I'm so sorry." Ordinarily, I'd have scurried for napkins, but I didn't want to leave my tea unattended. I put on a dithery act and even wrung my hands for effect.

"It's not a problem." Her peeved tone belied her words. "I'll be right back." She got up and headed for the rest room.

"I'll get you a refill, Susan."

"Okay."

Once Susan disappeared into the rest room, I dumped half my tea into the philodendron behind me. I offered a silent apology to the poor plant, hoping it would survive whatever substance Susan had added to my beverage.

No one seemed to notice my staged spill.

I checked to make sure my recorder was still working before getting Susan's refill. While I waited for her, I thought back to my experience at the Moonshine Inn, the rowdy redneck bar I'd infiltrated while investigating the death of my cousin's wife. I'd successfully played the part of a redneck queen. If I could pull off that feat, I could get through a discussion with Susan. My confidence level soared and, by the time a still-damp Susan returned from the rest room, I had assumed a relaxed, not-a-care-in-the-world demeanor. I felt well on my way to getting an acting award. A Razzie would do.

Settled back on the sofa, Susan glanced at the mug in my hand. No doubt the depleted amount of liquid in my mug explained the self-satisfied smile that hovered around her lips. What did she expect to happen next? I felt at a disadvantage not knowing what I was supposed to do. Was I to die immediately or simply nod off?

"How's your tea?" Susan asked.

"Oh, really good." I took another faux sip-and-swallow combination. "I love this flavor. Try some." I pushed the mug toward her.

"Oh, no." She moved a hand from side to side. "I'm not a tea drinker."

Not a drinker of this tea at any rate, I thought.

Susan sipped her coffee and gave me a mischievous smile. "Roseanne Dempsey says you talked her into revealing that I wrote the story you rated. Tell me about this panel you're planning."

Damn that Roseanne. I should have told her the panel was a surprise. After improvising a description of a panel topic on creating mood and tone in short stories, I said, "You did such a great job with your story, Susan. Tell me, what inspired you?"

"Well, I—" Susan took another sip before continuing. "I have something to get off my chest." She shot me a playful look.

Was she ready to confess? Good in one regard, not in another. Likely she intended her words to be the last I'd hear. She felt safe because she had plans for me—plans I needed to thwart. What were her plans, anyway? Did she expect me to fall asleep, allowing her to whisk me away to some location from which I'd never return? She wouldn't be daft enough to kill me right here in Sweetbrew—would she? I didn't even know if she actually added something to my tea. But I'd best assume she had.

Susan took a deep breath and said, voice quaking with emotion: "Oh, Hazel. I have a heavy heart."

First her chest, now an alliterative reference to her heart. Did she plan to go through her whole body, organ by organ, before admitting her guilt?

"Get on with it," I silently urged. I might not have much time if I had to stage a succumbing to some unknown substance.

I waited, pretend-sipped, swallowed, and prayed that the recorder would continue to do its job.

Finally she blurted, "I killed Randy. Randy Zimmerman." In case I couldn't keep track of the murdered Randys.

"What?" I tried to look astonished and sleepy at the same time.

Susan snorted. "Don't look so surprised, Hazel. Matt told me about your conversation last night, about how Randy came up with a little story idea about greed and murder. Matt asked me if my father had another daughter. I assured him he didn't.

"Then there was the thing with Roseanne and the panel. And Christina Bigelow—I overheard her talking to someone at the memorial service. She was so devastated and went on and on about Randy's research project. When I saw her today at the library, I figured she was passing you information."

"She was supposed to be in the class today," I murmured.

"Matt's told me all about your great detecting skills. Plus you have to clear yourself of suspicion. Matt is determined that you killed Randy because he laughed at you, mocked your writing. Lorraine was his second choice of suspect."

"But why did *you* kill Randy?"

"Because he wanted me to marry him."

"He wanted you to marry him? Why would you kill him over that?"

"I didn't want to marry him."

Susan's matter-of-fact delivery chilled me. Matching her tone, I asked, "Want to tell me about it?"

"Sure. But first, let me make one thing clear: it was an accident. I —I overreacted."

"Oh?"

"It was a crime of passion. He made me *so* mad."

"Yes, Randy could do that."

I lowered my eyelids halfway, trying for a sleepy effect.

"That Saturday night, I went to Randy's house on my evening walk. No one saw me. I knew Joyce was away. I went to ask him to divorce Joyce. Then she and Matt would be free to marry."

"Is that when Randy proposed to you?"

Susan hooted. "*Proposed.* You make it sound like he got down on one knee, dazzling me with diamonds. To answer your question, yes, that's when he popped the question. Not what I expected, not by a long shot."

"I bet it was a surprise. After all, you anticipated being free to marry Robert Crain."

Susan looked at me like I was a not very bright child. "Robert Crain?"

"Yes. Weren't you in love with him?"

"Hell, no," Susan said with a laugh. "Years ago I was, but not now. No, I wanted to marry my ex. He's getting out of prison soon. I always liked bad boys, even at my age. Robert's such a goody-goody. Your detecting skills went awry this time, Hazel."

Susan paused, regarding me with a smirk, before continuing. "Randy and I kept company for a while. But you knew that, didn't you?"

"It sounds familiar. Why did you break up?"

"He met Joyce and that was it for me. Joyce and Matt had been seeing each other, but she dumped Matt. Musical couples. I guess that's what got me thinking about swinging couples."

"Did you—"

Susan rolled her eyes. "No, Hazel, we didn't do any swapping. If I'm going to be a fiction writer, I need to make up stuff. Anyway, Matt and I wound up together, almost by default. I guess we were each other's consolation prizes. I realized soon after marrying him that he was a big mistake."

"So you didn't love Matt?"

Susan laughed. "No, I didn't love my husband. Especially once I found out he wanted to divorce me. My prospective fortune changed his mind about that."

"Go on." I made a weak go-on gesture with my hand as I maintained the pretense of trying to keep my eyes open.

"It didn't take long for Joyce to start loathing Randy and me to start loathing both Matt and Randy. I wasn't too hot on Joyce, either. But it was clear that Joyce and Matt were hot on each other. Clear as day."

"But you just said your inheritance made Matt change his mind about divorcing you."

"I plan to offer Matt enough money to make divorce appealing. If that doesn't work, well . . . I'll figure out something."

The gleam in Susan's eyes reminded me of Barbara Stanwyck's gleam in *Double Indemnity* when Fred MacMurray killed her husband just out of camera range. An association that suggested Susan's idea of "something" involved killing Matt. Another chill rippled through me and my mouth felt as dry as if I'd traipsed through a desert for days. A sip of tea would help—not this tea, though.

"Besides," Susan said. "There's Joyce's new bad-boy lover in the picture, gumming up the works. Although he may just be a diversion. He was pretty hot, didn't you think?"

Declining to comment on Mick Jacoby's hotness, I asked, "Back to that Saturday night—did you tell Randy you didn't want to marry him?"

"I did."

"And?"

"He laughed."

"No surprise there," I said. "Now tell me the real reason you killed him. He threatened you, didn't he? He found out about your father's other daughter and threatened to tell her she stood to gain a hefty inheritance. He also threatened to tell Matt. But he wasn't asking for hush money, was he? He wanted you to marry him. He'd long had a thing for you and wanted you back—whatever it took to get you."

Whew. Pretending to nod off and presenting someone with a motive for her crime were tough to manage simultaneously. Dangerous, too. But Susan seemed too wrapped up in her confession to notice my alertness.

She looked up at the ceiling, perhaps seeking inspiration from the heavens. "How many women do you know who get blackmailed into marriage?" She didn't wait for my response, not that I had one. "And he laughed at my probably shocked expression."

"He knew you wouldn't want to share your inheritance with your half-sister."

"Well, no. Would you?"

"So you're no longer denying her existence. When did you find out about her?"

"Recently. The will. My parents never mentioned a daughter."

"Strange."

"My parents didn't talk much. To me, or to each other."

"But do you know if she's living?"

Susan gave a half laugh. "Oh, Deborah's living all right."

And next on Susan's hit list.

I envisioned Susan contacting Deborah Godsey Travis, suggesting they get together for a nice sister's lunch—Deborah's last.

Susan held up a hand, signaling an end to discussion about her family. "Let's get back to Randy: he'd been drinking. So had I. When he wouldn't stop laughing, I took that stupid sculpture and swung it at his shoulder, but he ducked and I got him in the back of the head. I panicked. Ran. Well—" Again that playful look that made my skin crawl. "First, I cleaned up everything, then I skedaddled. Again, no one saw me."

"Did you cut through the back yard?"

"I did. The same way Matt and I always went to their house. Matt did the same thing when they were boys."

"And I bet you dropped a Starbucks receipt."

"Starbucks receipt?"

"Yes, it was from earlier that day. Caffe mocha. Paid in cash."

"I vaguely remember that. Good thing I paid in cash."

"Didn't Matt wonder where you went?" I let my eyes close completely and slowed my speech. "Especially when he heard the news?"

"Well, he certainly didn't think *I* killed Randy. Matt didn't even know I'd left the house. I gave him a wee little pill in his food. In no time he was sound asleep on the sofa."

I wondered if that wee little pill wound up in my tea. And in the philodendron.

"When the police talked to us Matt said we'd been home all night. As far as he knew, we were." Susan sounded quite pleased with her deception. Her amused demeanor turned flinty as she added, "All would have been fine until Claudia got you and Lucy in the act."

My eyes popped open, but I quickly shut them. Slurring my words, I said, "Claudia? What are you talking about?"

"Remember the day Claudia met the two of you here? And that big woman, she lives next door to Randy and Joyce, she blasted Claudia. Something about her leaving a kid in her car."

"Oh, my God! That was you. You were sitting over there—" I pointed to the table occupied by the same-sex couple and their wedding planner— "You had on a rose-colored pashmina. And glasses. And messy hair. What, were you eavesdropping on us?"

I pictured Susan in a rose pashmina in one of her Facebook photos. Was it the same one she wore that day she masqueraded as a frumpy neighborhood denizen out for a caffeine fix? Why hadn't I noticed the little things, like pashminas, until now? Would it have changed anything if I had? It wasn't a crime to wear one of those pretty shawls.

Susan smiled over the rim of her mug.

"Matt told me you were meeting Claudia here that day. And he told me that you solved the murder of a woman Randy had a torrid affair with years ago. I had to check out what you all knew." She sounded like she was explaining a simple concept to a child.

"It was you who followed Lucy and me home from the library, wasn't it? But you weren't driving the same car you have today." I gestured toward the window behind me, and the parking lot beyond. "You'd had an accident, and you were driving a loaner."

"Right you are, dear Hazel."

"You also sent me that threatening note."

Susan laughed. "I wasn't sure if the tailgating thing would scare you off, so I ratcheted things up a bit. Didn't you love that message I composed with cutout letters? Such a cliché!"

"And Lorraine. Why did you kill her?" Claudia's advice to mystery writers came to me: "During the sleuth's confrontation with the killer, convey emotional reactions like panic and fear." So far, I'd remained calm throughout this particular confrontation. Between listening to Susan and guessing the appropriate reaction to the unknown substance in my tea, I felt hard-pressed to respond the way a normal person would under the circumstances. I made a mental note to tell Claudia to think about a broader range of emotional reactions—providing I survived.

"Lorraine was hot on the heels of Randy's killer. She told Matt that. Climbing family trees. She invited me over to her place to show me how she researched on the genealogy sites. We'd talked about it at the gym. When I arrived, she rather smugly told me she knew about my ex being in prison. I didn't care if anyone knew about that, but how long would it have taken for her to find my dear half-sister? Not long, I figured. Who knows what blackmail scheme she'd come up with? Lorraine had to go." That self-satisfied gleam appeared in her eyes again.

"So how did you do it?" I asked, picturing the scarf around Lorraine's neck.

"You found her, so you know how I did it. I came prepared with a long scarf. Much like this one." She pulled on the tassels that edged the scarf she wore around her neck. Did she intend to use it to murder me? She lifted her arm and flexed a bicep, a not-so-subtle reminder of her superior upper body strength. But I had my own weapon—I stole a glance at my roach killer boots.

"I'm guessing Matt got another wee little pill that night?"

Susan didn't answer, but I saw her smile through my hooded eyes.

"Some guy saw a woman with long, blond hair outside Lorraine's place. Was that you? That day Lucy, Claudia, and I saw you here—you had on a blond wig, didn't you? From your chemo days?" When Susan nodded, I said, "You were trying to look like Joyce, I bet."

The middle-aged woman sitting nearby stood. Walking with a slight limp, she took her phone and went outside. Since she left her laptop, headset, and a couple of other gadgets on the table, I guessed she'd be back.

Susan didn't offer a sarcastic comment on my stellar detective skills. Her voice took on a singsong quality when she said, "You know something, Hazel—I really, *really*, hate to be laughed at. Maybe if Randy hadn't laughed at me, he'd still be alive. I bet he never expected that laughing could kill him."

FIFTY-EIGHT

Would Vince ever show up? I still didn't know who Billy was, but surely a customer would lend a helping hand, if needed. Blanche DuBois always depended on the kindness of strangers. But taking inspiration from the unstable character in *Streetcar Named Desire* probably wasn't a wise course to follow.

Susan leaned toward me. "Hazel, you know you need proof that all this happened. And you won't get away from me alive."

Uh oh. Time to ratchet up my performance. I slumped into a reclining position, resting my head against the arm of the sofa. Likely I wasn't doing this in any natural way. But would Susan know what the natural way looked like?

"Oh, dear. I must get you home." Susan yanked on my arm and pulled me to my feet. I wobbled a bit in my roach killer boots. When she bent to pick up my purse from the floor, I delivered a kick to her shin, following up with a shove that sent her backward, landing at the feet of the wedding planner who jumped up with a shriek. Moving quickly, I straddled the screaming Susan and held down her arms.

"Billy!" I bellowed.

"Don't worry, Hazel. The police are on their way."

The two men interrupted their wedding planning and took my place restraining Susan, who continued to scream and curse.

The voice of assurance belonged to the tech-savvy middle-aged woman who'd been sitting near us, operating various devices. As she limped toward me, I asked, "Are you Billy?"

"I am. I have her confession recorded."

The door to the café burst open to admit Vince, Fish, Garcia, and an officer I didn't know.

"Well, well, well, Ms. Rose." Fish grinned. "Fancy meeting you here."

FIFTY-NINE

Greta Popp went to considerable expense to thank me for finding her daughter's killer. Pots of poinsettias in vibrant reds decorated the community room of River Edge Retirement Villa. White lights and gold ornaments adorned a ten-foot tree set in a corner. Platters of hors d'oeuvres and pastries filled the tables. Bottles of wine and a dispenser filled with water and lemon slices satisfied the thirst of the group gathered to honor Lorraine's and Randy's memories and help Mrs. Popp find closure.

Along with Lucy, Vince, and Eileen, guests included Claudia, Ruby Landis, George Monahan, Gail Bayer, Kat Berenger, and Sherry Guanzon. They clamored for every detail of the drama starring Randy, Lorraine, Joyce, Matt, and Susan. My audience hung on my every word, making me feel like a storyteller at a campfire. Beyond an occasional "Yikes!" "I'll be," "Who would have thought it?" and other exclamations of surprise, shock, and wonder, no one spoke until I finished. I made sure the various players, like Vince, Lucy, and Eileen, shared the credit for nabbing the killer.

Susan Rowan confessed to murdering Randy and Lorraine. At her arraignment the charges included first-degree murder and attempted abduction. An analysis of the tea she had doctored and, thankfully, I hadn't consumed, showed a hefty dose of Rohypnol, a.k.a. the date rape drug. The trial date was set for some time in February. The police took the recordings Billy Ruffalo and I produced, but, with Susan's confession, they weren't necessary.

Billy Ruffalo, my guardian angel in human form, was a former Richmond PD detective who'd left the police force after being shot in the leg during a chase, explaining her limp. Billy now owned Café Sweetbrew. Vince and Dennis had mentioned Billy when we had brunch at Joe's Inn a few Sundays back and I'd forgotten the conversation.

Billy had seemed preoccupied with her various devices, paying no attention to Susan and me. But the skills she'd no doubt developed as a detective—observing, but appearing not to—would stay with her forever. Based on her name, I had expected her to be a man—I needed to broaden my thinking.

When Billy came through the doors of the community room, the two of us embraced. "You have my undying gratitude," I said.

At the food table, Billy and I speared bite-sized items with toothpicks while she gave me her account of that harrowing day. "Vince texted me, asking me to keep an eye on you until he could get to the café. He wasn't sure about Susan. So I googled you, saw your picture, found you by the window, and parked myself close enough to record your conversation. When you dumped your tea in my plant, I knew something was up— either you didn't like the tea, or you thought Susan had doctored it."

"How did your plant do?" I asked.

"I had to repot it, but it should be fine. Thanks for the replacement plant." Billy brushed back her shoulder length cloud of hair. "I need to get going, but before I do, let me give you some advice. Think long and hard about this dangerous business of nabbing killers. Is it really worth it?"

Having no ready response, I repeated my expression of undying gratitude and wished her well with Café Sweetbrew. We hugged again and she left.

Joyce Zimmerman did not accept the invitation to the gathering that I sent via Ruby. According to Ruby, Joyce responded with uproarious laughter. Perhaps she'd picked up the cackling habit from her dearly departed husband. She also failed to thank me for discovering his killer.

Writing THE END to the probe into Randy's and Lorraine's murders filled me with a spirit of generosity, so, even though Ruby Landis had been a pain in the butt the past few weeks, I had invited her to join us. When she arrived, she leaned close to me and said, "Joyce is going to sell the house here in Richmond and go back to California." Her pale blue eyes gleamed when she added, "*With Mick Jacoby.*"

"Not exactly the grieving widow, is she?"

"Not hardly."

Claudia, laughing at something George Monahan was saying, took a glass of wine from the drinks table. The day before, she confided that she and her husband were divorcing. As it turned out, Claudia hadn't saved my sister Madeline from drowning all those years before. When I told my sisters that I'd paid the family debt, they both informed me that another neighbor had rescued Madeline, and that Claudia had cowered nearby. They didn't even remember the real hero's name.

"Great," I grumbled to Vince. "I've been misled for decades. Now I owe a debt to someone else. I don't even want to know who. Good thing I never mentioned the incident to Claudia."

Lucy finally confronted Dave, who maintained that Arianna had come on to him and texted that one sexy photo of herself. When he told her to stop, she had and turned her attention to one of the firm's partners, who fired her. Something made me doubt this account, but I didn't share my feelings with my cousin.

"Have you talked to Trudy?" Claudia appeared before me,

balancing a plate of mini sandwiches and her nearly empty wine glass. "How's she doing with the whole Randy thing?"

"She feels bad, even if he was out of her life." I popped an olive in my mouth.

"But he was in her life for a long time."

"Yes. She's happy Susan is behind bars."

"Does Susan's half-sister know about her dad's death and that she stands to inherit a fortune?"

"That's something for a lawyer to take care of," I said.

When Lucy and Eileen joined us, Claudia said, "Oh, good. You're all here together. Is it okay with you if I join your book group?"

"Of course," we chorused.

"We'll start up again in January," I said. "Trudy and Sarah will be back by then."

"About—" Claudia hesitated for a moment. "About the writing class—we're pretty stripped down now, just the three of you. I doubt that Matt will show up tonight. Do you all want to continue?"

"I do," Lucy said. "We only have a couple of sessions left."

"Hazel's firsthand experience will enhance the class," Eileen said. "After all, how many mystery writers solve actual murders?"

We all laughed. A good kind of laughter.

Not the kind that could get you killed.

THE END

ACKNOWLEDGMENTS

I am grateful to the following:

Jeni Chappelle, for her excellent suggestions which made this a better book.

My readers, for their sharp eyes and invaluable feedback: Betsy Ashton, Thomas A. Burns, Jr., Phyllis Entis, Julie Fasciana, Jean Harris, Glen King, Amy Reade, and Heather Weidner.

Margaret Howard, Manager of the Bon Air Branch of the Chesterfield County Public Library. Her advice on library practices gave me the authentic detail I needed.

Sisters in Crime Central Virginia and James River Writers, for their support and first-rate programs.

Steve and Janice Nuckolls, for lending me their lovely home.

The many restaurants, cafes, and bookstores of Metro Richmond featured in this book. All are real, but I gave some pseudonyms and alternative locations.

My readers, for their encouragement and enthusiasm.

Book groups everywhere, for their love of the written word.

Olive and Morris, for making me laugh.

Glen, for his love and support.

Hazel Rose Book Group Mysteries:
Death Turns the Page
Murder at the Moonshine Inn
Laughing Can Kill You

ABOUT THE AUTHOR

Maggie King is the author of the Hazel Rose Book Group mysteries. Her short stories appear in various anthologies, including the *Virginia is for Mysteries* series, *50 Shades of Cabernet, Deadly Southern Charm, Death by Cupcake, Murder by the Glass,* and *First Comes Love, Then Comes Murder, and Crime in the Old Dominion.*

Maggie graduated from Rochester Institute of Technology. She is a member of Sisters in Crime, James River Writers, and the Short Mystery Fiction Society. She has worked as a software developer, retail sales manager, customer service supervisor, web designer, and non-profit administrator. She has called New Jersey, Massachusetts, and California home. These days she lives in Richmond, Virginia with her husband Glen and mischievous cat, Olive. All these jobs, schools, and homes have gifted her with story ideas for years to come. www.maggieking.com.

Connect with me

Facebook Facebook.com/maggiekingauthor
Instagram instagram.com/maggiekingauthor

Sign up for my quarterly newsletter at maggieking.com for news, views, and giveaways.